CASIDDIE WILLIAMS

Annie You're Okay

Life is a journey that takes many twists and turns. Without knowing it was happening, a side character quickly took on a central character role and won my heart.

I dedicate this book to all the side characters who deserve every ounce of main character energy they keep locked inside themselves. LET IT SHINE!

Contents

Preface

CONTENT NOTICE:

Thank you so much for picking up Annie You're Okay. I am so honored that you have chosen this contemporary romance as your next read. However, I want to make you aware of a few triggers and heavy topics that run through this book before you dive in.

This is an 18+ contemporary why choose/polyromance where the main female character has more than one love interest and does not have to choose between them. The three main characters share a relationship and love each other equally. There are several BDSM and Domme/sub scenes throughout this novel including but not limited to shibari, rough play, kinky play, and role switches. Scenes range from exposition to explicitly detailed.

These characters go through a traumatic emotional journey together including dealing with mental and physical health issues, possible infertility and character death. This novel in no part is a guide on how you should take care of your mental and physical health. How the characters deal with mental and physical trauma in this book may differ from how you or someone you know has dealt with the same trauma.

YOUR MENTAL HEALTH MATTERS and this novel is not here to lessen that fact. I hope you enjoy reading Annie You're Okay, and the journey they take towards healing.

Substance Abuse and Mental Health Services: SAMHSA (800)662-4357

Acknowledgement

A huge thank you to YOU for choosing to pick up this book and read the journey of the crazy characters in my head. This book took me on a roller coaster of emotions and challenges from the start. The characters and relationships bloomed farther than I could have ever imagined. Now, to the good stuff.

Oh, my Alphas. What can I say? Thank you doesn't seem like a strong enough word to my Comma Queen, Beth. From the obsessiveness of your commas to your quirky comments and texts, I love it all! It was never a dull moment waking up to the dozens and dozens of corrections each morning. Thank you!

Alpha K.K. Your off-the-wall ideas and memes became some of this book's greatest chapters. Triple D's! You always managed to turn my no's into maybes and, eventually, okay fines, and I was always happy I did it. Thank you!

To my Beta, Author N. Slater (seriously, go check her out!) Your insight was invaluable, but nothing compares to the play-by-play of all your favorite moments in Annie's book.

To my ARC readers. Hearing how your emotions took the

same roller coaster as mine has been amazing. I'm so excited you were as touched by Annie's story as I was.

To The Mercantile in Rock Hill, SC. Thank you for putting up with me sitting for hours writing about these wonderful characters while drinking your coffee and talking the ears off your baristas.

Thank you to my friends and family, who continue supporting me on my writing journey. I will forever appreciate you!

I

You're Enough ~ Book 1

Annie's book is the first in a series of characters who find themselves in emotionally traumatic situations, and follow their journeys to healing.

1

Annie

I'm fucking naked. Well, I might as well be. The breeze threatening to make this a Marilyn Monroe moment is not helping my dilemma. This is all Candy's fault. All I wanted to do when I got home from work was take a hot bath, drink a glass of wine, and read a book. Fucking Candy. Of course, she couldn't let me have an evening of peace. She had to get into trouble. How the hell did I get here?

I knew immediately as I walked in the front door that Candy had gotten into trouble while I was at work. She stands before me at the entrance to the house, attempting to look sweet and innocent. The powdered sugar on her face tells another story. In fact, the trail of powdered sugar leading from the kitchen to the living room, trailing across my maple floors, and all over the charcoal gray sectional tells a very different story. I must have left the pantry open. She's earned her name honestly.

"What did you do now, girl?" Her small tail thumps on the floor echoing off the vaulted ceiling, so proud of herself

3

for her messy accomplishment. I follow the powdered sugar trail like a scavenger hunt to find the exploded bag under the dining room table.

"I thought Doberman Pinschers were supposed to be intelligent dogs?" In response to my question, she tilts her head to the side and then walks away. I grab my phone out of my purse to text the pet sitter, who should have come by and taken Candy for a walk this afternoon.

Me: Hey, Emily. How was Candy's walk today? She made a mess out of the living room.

Emily: Sorry, Ms. Poulsen, I quit.

Quit? What? I hit the call button on the phone screen, and the number goes straight to voicemail. I make several more attempts with the same result. Dammit, she must have blocked me. This is not what I need right now. I need to clean up this mess, but first, I need to change. I guess the bath will have to wait a little longer.

I take my red bottom heels off before I walk up the stairs to my bedroom. I'm mentally exhausted today. Who would think staring at a computer screen all day would leave me this bone-tired? Placing my shoes in my closet on the shelf next to their companions, I take a moment to appreciate my collection. I have heels in every color imaginable. I'm not a short woman at 5'7", but being a female in the corporate world already has me at a disadvantage. Wearing 5-6 inch heels and putting me at or near eye level with my subordinates gives me an edge.

I strip off all of my clothes and separate them in the baskets for regular and "dry clean only" laundry. I have nowhere else to go tonight, and I'll be cleaning up the sugar mess downstairs, so I throw on an oversize white t-shirt, toss my too-long blonde hair up in a messy bun, and make a mental note to call my hairdresser.

Candy doesn't greet me when I come back downstairs, and I assume it's because *she* doesn't even want to look at her mess anymore. She must be outside in the backyard. That doggy door was the best investment. I look out the window to confirm my suspicions and notice that my rose bushes have been pruned. The gardener must have come by a day early.

Taking out the cleaning supplies from under the sink and grabbing the broom, I start to make work of the sugar apocalypse. I hear Candy begin to bark and realize the sound isn't coming from the backyard anymore. I rush to the front window to see her charging down the driveway toward an unsuspecting person walking a small dog across the street. *Shit.*

Without thinking about what I'm wearing, I whip open the front door and chase her yelling and screaming down the driveway.

"Candy. *Kommen.* CANDY. STOP!" She successfully crosses the street without incident, but I can't say the same for the man and his dog. Despite her size and intimidating stature, Candy is a lover, but without knowing her, you'd have no idea she wouldn't hurt a fly.

Hearing my screaming and seeing the charging dog, the man picks up his small fur ball and crouches down, braced for the attack. Except the attack is more of an impact, and the three of them go rolling across the grass when Candy pounces. By the time I reach them, Candy is licking the man's

5

face and bouncing back and forth, trying to get the terrified dog to play with her.

2

Cole

The weather is so beautiful tonight. It's a great temperature to be outside with Lucy. She's the smallest dog I walk; a feisty, fluffy, tan Pomeranian. The Chicago weather has been rainy lately, and we haven't gotten to walk the neighborhood as much. She stops to smell a tree, and I hear a woman's voice screaming. I can't make it out at first, and I'm looking around, trying to find the source, when I see a large brown dog charging at us.

"Candy. *Kommen.* CANDY. STOP!" The woman is yelling, but the dog isn't making any attempt to stop. I scoop Lucy up off the ground, crouch, and curl around her. Closing my eyes, I'm wondering when the pain will start when we're suddenly rolling around in the grass. My face feels wet, and I worry it's blood until I open my eyes and see a large Doberman licking my face, trying to get us to play. Lucy wiggles out of my arms and nips at the dog's legs in a playful manner.

The screaming lady reaches us, and I stop watching the dogs play to take in her appearance. She's panting and sweating, and her hair, which I assume was once on top of her head, is now flopping around at the side of her neck and glued to her temples. She's bent over with her hands on her knees, attempting to catch her breath. I see her feet are bare, and her toes are painted a vibrant red. The t-shirt she has on barely covers whatever she's wearing under it, and unless she has on the tiniest shorts in the history of shorts, I don't think she has any bottoms on.

She tries to speak but is so out of breath from her sprint that it just sounds like wheezing. She holds up one finger in a gesture that says, "Give me a minute." I turn back to the dogs, who are happily playing on the plush green lawn, and give her a moment to compose herself. Finally able to speak, she stands up and addresses me.

"Oh my god, I'm so sorry. If you haven't already noticed, Candy is a big teddy bear. Her breed has a bad reputation, but that's all in the training. Candy thinks she's a lap dog, and you can't tell her otherwise. And as you can clearly see, she loves to play."

"It's no problem. I had made my peace with death as my life flashed before my eyes while she was barreling towards me." The woman gives me an unamused smile. Okay. Tough crowd. I stick my hand out to her. "Hi, I'm Cole." She places her hand in mine, and I almost wince at the strength of her handshake.

"Annie." One syllable is all she gives me in a no-nonsense tone. She's watching the dogs play as a breeze sweeps by and catches the hem of her shirt. She instantly places a hand on the front and back, holding it down. I watch as she attempts to keep the bottom of the shirt in place and notice the angle of her front hand pushing the side of her right breast in and upwards. The cool chill from the breeze has made her nipples hard, and I can see the slightly darker outline of her plump protruding areolas through her white shirt. A throat clears, and I look up to see her staring at me, staring at her breasts.

"I didn't sign up to be objectified today. That's on Friday's schedule." *Shit.*

"I'm so sorry, Annie. That was rude of me." She crosses her arms over her chest. Luckily for her, the breeze has stopped, so her arms are free to cover herself.

"Candy. *Kommen.*" She snaps her fingers with her commanding tone, and the once goofy, playful dog stops in her tracks and comes to sit directly next to Annie. That was impressive. "My apologies for my dog startling you. The gardeners came today, and they must have left the gate open. I hope you aren't hurt in any way."

"Nah, just a bruised ego."

"Alright, well, have a nice night." At her dismissive words, she walks back to the house, Candy on her heels, and disappears into the fence.

3

Annie

The following morning I didn't have any meetings, so I decided to work from home for the day. I have to call my hairdresser and find Candy a new dog walker. Without her midday exercise, she's like an over sugared-toddler by the end of the day.

"Hello, Nicole speaking. How can I help you?" She's always over-the-top cheerful, but her hair skills are exceptional, so I deal with it.

"Hi Nicole, it's Annie Poulson. I'd like an appointment at your earliest convenience."

"Oh, hey, Annie. Let me check my schedule." I hear typing in the background. "I actually had a cancellation this afternoon at 3:30 if you're available?" Now it's my turn to check my schedule. I have a meeting at 2:30 today but nothing after.

"I can fit 3:30 in my schedule. I'll see you then. Thank you." I hang up before she can speak again. Saying goodbye is just unnecessary banter when you know the conversation has ended.

I make a few phone calls to the local veterinarian's offices seeking recommendations for a dog walker. None of them had any immediate ideas but will call me back if they have any references. Candy needs someone who is an alpha to walk her, or she won't listen. I'm surprised she got along so well with Emily. I think there was more of a mutual respect between them. I also think she stocked her pocket with her homemade yogurt melts. Even I enjoyed those treats on occasion.

Around noon I can hear Candy pacing downstairs with boredom. Her nails click on the marble kitchen tile, then the tone changes as she crosses over onto the hardwood floor into the living room and back around. Fucking, Emily. It's around the time she would come to take her out. Even with the doggy door and free access to the backyard, she needs her mind stimulated as well as her muscles.

I recheck the time and close out the file I've been working on, deciding I'll take her for a walk to the local dog park and let her get some energy out. She hears me shuffling and trots into the room with hope in her brown eyes.

"Yes, yes, Candy. I'm taking you for a walk. Calm down." I take her pink leash off the hook at the front door, and we head off on our walk. She's the picture-perfect trained dog when she's on leash. She walks diligently at my side, and only I notice when her attention strays to passing dogs.

The walk to the dog park only takes about 10 minutes, and thank goodness there are only a few other dogs playing. I open the double gates of the large dog area and let her off her leash. This particular dog park utilizes nature to stimulate the dogs. There are several large boulders for the dogs to climb, a wooden bridge to walk over, and large tree stumps to jump and sit on. Candy loves it here.

She takes off running towards a German Shepherd we've seen here before, so there are no worries about traumatizing its owner as she charges at them. I wave at their owner, Spencer, I think. That's either the dog's name or hers. She speaks to the dog in German, so I'm unsure and don't care enough to clarify.

I follow up on some emails and order lunch to be delivered while Candy plays. When it's time to leave, I call for Candy to come, and she's instantly at my side. I clip her leash back on, and as we reach the gate to leave, I pause to let someone in with a black and white Great Dane. Candy's ears perk up, and I look down the leash to the owner of the other dog. The same man she trampled yesterday.

"Annie?" He remembers my name. I should remember his, but my embarrassment over my appearance was so mortifying my only goal was not to flash the entire neighborhood.

I look back at the large Great Dane he's walking, and he misunderstands the confused look on my face because he introduces himself again. Only, my confusion is for the change in dogs, not the recognition of him. He sticks his hand out, "It's Cole. Your dog ran me over yesterday outside your house." I take his hand and give it another firm shake.

"Sorry again about that. Have a nice day." I walk into the gate's antechamber, and Candy lets out a slight whine. "Come, girl." She looks back at the man who's letting his dog off the leash and then walks through. Closing the gate behind us, I pause and take my first good look at the stranger whom she seems to have taken a liking to.

He's tall, maybe 6'1", but that's no match for my daily heels. His handshake was firm, complimented by his broad shoulders. A sleeve of colorful tattoos is visible on his left arm, but nothing on his right. Dark luscious hair cut short on the sides and is longer and swoopy on the top. I'm not sure swoopy is even a word, though it accurately describes his hair. But, what makes me pause and my breath hitch is his crystal blue eyes. Even from ten feet away, I can see them. They're as clear as a tropical ocean, and I want to swim in them.

How did I miss them yesterday? Simple, they were lowered and staring at my hard nipples. I turn around, open the second set of gates and exit. I glance back at him, and he catches me looking and gives me a knowing smirk as the gate swings shut.

4

Annie

"...and you wouldn't believe what he said to me..." Nicole hasn't stopped talking since I got in her chair. I've been appropriately smiling and nodding to the best of my ability, but she isn't the type of person to get the hint I don't want to talk. She gives the best scalp massages, and when I leave here in two hours, I'll feel like a new woman, which is the only reason I put up with her gabbing. "...Candy?"

"I'm sorry?" My eyes flash to the mirror at the reflection of the curly blonde-haired woman with her hands in my hair. Her eyes remind me of the man from the dog park today, a clear blue color. I've never noticed that before. But she was talking about my dog, and I wasn't even paying attention, so I should probably engage in conversation.

"How have things been with Candy? Any new wild and crazy antics?" Our dogs are the only conversation that I ever engage in. She has two dachshunds, Java and Beans. They are sisters and seem to get into as much trouble as Candy.

"I'm on the hunt for a new dog walker again. Emily quit without any notice or reasoning yesterday and then blocked me." I've gone through my fair share of dog walkers. Candy is very high energy for anyone unwilling to learn her commands. Someone can't simply walk her; she needs direct instructions.

"Girl, I've got you." She has an enthusiastic smile on her face as she grabs one of her business cards and writes down a number. "This is my brother, Coleman. He just moved here, and he walks dogs as a side business. I bet he would love Candy."

I take the card from her hands. If her brother is anything like her, Candy will walk all over him. "Um, thank you."

"He used to work for one of those dog-walking apps, but since he moved here, I've been recommending all of my clients to him, and he's building his own small business." Okay, that sounds a bit more promising. "Hey, aren't you an app developer? Maybe you can help him make one for himself?"

"I own a software company. I don't do any of the development anymore, and we don't usually do anything that small scale either." If she only knew what I actually did.

"Oh, well, no biggie. But you should still give him a call or a text. I'm sure he could help you out with Candy." I go back to half ignoring her as she finishes my hair.

"Thank you, Nicole. It looks amazing as always." She truly does an incredible job. My hair always looks vibrant and healthy when I leave. Even though I cut off six inches, my hair is still halfway down my back.

"You're very welcome. See you in about six weeks, and give my brother a call." I smile and nod as I walk out of the salon. Pulling my phone from my purse, I decide I need to release some stress.

Me: Hey, Darling. I need to see you. Are you free tonight? I miss you.

    Blake: I miss you, too. I am, in fact, free tonight.

    Me: See you at 7.

    Blake: I'll see you then!

That gives me plenty of time to take that bath I didn't have last night. I'll give Nicole's brother, Coleman, a text as well. Even if it's just temporary, I need someone to walk Candy because I have a meeting I can't miss tomorrow.

Me: Hello, Coleman. My name is Danika. Your sister gave me your number. I'm in need of a dog walker. Are you available tomorrow at noon? I'm in the Hinsdale area and have a full-sized Doberman.

    Coleman: Yes, ma'am, I'm available. If you send me your email address, I can send you a contract to review and sign along with my rates and liabilities. Are you looking for a one-time walk or a daily contract?

    Me: I need a permanent walker but want to ensure it's a good fit.

    Coleman: Absolutely, I understand. I'll send the contract over for you to fill out as soon as possible.

I send Coleman my email address while I start my bath. As promised, he emails the contract, and I read it over while I soak. It's relatively standard, and his rates are fair. I fill it out and send it back.

5

Cole

That blonde bombshell was checking me out at the dog park. That's the second time I've run into her in as many days. Today she wore tailored navy slacks and a light pink silk blouse with heels that made her nearly as tall as me. Her golden hair and makeup were done, and I almost didn't recognize her. Today she looks stunning, a force to be reckoned with. But, she was just as beautiful yesterday, fresh-faced and in only a T-shirt. This woman has been nothing but cold to me, and I don't know why I find that so enticingly attractive.

Nicole texted me earlier to let me know she referred me to another one of her clients and to be on the lookout. She's been vital in growing my dog-walking business, and I really appreciate her. Dog walker by day, game tester by night. Life is working in my favor lately.

I've lived here a little over a month, and I'm ready to get out of my sister's guest room. Her dogs, Java and Beans, are adorable, but I can't sit anywhere without having a dog in my lap.

After I brought Titus, the Great Dane, back to his house, I came home and worked on the latest video game the developer sent me to test. It's another first-person shooter that needed updates because of glitches.

My phone buzzes on my desk, and I see it's an unknown number.

Unknown: Hello, Coleman. My name is Danika. Your sister gave me your number. I'm in need of a dog walker. Are you available tomorrow at noon? I'm in the Hinsdale area and have a full-sized Doberman.

I wish my sister would stop insisting that she use my full name with her clients. Not even our parents call me Coleman anymore. I check my schedule and see that Lucy the Pomeranian is scheduled for 10 AM tomorrow in the same neighborhood. This works perfectly. I respond back to Danika and email her my contract before I continue working on my shooter game.

The following morning I head to Hinsdale and take Lucy for her walk. The small neighborhood is full of older upscale houses. Mature trees line the streets and lend a lot of shade in the heat of the summer. I make sure Lucy has a full dish of water, and I enjoy some cool air conditioning before I pull up Danika's contract in my email.

"There's no way?" I hadn't looked at the email to see the address because I know the streets here relatively well, and she couldn't be more than 10 minutes in any direction. The town is that small.

Name: Danika Poulsen
Pet Name: Candy
Breed: Doberman Pinscher

Special Instructions: Responds to English but behaves better to German commands: sit-*Sitzen*, come-*Kommen*, stay-*Bleiben.*

I map the address, and I'll be damned, it's my bombshell's house. I guess Annie is a nickname. Her entry instructions say to ring the doorbell, and she can disengage the front door lock from her phone. I wonder if she has a camera because I have a feeling seeing me on her front steps will shock her.

·ᴎᴎ·ᴎᴎ·

Promptly at noon, I ring her doorbell camera and wait. I hear the speaker crackle, "Hello, Colem- Cole? Is that you? What are you doing at my house?"

"Hi Danika, I'm actually Nicole's brother. I'm here to walk Candy." The cracking stops, and a moment later, my cell phone rings with an unknown number.

"Hello, Cole McGrath speaking."

"Coleman. Cole? You're Nicole's little brother? Nicole, my hairdresser?"

"Yes, ma'am, one and the same. I realize this is a strange coincidence, but I'm happy to walk Candy for you." There's silence on the other end of the line, and I pull my phone away from my ear to see if she's hung up. The timer is still counting. "Danika?"

"Yes, I'm here. I'm just processing this coincidence. I didn't even know Nicole had a brother until yesterday." I hear the whirling of metal as the front door lock turns. "Her leash is hanging up next to the front door. I'll lock the door when you leave, and you can ring the bell when you return, and I'll unlock it again."

19

"Sounds wonderful. Thank you, Danika. You signed up for an hour of outdoor time, so that's about how long we will be." I place my hand on the doorknob to open it, but before I can, I hear her mumble something. "I'm sorry?" I honestly thought she had hung up without a goodbye. Those don't seem to be her thing.

"You can call me Annie."

"Okay. I'll make sure to wear out Candy for you. Enjoy the rest of your day." This time she does hang up; the screen is black when I look at my phone.

6

Blake

Danika: Hey, Darling. I need to see you soon. Are you free tonight? I miss you.

Seeing that text sent a thrill up my spine. I've missed Annie. I need to scene with her badly. My daily life has been stressful, and the anticipation of the relief I know I'll be getting tonight already melts some of the stress away.

Being a receptionist for a high-powered attorney has as many downfalls as it has perks. Always wanting to succeed, resulting in long days, being one of the downfalls. I need to let go tonight.

At 6:55, I enter Danika's house with my personal security code and go straight to her bedroom. This room always feels clean and inviting, with various shades of gray and white decorating it. The velvety rug and oversized chairs in the corner complete the feel of comfort.

I remove my clothing to her liking, grab my pillow and place it on the floor at the foot of her bed. I kneel down and take a deep, cleansing breath. I go over my mental checklist:

Knees together, shoulders back, chest out, hands in my lap, head down.

A few minutes later, I hear the soft click of the door as it shuts behind her. A drawer opens and closes near me. Her bare feet walk past, and I feel the heat radiating off her body as she steps up behind me. A brush slowly moves across my long locks, and I sigh as the sensation sends a chill down my spine.

"I've missed you, *Mijn Diamant.*" I don't respond because she hasn't asked me a direct question, and I don't have permission. She brushes the knots out of my hair, then braids it down my back and secures it with a hair tie. I can feel my nerves humming with anticipation as her fingers wisp over my bare shoulders. She walks around to stand in front of me and gently lifts my chin, signaling me to stand.

I take a quick perusal of her body without lifting my head. A bra and panties are her standard outfit when we scene, and she looks as breathtaking as ever in a red matching set. *I love her in red.*

I stand before her, hands clasped behind my back, in nothing but my thong. A new yellow one that I bought today just for her, because I know it's her favorite color. Her eyes peruse my body, and I see the heat flash in them when she notices the tiny yellow scrap of lace fabric.

"Did my good girl do some shopping just to please me?" She noticed, and I gave her a small smile with a nod. She's asked me a direct question, so I have permission to speak.

"Yes, Danika." My words come out breathier than I expected. As I answer, I look into her eyes, the only time direct eye contact is allowed. This close, I can see the gold flecks in her honey browns.

"Five days is far too long to go without seeing your beauty, *Mijn Diamant*." Her fingers leave a burning trail of fire as they cross my collarbone and down my arm. My eyes flutter closed at the delicate touch.

A sharp cracking sound cuts through the air when she smacks my left nipple. I convulse forward with a gasp as she palms my breast, taking it into her hot mouth to soothe the pain. Popping off, she licks the other, swirling her tongue until it peaks in her mouth.

"Good girl," she purrs before devouring my mouth with hers. I taste the subtle hints of the red wine she must have drank before I got here. Her hand grabs my braid and tugs, lifting my chin and opening my mouth wider to deepen our kiss. "Lay on the bed, hands above your head."

Climbing on, I arch my back and over-exaggerate my hip sways as I crawl to the middle of the king-size bed. The pale gray duvet feels like I'm lying on a cloud as I raise my hands above my head and wait. The bed dips next to me, and I feel the coolness of the silk as my wrists are bound together, then tied to the hidden hooks in the headboard.

The bedside table opens, and I hear the metallic clink of the trauma shears as she places them on top. She moves to a lower drawer and takes out two bundles of bound rope.

"Remind me of your safewords, BlakeLynn." I love the refresher we go through every time we play.

"Yellow means everything is good." Her favorite color. "Orange means I need a moment, or I'm unsure." My favorite color. "Red means stop." That's an obvious one.

"Confirm the trauma shears are out and available."

"The trauma shears are available on the nightstand."

"Such a good girl, as always." I'm graced with a kiss on my

inner thigh as she settles between my legs with the two sets of rope. She unwinds one of the ropes and makes a six stranded loose column around the base of my left ankle. My ankle is pushed back until my knee is bent and my heel is touching the base of my butt. She begins to wrap the rope from the outside of my thigh around to the inside and continues spiraling it up and around my leg towards my knee. Once four spirals are created, a hitch knot is placed along each layer of ropes. When all the knots are completed, she repeats the process on my right leg. For the final step, she grabs two smaller ropes from the drawer and ties each leg to the outside of the bed, leaving me wide open to her and unable to move.

"Knot name?" she demands.

"Spiral Futomomo, Danika."

"Excellent memory, *Mijn Diamant.*" Danika hosted a Shibari party a year ago, and we learned how to tie knots properly and play responsibly.

"How many?" I know what she's asking without her even saying the word. This is the million-dollar question that has no correct answer. If I give too high of a number, she'll try to meet it. She'll punish me and make it higher if I give too low of a number. I'll go with something safe.

"Eight, Danika." Eight seems like a good middle number. Our record is lucky number 13 before I passed out from complete exhaustion.

"Hmm." Her fingers drift up and down my inner thigh, bumping over each layer of the rope. "I think you can handle nine." Nine orgasms. I need this sweet torture that only she can give me. My clit is already pulsing, waiting for her to touch me. She reaches down again to the bedside table and grabs several different vibrators. We have an extensive

24

collection. It's our favorite kind of shopping trip.

A slender finger moves my thong aside, slides through my pussy lips, and circles my clit. "Oh, *Mijn Diamant*, it appears you've missed me as much as I've missed you. You're already soaked, and I haven't even touched you." She crouches lower, spreads my lips between her fingers, and blows cold air onto my inflamed clit. The ties on my legs tighten as I involuntarily flex inward, leaving a delicious bite of pain.

"You seem so worked up. Should I make the first one quick so you can get some relief?"

Without thinking, the word "Yes," rushes through my lips. That was the wrong answer. I should have said the opposite if I really wanted to make it quick. She removes her hand from my clit and crawls up my body.

"Tsk, tsk. Too eager, little girl." She takes my bottom lip in hers and lightly sucks before moving to my jaw, then down my neck. Continuing lower, she spends a considerable amount of time nipping and teasing my nipples. While her mouth worships my breasts, her knee is between my legs, grinding a steady rhythm into me. A knot low in my belly is already tightening. Danika knows my body so well she can tell how close I am based on how my body is reacting. "Beg for it."

"Please. Please, Danika. Please let me come." She bites down on a nipple and grinds harder into me with her knee, and my first orgasm crests. My back arches off the bed, and I throw my head back in pleasure.

"Count," she demands as she crawls down my body. She hovers over me between my legs, waiting.

"One." Before the word is entirely out of my mouth, she sucks my clit between her lips with a long pull. Sliding two fingers inside me, she immediately starts making the "come hither" motion on my g-spot. Before my first orgasm has subsided, I'm convulsing again with another.

"T-two," I stutter out. Still not letting up, she lowers her mouth to my entrance and starts spearing me with her tongue while using her thumb to flick my overly sensitive clit.

"Fuck, *Mijn Diamant*, you taste like the only meal I ever want to eat. Come on my tongue one more time." She increases the pressure on my clit, and I squirm the best I can with all the restraints. She replaces her thumb with her mouth, and her tongue flicks my clit at an almost punishing pace. Tears spring to my eyes at the intensity of the orgasm building. I'm holding my breath as the sensation mounts. Seeing my tension, Danika mumbles between my thighs.

"Breathe and let go." It's not a suggestion. It's a command. Releasing a shaky breath, Danika inserts three fingers, and the fullness shatters me. I'm screaming and sobbing. My hips bucking into her mouth as my butt cheeks spasm. Her tongue caresses me until my orgasm subsides.

Crawling up to see my face, she kisses away the tears on my cheeks, telling me what a good girl I am. With gentle fingers, she smooths away the hair that's clinging to the sweat on my forehead.

"Count"

"Three, Danika."

"Color?" Always checking in.

"Yellow." She nips at my earlobe and then seats herself back between my legs. Kissing tenderly up my thighs, she slowly unties her knots one by one until I have full movement of my legs again. She hands me a purple vibrator that has both internal and external stimulation.

"Use this while I massage your leg muscles, but don't come

unless you ask." No response is needed. It wasn't a question. This vibrator is my most and least favorite at the same time. I'm already so overstimulated that it won't take long to ramp me up again, but it also always produces intense orgasms. Considering I still have six more to go, I appreciate that we're using this one closer to the beginning than the end.

I insert the vibrator, and she instructs me to use the second setting. It's equivalent to a medium speed. The clitoral stimulation flicks up and down while internally, it vibrates, and little pearls twirl around inside the shaft. I'm trying to concentrate my focus on her firm hands massaging my calf muscles, but this vibrator is making it extremely difficult. My toes start to tingle, and my breathing increases.

"Please, may I come, Danika?"

"Not yet." I groan as my thigh muscles start to quiver. The intensity is building, and I'm holding back as best I can.

"Please, Danika." I'm so close to exploding.

"No. Turn it off." I let out a whimper as I turned the vibrator off. My chest is heaving with the exertion of my rapid breathing. I'm panting with need as she continues to massage my legs.

7

Annie

Seeing the blush across her chest and up her neck as she pants before me is the main subject of many of my erotic fantasies. She held back that orgasm longer than I expected she would, which will only make the next one more intense. The whimper that escaped her lips when I told her to turn it off has my clit throbbing.

I run my hand up her milky skin. It's such a contrast to her raven hair and bright brown eyes. Brushing my fingers over her lower lip, they part as she sighs. Her breathing is almost back to normal. I reach down and turn the vibrator on full speed. A guttural sound pours from her lips before she starts to beg.

"Please. Please, Danika. Please let me come. Oh god, pleeeeease." That's the begging I was waiting for.

"Come, *Mijn Diamant*. Come for me." Her body convulses around me as her back lifts off the bed, pleasure taking over her entire body. "Count, and don't stop until you have another one.

"F-f...fooour." She barely gets the word out. Lifting her

right leg to her chest and holding it there for her, the new position changes the angle of the vibrator. Her mouth opens in a scream, but no sound comes out; all the air is stuck in her lungs and I watch as her stomach muscles contract, and another orgasm takes her over.

I turn off the vibrator and slowly remove it. "Count."

"Five." The word is a whispered sigh from her lips. I reach up and untie her hands and massage her wrists. Using the same silk, I blindfold her.

"Don't move. I'll be right back." Quickly I make my way to the kitchen and return to the room with a cup of ice, and a few extra supplies. Placing a piece in my mouth, I bend down and take her nipple between my lips, swiping her peak as she gasps with the temperature change. Releasing her, I suck in her other nipple, and she gasps again. We love sensory play, especially when blindfolded. I see her hands moving toward me, and I warn her before she gets too far.

"Be careful, little girl. Don't make me have to tie you up again. You don't have permission to touch yet." Her responding moan is a plea of desperation and longing.

I put another piece of ice in my mouth and bury my face between her thighs. The alternating sensations between stroking her with the cold ice and licking her with my warm tongue has her making the most delicious sounds. She doesn't shy away from being vocal about her pleasure, and that's precisely the way I like it. The more noise she makes, the more pleasure it brings me.

Once the ice has melted in my mouth, I continue to lick her languidly, allowing her next orgasm to be more for relief than intensity. When she fully comes down, I remove her blindfold.

"Count and color."

"Six and yellow." She's never needed to use red, and I never expect she will. There have been a few oranges, especially in the beginning when we first started practicing with the ropes. It takes time and patience to ensure you aren't tying them too tight.

"Would you like some water?"

"Yes please, Danika." I pour the bottle of water I brought back from the kitchen over the remaining ice and hand her the cup. She whispers her thanks and drinks until the glass is empty.

"You still owe me three more, but how about we take this to the bathroom? I can get you clean and dirty at the same time." Even though I've asked her a question and she has permission to speak, she still chooses to smile and nod in response. She knows it's a courtesy question and will do what I ask of her.

Standing, I offer her my hand, and she accepts it. I lead us into the bathroom and turn on the shower. This is one of my favorite rooms in the house. The black and white checkered patterned floor, black and white marble countertops, and glass shower are the focal points in the room. Everything else around us is white, and the accents are red. The entire space has a romantic feeling.

Facing Blake, I brush my knuckles across her cheek. I pull a makeup wipe from the package and gently remove the streaks of mascara from her face. She smiles sweetly at me for the gesture. I kiss her forehead and lead her into the shower.

"You have permission to touch-" She raises her hand to grab my hips, and I lift a hand halting her movement. "-But, you have to ask first."

"Yes, Danika. May I kiss you?"

"Please do, Little One." I allow her to come to me since she asked. When her mouth presses with mine, I grab her wrists and place them on my hips where she wanted them. Her body melts into mine. While we kiss under the steamy water, I reach behind her, remove the hair tie and unbraid her hair. Without breaking our kiss, I grab the vanilla scented shampoo we both love, pour some into my hand, and gently massage the gel into her hair. She sighs into our kiss and I pull her back to rinse her hair.

"May I?" She asks while lifting the shampoo bottle.

"Of course." I give her my back, and she massages my scalp as I had just done to her. I lather the loofah with body wash. Once my hair has been rinsed, I run the sponge over Blake's body, paying special attention to her breasts and inner thighs. Guiding her to sit on the shower bench, I drop to my knees and begin to work on orgasm number seven.

"Danika, may I play with your hair?" She knows that's my weakness and why permission is required. I'm already half-melted from her shampooing.

"After this orgasm. If you want to touch me so badly, show me how quickly you can come for me." She leans back against the shower wall and closes her eyes. Her breathing evens, and I can tell she's concentrating. She's focusing on my tongue gliding over her engorged clit, and my fingers as they slip inside her wanting pussy. When her next orgasm hits, her moans bounce off the shower walls, echoing her pleasure. As she comes down, her fingers thread into my hair. I can tell she notices I got a haircut, but she won't speak out of turn.

"Count, *Mijn Diamant*."

"Seven." Always so obedient.

"Give me another." Her grip on my hair tightens, making my

scalp tingle, and I'm losing my resolve. I allow her to adjust my head to the angle she needs to reach her next climax, while her fingers continue to brush through my hair. Once she's counted her eighth orgasm, I switch our positions, pushing her to kneel before me as I sit on the shower bench.

"Make me come while you make yourself come. I want to orgasm together."

The moment her hot tongue touches my pussy, I groan with relief. Causing Blake pleasure is my own personal edging. With her tongue on my pussy and her fingers teasing her clit, she reaches up with her free hand and rolls my nipple between her fingers. Our moans of pleasure echo against the bathroom walls.

"I'm close," I tell her, but she already knows. She knows my body as well as I know hers. She increases the speed of her tongue to match the speed of her fingers. Our bodies convulse together as we both come.

She stands, and I follow her. "Nine," she says as she pecks me on the nose, wraps her hands around my waist, and grabs handfuls of my ass cheeks.

"Blakey, what do I need to do to get you to quit your job, move in, and make you a kept woman?"

"Hmmm, that sounds so tempting, Annie. But you know I love the work I do."

"But I love *you,* and I want to see you more. That mean old attorney keeps you so late sometimes. It's interfering with our sex life, and you know you don't have to work. I'll always take care of you."

"I love you too, Lady Billionaire, and you already take care of me. I wear your permanent bracelet because I belong to you." I grab her wrist from around my back and kiss her knuckles. Then I toy with the bracelet that I also wear. Kissing the jewelry and continuing to kiss down her arm, I whisper in her ear.

"BlakeLynn Rogers, move in with me?"

"Annie." She says my name as a sigh. I tilt her chin up to look into her beautiful brown eyes.

"I'm serious, Blake. You can continue to work if you want to. Even though you don't have to, and have refused to work in my building despite my many offers. But I want you to come home to me every night. I want to wake up to you every morning. We've been together over two years, and although this started out as a mutual arrangement for us both, it's clearly developed into a real relationship, with playtime as a perk." She's staring intensely into my eyes, looking for a sign that I'm not serious, but she won't find it. We've joked and tiptoed around the idea for months, but this is the first time I've officially asked her.

"You really want to add my chaos to your calm?"

"I love you, and I love your chaos. If I have to have the housekeeper come daily to clean up after you, I'll do it." And I will. A bright smile stretches across her lips.

"Let's go to bed, roomie." She turns off the shower while giggling.

"We may need to reevaluate that nickname." Stepping out, I stand flush to her back, reach my arms around her and grab handfuls of her breasts. "We are many things, girlfriends, lovers, Domme and submissive, but 'roomies' isn't one of them, *Mijn Diamant.*"

8

Cole

S tanding in front of Annie's house, I ring the bell expecting to hear the lock disengage like every other day, and it does. What I didn't expect was for the door to open. Confused, I check the screen on my phone, confirming it's a weekday. It is, indeed, Friday, and I'm here at my usual time. I've been taking Candy for her walk every day for almost two weeks.

"Candy, *Bleiben*." I look at the open door, startled to see Annie standing there. She looks different every time I see her. Today she's wearing skinny jeans with holes and a basic white v-neck shirt half tucked in. Casual and sexy. I wonder how she would look in one of my T-shirts?

"Cole." Her tone is flat as if she wasn't expecting me.

"Hi, Annie. I didn't know you'd be home today. Did you still need me to walk Candy?"

"Yes, sorry. I took the day off. Please, come in. She still needs to go for her walk. I have a lot going on right now." Stepping inside, I see caterers setting up for a buffet, a bar area being stocked in the corner, and landscapers and pool cleaners outside.

"Having a party?" She peers at me with an agitated look in her eyes. Maybe I shouldn't be asking questions. The help should be seen and not heard. Got it.

"Yes. My partner just moved in with me, and we're having a little gathering."

"Congratulations. Will you still be needing me to walk Candy?"

"Yes. Of course. We both work full-time jobs." Her answer is clipped, and I get the hint that she's done chatting. "Candy, *Kommen*." Candy trots to us. Seeing the leash in Annie's hand, she sits without being told, and Annie hands the leash to me.

"Will you still be here when we return in an hour?"

"Yes, just ring the bell, and I'll retrieve her from you." She dismisses me by walking away. Our walk is uneventful, and when I return her home, Annie barely says "thank you" and closes the door quickly.

I have to come back to this area again tonight. Lucy's parents are going on a date and asked me to walk her twice today. I need to stop at the liquor store now because they'll be closed by the time I get back from walking Lucy.

Pulling into the parking lot, I'm greeted with a gorgeous ass in a slim-fitting gray skirt and heels sticking out of a trunk. A shopping cart full of wine is leaning against the little blue car, and it appears she's trying to get it all in the trunk.

"Ma'am, can I help you with this?" I accidentally startle her causing her to jump and hit her head on the inside frame of the trunk. "I'm so sorry. Are you okay?" Removing her head from the trunk, she braces her hand on her hairline above her right temple, where she must have hit it. Now that I can see her upper half, she's stunning. Her white blouse is a stark contrast to her dark brown hair. Her frame is petite but, holy hell, are her tits big. My instant attraction for this woman has me needing to adjust myself in my pants discreetly.

"I'm okay. I just wasn't expecting anyone to come up behind me." She rubs her head a little and then removes her hand, looking at her palm. There isn't any blood, so hopefully, she didn't hit it too hard.

"Sorry again. My offer to help load is still available. It would make me feel better after causing you to bump your head."

"Oh, sure. That would be great. Thanks." I help her pack the rest of the cases of wine in her car and make sure the trunk closes securely.

"That's a lot of wine. Having a party?" She smiles at me and nods. It lights up her face, and she looks impossibly more beautiful.

"Yeah. My girlfriend and I are having a little celebration tonight. This is the only liquor store that carries her favorite wine, so I thought I'd surprise her with it." She said her "girlfriend." Does she mean girlfriend, as in best friend or lover? That "G" word is so interchangeable now it's hard to tell.

"Sounds like fun. I hope you have someone to help you unload this when you get there."

"Oh yeah. I'll grab a caterer. Thanks again. You've been my white knight."

"Nah, just your friendly neighborhood dog walker. You're very welcome, and have a great evening." Must be a good night for a party.

9

Annie

*You are cordially invited to an evening of
Masks, Margaritas and Mexican.
Your Hosts: Danika & BlakeLynn
Time: 8 PM
Attire: Masks are mandatory, all other clothing optional.
Drinks & Dinner will be provided.
Swimming is naked only.
Condoms and Lube provided.
Feel free to bring your own toys.*

"Are you ready for me?" Blake wouldn't let me see her outfit before the party. She insisted she wanted to surprise me and has been in the bathroom for an hour getting ready.

"Of course I'm ready. I'm dying out here waiting." The bathroom door opens, and I'm glad I'm standing next to the bed. She's so breathtaking my legs give out, and I crash onto the mattress.

"You look like a Greek goddess." My eyes roam over every

inch of her. The dress is a red sheer material and revealing in all the right places. She spins for me, and I'm glad I was already sitting. The top is halter style and completely backless. The front is two vertical strips of fabric that barely cover her breasts, leaving an open line down past her navel. The bottom goes straight to the floor with a slit on the front of each thigh that opens past her hip bones.

"Do you like it?"

"I don't know if I want to forget about the party and worship at your feet for the rest of the night or drop to my knees and ask you to marry me?" Her breath hitches at my admittance.

"Annie, you can't say things like that to me. You'll get a girl's hopes up." She puts her hands on her hips and gives me the cutest little pout.

"Oh, *Mijn Diamant*, get your hopes up. It's coming, but it won't be tonight. You will belong to me mind, body, soul, and on paper." Her eyes well up, and a tear slips down her cheek. I stand, crossing the room to her, and wipe it away with my thumb. "Shhh, Little One. Please don't cry."

"These are happy tears. I love you so much, Danika Liv Poulsen. I can't wait until the day I'm yours." She throws her arms around my neck and pulls me tight, burying her face in my neck. I rub her back in small soothing strokes and hum in her ear.

"Hmmm, I love that song."

"I know you do. Now are you ready to greet our guests?" It's 8:30, but I always like to make a fashionably late entrance to my parties.

"Let me take a look at you first. I was too busy watching you ogle me that I didn't get a good look at your outfit. Stand back and let me see." I take a step away and do a slow spin. My top

38

layer is a black lace and mesh babydoll-style dress. It sits off the shoulders, held up by tiny spaghetti straps. Underneath I'm only wearing a black thong, and I've paired the outfit with black six-inch strappy heels. "Fuck Annie, do we have to go to this party? You look like a gift I want to unwrap."

"Yes, Darling. We need to get downstairs. We can unwrap each other later." She sticks out her bottom lip, and I nip at it. "You're adorable, but that pouty lip doesn't mean you're going to get your way. Besides, I have a surprise for you downstairs." She perks up. I know how much she loves a good surprise.

"I have a surprise for you, too. Let's put our masks on and go down." She has a bright smile on her face. I love when she's happy.

We secure our matching black lace masks on each other and make our grand entrance. My party planner is worth every expensive dollar that I pay her. The sight before me is exquisite. Black and red fabric drapes the walls, and the lights are low and seductive.

"Is he…" A server walks past us carrying a tray of margaritas, and Blake finally gets her first look at the staff attire. All the men are wearing silver bow ties and chastity belts. "Is that a-"

"Chastity belt," I answer for her. "Their dicks are locked up in cylindrical cages for the night."

"Who has the keys?" I give her a devilish smile.

"No? You do? Does that mean we get our choice of who to play with?"

"Unfortunately not, Darling. The staff is off-limits until the party is over. Afterward, though…" I can see the gleam of excitement in her eyes.

Every staff member who walked into this house tonight was paid handsomely, as well as the ironclad NDA that they've signed. The guests also sign an NDA, and phones are left with the doorman. Our home is a free environment with no worries of exposure.

"What are the women wearing? And is this my surprise? Because if it is, it's amazing."

"The women are wearing pasties and thongs. Only the door attendant is covered. Well, if you consider silver boy shorts and a bow tie covered. And no, this isn't your surprise. It's outside. Let's go see."

"Wait, first, let's stop at the bar. That's where your surprise is." She takes my hand and leads me to the bar in the corner of the living room. Several of the larger pieces of furniture have been moved off to the side, and beds have been arranged around the rooms encouraging open play. There are bowls scattered around with condoms and individual packets of lube. Off the living room, a silk dancer is twirling from the vaulted ceiling, and several feet away from her, a pole for dancing has been installed.

Every man here was personally selected from the local escort service, and their bodies were made for the covers of romance novels. The handsome man tending the bar has eight-pack abs, bright blue eyes, and a smile that could melt panties a mile away.

"Could we please have two glasses from the secret collection?" I give her a questioning look. "Trust me," she says and winks. The bartender nods and starts uncorking a bottle.

"You didn't?" I'm shocked at the bottle he's holding.

"I did. Louis Jadot 2019 Grand Cru Burgundy wine. Only the finest for my finest. I had the store purchase three cases for us, so you can decide to share or keep them all for yourself."

"*Mijn Diamant*, the price. It's too much. Why would you

do that?" This particular wine is $500 a bottle plus shipping because no one around here carries it. Only one liquor store knows where to order it from.

"Because I love you and wanted to do something special for you. And I have almost no bills since moving in here." Soon she will have no bills at all. I plan to buy her a new car and join our cell phone accounts. I kiss her tenderly on the forehead in thanks.

"I love you, too. Now my present seems silly compared to yours. This was so thoughtful."

Leaning into me, she whispers in my ear. "Unwrapping you from this barely there scrap of fabric that you're calling a dress is the only present I need from you." She lightly brushes the knuckles of her hand across one of my nipples, and I shutter.

"Let's go greet our guests, or we may end up leaving before the party truly starts." We take our wine and I instruct the bartender not to serve it to anyone else. Linking our hands, we make our rounds and say our hellos to the guests.

When we finally make it to the backyard, the sun has gone down, and the strings of light illuminating the backyard create the perfect ambiance for the activities going on. There are several people in the pool indulging in themselves as well as people scattered on the outside patio furniture in various stages of undress. I point in the direction of Blake's surprise, and her face lights up when her eyes finally land on the performance on the far side of the deck. I hired the Shibari teacher to come and give demonstrations during the party.

She spins towards me with all the joy of the world on her face. "Can we, please? Please, Danika. Pleeeeeeeease." Her hands are folded in prayer, and she's bouncing in front of me.

"Calm down, Little One. This is your surprise. I wouldn't have him here if we weren't going to participate. We'll need to lose some layers." She unties the halter on her dress before I could finish the word. "You're so fucking beautiful." I can't stop the words as they spill out of my mouth. She's standing completely naked in front of me, and if I weren't so excited to learn some new techniques myself, I'd indulge in her right out here in front of everyone.

"Just as beautiful as you." She reaches for the spaghetti straps on my top and slowly peels them off my shoulders. The fabric slips off my arms and down my body, until it pools at my feet.

"Good evening, ladies." The Shibari instructor greets us as we walk over to him. "Ms. Poulsen, Ms. Rogers, it's a pleasure to see you both again. I have something special prepared for you if you're ready."

"Thank you for coming, Beck. It's nice to see you again as well. We're ready whenever you'd like to start."

"Excellent. What I have to show you tonight is called the Rope Dress. Are we still wrapping Ms. Rogers?"

"Yes, oh yes. We're wrapping me." I look at her and laugh. Blake is a bit eager to be tied up. Beck hands me a large bundle of black rope.

"Wonderful, Ms. Rogers. Can you please confirm that the trauma shears are out and visible."

"Yes, Beck, I see the trauma shears," Blake confirms.

"Perfect. Now as always, Ms. Poulsen, I'll demonstrate on the mannequin, and you can follow me on your gorgeous model. Start by finding the bite of your rope, the middle. Bring the rope over her head and tie a knot with about a two-inch loop between her shoulder blades. Now, come to the front, and you want to create a series of five knots in the front. One just above the collarbone, one between her breasts, one at the center of the rib cage, and one at the belly button. The fifth knot you are going to tie to line up over her clitoris, it's called the happy knot." He winks and smiles.

Beck is a patient teacher and gives very detailed instructions while he demonstrates. He's sent me videos of techniques when I want to try something new with Blake. Once all of my front knots are in place, we move on to the next part.

"That looks wonderful. Next, pull the rope through Ms. Rogers' legs and up her back. Thread it through the loop we made in the beginning." He pauses to watch me before moving on. "Now comes the part that makes this binding beautiful. Separate the ropes and bring them individually around to the front of her body. Pass under her armpits, and we are going to thread the rope between the top two knots and loop it back." He shows me where to thread, and as we wrap both sides back around, a beautiful diamond appears across the top of her chest from the tension on the rope.

"*Mijn Diamant*." We continue wrapping the rope from front to back while creating friction knots down her spine. Once done, she has four diamond shapes running along her center. The rope is wrapped above and below her breasts, a set across her waist, and a set at her hips. We finish off the bondage by securing the rope at the base of her spine, and when she turns around, my heart skips a beat. She is a vision.

"You are breathtaking, Little One. How does it feel?" Her eyes heat up.

"It feels like I want to drop to my knees and worship you." Her chest is heaving from her arousal.

"Is that so?" I lean into her ear. "You don't have permission." She whimpers, and I smile to myself. "Let's show you off a bit first. Color and knot name?"

"Yellow and a Rope Dress."

"Mmm, good girl."

10

Cole

I probably should have started my walk with Lucy a little
earlier. I underestimated how long we were out, and it's
dark now. It's not bothering me, but Lucy is scared of
all of the noises that the night brings, and I've had to carry
her the last few blocks. Small dogs can be such scaredy cats.

We pause outside her door when fireworks start nearby.
Lucy trembles in my arms, so I bring her back inside and
make sure she's all tucked away and safe. Driving away from
her house, I see something running down the street. Initially I
thought it was a deer, but as it gets closer, I see it's a large dog.
A large familiar dog. I roll down my window and whistle.

"*Kommen.* Candy, *Kommen.*" I pull over and put my car
in park as she reaches my door. "What are you doing out
here, girl? Where's Annie?" I open my door and look around
expecting to see a frantic blonde woman in a white t-shirt
chasing after her again, but the street is silent.

"Hop in, Candy, I'll take you home." I open the door wider,
and she climbs in. Did someone leave the gate open at her
party? Bright bursts of red and blue flash in the air, and she

45

whines.

"Do the fireworks scare you? Did you jump the privacy fence?" I wonder if Annie even knows she's missing?

Pulling up to her house, I have to park down the road. Cars fill the driveway and line either side of the street for at least a block. She must throw a really good party to have all these people here.

Candy walks diligently at my side. Lucky for her, the fireworks seem to have stopped. We reach the front door, and it opens before I can ring the bell. A bulky man in tiny silver stripper shorts, more abs than I can count, a silver bow tie, and nothing else, looks me over.

"Good evening, sir. Please leave your phone on the table. You can remove any articles of clothing that you'd like and leave them on an empty shelf on the wall over there." He gestures to a row of shelves that were not here this afternoon when I walked Candy. In fact, if I didn't know any better, I'd assume I was in the wrong house. Nothing around me looks the same. "Sir? Are you coming in?"

"Oh, yes. Thank you. *Kommen*, Candy." She walks in and stops at my feet.

"I'm sorry, sir, we can't allow you to bring your pet in here."

"This is the homeowner's dog. Ms. Poulsen's dog, Candy."

"Ah, I see. Then proceed. If you've forgotten your mask, there are several extras on the table over there."

I walk over to the wall of shelves. Looking around, I see that most of the guests are naked or close to it. What kind of party is this? What the hell is on that guy's dick? Fuck. Is that a cage? Okay, I've safely delivered Candy back home. I should probably leave before anyone questions who I am and why I'm here.

"Drink, sir." I'm startled by a naked man with a cock cage and a bow tie carrying a tray of drinks.

"What are they?" The tray has several different colored drinks. Green, red, and purple, all adorned with fruit.

"These are margaritas, sir. If you'd like something different, there's a stocked bar in the corner of the living room." He points through the sea of naked people, and I see the bar. I also see a woman hanging from the ceiling and something that sends my heart soaring. A pole. It's been so long since I've seen a good one. My muscles twitch with anticipation.

"I think I'll head to the bar. Thank you." As instructed, I leave my phone on the table and strip down to my dark gray boxer briefs. While tying a mask around my face, I think to myself how happy I am that I worked out this afternoon between my walks. My muscles are still holding tension, and I look more ripped than usual.

On my walk to the bar, I pass several more men in cock cages carrying trays of drinks and what look like small tacos and various other Mexican-inspired appetizers. I've also seen a few women wearing thongs and pasties carrying similar trays.

"Good evening, sir. What can I make for you?" Another cock cage and bow tie. I guess that's the uniform attire for the help tonight.

"Gin and tonic, please. Bombay if you have it."

"Of course. Just a moment." I turn my back on him and take another look around the room. Spread across the counters are glass containers filled with condoms that the guests are clearly partaking in because several people and small groups are having sex all around me. Light music plays on the speakers, and everyone seems to be enjoying whatever activities they are indulging in.

I turn around as the bartender slides my drink towards me. I make an exaggerated patting motion on my hips. "Sorry, man, my wallet is back at the door."

"The bar is complimentary, and Ms. Poulsen takes care of all the tips. There's no need for money here. Or anywhere in the house."

"Okay, noted. Speaking of which, have you seen Ms. Poulsen?"

"Last I've seen, she and Ms. Rogers were outside during the fireworks.

"Okay, thank you." I turn to walk away but look back at him. "What's the deal with the pole?"

"The deal?" His brows knit together in confusion.

"Yeah. The girl is spinning around on the fabric from the ceiling. Is there someone assigned to the pole, too?"

"No, sir. The pole is for guest use."

"No shit. Okay, thank you." I reach out and slap the side of his shoulder in thanks. He grimaces at my action.

Slowly I make my way over to the pole. I run my finger along the cool, smooth length of the bar. I take a tentative spin around to test the stability and find it's a spinner, just the way I like it.

11

Blake

The Rope Dress was incredible. The feel of Annie's gentle fingers all over my body as she tied each knot, wrapped each strand around my body. Just thinking about it while we're watching our fireworks display has my heart pounding and my stomach fluttering.

The fireworks were a surprise for our guests. Annie loves them, and has them as often as possible at her parties. We try to be respectful of the neighbors. Despite Annie's bottomless wallet, she chooses to live in a small suburb, albeit the most prominent house in the entire town. Knowing house style isn't my thing, so I don't know if it's Modern, Colonial, or Victorian. What I do know is it's gorgeous, and she hired the best contractors and designers to bring her vision to life. It's painted dark blue, and all the exterior accents are wood. Despite the size of the house, she wanted to blend in with the neighborhood.

When the fireworks end, Annie unties me, and we redress. As much as we'll tease each other all night, we don't usually play at our parties, at least not until much later in the night.

We like to make sure all of our guests are enjoying themselves, and if we disappear, we may not come back. Watching everyone else pleasure each other is a form of foreplay and edging for us.

We're chatting with Beck about some other bindings, when we notice a small commotion coming from inside the house. No one from security has notified us of any problems, so this must be a good commotion. Someone or someones is putting on a show that's caught the attention of a crowd.

"Who do you think it is this time?" I nudge my arm against Annie's. She smiles at me.

"Hard to tell with this crowd. Let's go see." We walk hand in hand back into the house and work our way into the dining room area.

"Do you think the silk dancer is doing something fancy?"

"No." Annie motions toward the kitchen, where the dancer is talking with a server. "She must be on break. This is someone else."

We mingle through the crowd until we come to the center of the gathering group. Someone is on the pole. A male someone, and he's extremely skilled. His moves are defying gravity. His body is taut with rippling, tattooed muscles that flex at all the different positions. One moment he's making love to the pole upside down. The next, he's holding himself, suspended parallel to the ground, in the air by sheer arm strength.

"Close your mouth, Darling, before you drool," Annie playfully chides.

"Did you hire him? He's incredible." He just spun around the bar with his head below his feet in some crazy gymnastics move. He's doing front and back flips. I've never seen most of these moves. Annie and I took a beginner pole dancing class together a few times. It was fun and sexual, but we didn't learn anything like I'm seeing right now.

"Holy shit. How is he doing that?" He just did a 360° slow motion flip while pretending to climb stairs. His movement is fluid, and the package he's packing in those gray underwear looks impressive. "Who is he? Do you recognize him?"

"He looks familiar, but it's hard to place with the mask on and low lighting." Her brows are furrowed as she watches the Adonis in front of us put on a show for the crowd. But he isn't paying us any attention. It almost seems as if he's dancing for himself.

"I want him. Can we play with him tonight? If he can do that on a pole, imagine what he can do with our bodies?" Mister tall, dark, and muscled, can use my body as a pole any way he wants.

"Let's not interrupt him. We will speak when he's finished."

He somehow manages to last another five minutes. I can see his muscles spasming from the exertion. The bartender comes over and hands him a bottle of water which he hastily takes and empties. As we're about to go and speak with him, Candy trots up and sits at his feet. The man pets her on the head. They have an air of recognition between them.

"Are you sure you don't know him? Candy seems to." We walk closer, and Annie stops dead in her tracks.

"No fucking way. Holy shit." I've never seen her so rattled before.

"What's wrong, Baby?"

"It...it's..." Does she know the pole dancer?

12

Annie

How is he here? How did he get in? More importantly, where was he hiding that body, and how did he learn to dance like that?

Blake is staring at me with concern. I realize I have yet to speak out loud who he is.

"It's Candy's dog walker."

"Who? The pole dancer?" She sounds just as confused as I feel. I suddenly feel very exposed in my sheer dress. Taking a quick look at everyone, the crowd is primarily naked by this time in the night. All around me, people are enjoying their pleasure in whatever fashion or kink excites them. Beck has a couple tied together on the patio, and there are men wearing chastity belts everywhere. I am not shy about my preferences, but I diligently keep my private and personal lives separate.

"Yes. The pole dancer is Candy's dog walker. If you'll excuse me momentarily, I'll handle this." I walk towards Cole, and Blake links her arm in mine.

"Oh, no you don't. I'm not missing any of this action." I roll my eyes at her.

"Such a drama whore, Little One. Let's go."

Approaching Cole from behind, I tap him on the shoulder. He's conversing with a few of the other guests as he turns around, and his face goes white when he sees me. I place my pointer finger under his chin and lift, closing his mouth that's hanging open. He barely nods in response as his eyes widen, roaming my body.

"I feel like I should scold you, but technically I did tell you I scheduled my objectification for a Friday, and today happens to be Friday." Next to me, Blake giggles and kisses my bare shoulder. I kiss her forehead and turn back to Cole. "May we speak to you, please? Now." There's a pause, and his eyes flick between me and Blake.

"Y-yes," he barely croaks out. Then clears his throat and tries again. "Yes." We turn and head upstairs to my office. Unlocking the door with my security code, we walk in, and Cole's mouth drops once again.

"What is this place? Are you some evil mastermind, Annie? I've never seen a home setup like this before." I know what he's drooling over. Spanning half the length of my L-shaped desk are six large monitors and my custom ergonomic keyboard, designed specifically for me. I smirk at the look of awe on his face.

"Impressive, isn't it, pole boy? My Annie is a big deal." His gaze drifts from my computers to Blake's arms. She's standing behind me with her chin on my shoulder and her arms wrapped around me. Her fingers are roaming under my dress from the top of my thong upwards until she's grazing the bottom of my breasts and back again.

He meets my eyes, and he stutters again before lowering them back to Blake's as they roam my body.

"Um, y-yeah. Super impressive. What do you do, Annie?" I hate this question.

"I'm in software development." That piques his interest.

"I work for a software company helping test video game demos during development."

"Oh, Annie. Do you think our pole boy works for you two times over?" His eyes snap to mine, forehead scrunched in curiosity.

"What software company do you work for?" Blake and I both laugh.

"I don't work. I own. But I want to know how you got into this party and why you were dancing almost naked on my pole."

"Oh, that's easy. Candy." His response is smug as if it should answer all my questions.

"Candy, what?" I ask.

"I was in the neighborhood walking Lucy, the small dog that Candy really likes. As I was leaving her house, Candy came charging down the road toward my car. I think the fireworks spooked her."

"Candy got out?" Blake sounds just as shocked as I feel. "Did you know?"

"No, I had no idea. No one's been through the gate. I locked it for the evening."

"Maybe she jumped it," Cole suggests. *Jumped it.* That's always a possibility.

"Okay, that explains why you're here, but not any of the other questions." I'm more curious about the pole than I am about how he got into the party. Our doorman usually does an excellent job of keeping out the strays. Apparently, tonight was an exception.

"When I walked up to the door, the half-naked guy in the stripper shorts told me where to put my phone and clothes and to grab a mask. Then a guy in a cock cage offered me a drink, but I didn't want a margarita, so he directed me to another guy in a cock cage who served me at the bar."

Vibrating against my back, I can feel Blake trying to control her laughter. Her upper body is convulsing, and the dam finally breaks. Her laugh is boisterous and contagious, and I can't help but join her.

"Um, is everything okay? I'm not sure what's so funny?" Cole is looking at us like we've lost our minds, and I can imagine the sight we are. Two near-naked women laughing so hard tears are streaming down our faces.

"Tell...him." I manage to gasp out to Blake. She takes several cleansing inhales, trying to calm herself.

"You said..." The giggling is starting again, and she has to pause. "You. Said. Cock..." Full-on laughter. "Cock...cock..." Oh god. Now she sounds like a teenager laughing at the word Cock. Big inhale. Big exhale. "YouSaidCockCage." The words pour out of her mouth, all strung together.

"Okaaaaaay?" Cole doesn't understand our hysterics. I still can't manage to compose myself, but Blake does enough to speak.

"It's called a chastity belt, but a cock cage is *such* a better term for it."

"Ah, okay. Well, from a guy's standpoint, it's a cock in a cage. A cock cage."

Blake approaches Cole and places her finger on his Adam's apple. It bounces as he gulps. Slowly she moves her finger across his collarbone. When she reaches his pec, she swirls her finger around his nipple, and he growls.

"Oh, a feisty one." Continuing her exploration, she traces the ridges of each of his abs. They constrict at her feather-like touch. Her finger dips into his "V," and he growls again as she traces along the top of his waistband and then up the other side of his "V."

"Blake, Darling. You're teasing the poor boy."

"Mmm, but Annie, look at him. He looks delicious enough to eat. Can he be our dessert?"

"Little One, he's Candy's dog walker."

"I'll wear a collar, and he can walk me." I watch as Cole's pupils dilate. I gently grab Blake's wrist and remove it from his abdomen. Gripping her jaw, I turn her face to look directly at me.

"You wear NO ONE'S collar but mine, *Mijn Diamant*, and don't you forget that." I kiss the bracelet on her wrist for emphasis.

"Fuck me." My show of possession clearly entertains Cole, and his eyes aren't the only thing enjoying the show. A tent has appeared in his boxers. Blake smiles sweetly at him before devouring my mouth. I allow her to dominate the kiss for a moment before walking her backward to the wall and pinning her against it. A squeal escapes her at the pressure from my body. Releasing her lips, I bury my face in her neck, sucking and licking the sensitive skin. A throat clears behind me. I had forgotten he was here.

Turning my head toward him, I demand, "Where did you learn to dance like that?"

Startled by my question, he stares at me before blinking several times and answering.

"I taught myself. My mom got sick when Nicole was in college, and money was almost non-existent. I got a job at the local strip club and worked the ladies' nights." His lip tips up in the corner. "I know firsthand what it feels like to be objectified, Annie."

"So Nicole is your older sister. How old are you?" I know Nicole is in her mid 20's, and he doesn't look much younger than her.

"I'm 22. How old are you?"

"Oh, pole boy, tsk tsk. You never ask a lady her age."

"I'm 34. Blake is 29." I don't care if he knows our ages. I've accomplished a lot in my 34 years, and I'm proud of it. Cole reaches behind his head to untie his mask.

"If there isn't anything else, ladies, I'll head ho-"

"Wine Guy!" My attention whips to Blake.

"Trunk Girl?" What is going on here?

"Have you two met before?"

"Yes. No. I mean, kind of." Blake can't seem to give me a straight answer. She takes off her mask. "He helped me put the wine in my trunk earlier today."

13

Cole

It's safe to say, when I woke up this morning, I didn't expect to find myself in this type of situation. I'm standing in the middle of my boss's home office, sporting a raging boner, staring at her and her...girlfriend? Both of these women are gorgeous, and it's clear that Blake likes what she sees of me.

"Annie, is this your partner?" I didn't see anything wrong with the term earlier when she said it, but now that I know her partner is another female, I find it interesting. Is she ashamed?

"Aww, did you talk about me to our dog walker?" I wish they would stop calling me that.

"Cole, I'm sorry to hear about your childhood situation, but you should know I find you very talented." Was that a compliment?

"Baby, can we see what other talents he has?" Blake's personality is incredible. I'd love to get the chance to show her my other talents. I give her a seductive smile, and she winks at me. "Since she so rudely didn't answer your question, yes," she offers her hand to me, and I take it. "I'm Blake, Annie's *partner*. AKA her lover, her girlfriend, and on special nights her sub." Sub? That explains a lot of the dynamic I've seen in the short amount of time we've been in this room.

"Nice to officially meet you, Trunk Girl."

"Back at ya, Wine Guy." She releases my hand, but instead of dropping it, she trails her fingers up my arm. "Baby, are you sure we can't play with him?" She peers over her shoulder at Annie with a hopeful look.

"Darling, you know I don't mix business and pleasure. He's already crossed many of my boundaries just being here. That reminds me. There was a reason we came to my office." Blake has the sexiest pout on her bottom lip, and I want to bite it.

Annie clicks away at her computer while Blake and I stand and assess each other. I catch her staring at the tent in my boxer briefs. She licks her lips, causing my dick to visibly twitch, and she giggles and bites at her thumbnail.

"I don't think your Domme would appreciate you ogling my cock, sweetheart."

"Her Domme says she can look all she wants. But she knows the rules." Annie stands next to Blake and looks her directly in the eyes. "She has to ask permission before she can touch. Isn't that right, little girl?"

"Yes, Danika." Interesting. She seems to call her by her full name when they are in scene.

"And someone hasn't been given permission to touch but has been taking many liberties." *Fuck me sideways.* The temperature in the air has instantly changed. As if pulled by a string, Blake's back straightens, her hands clasped behind her back, sticking out her chest, and she dips her chin.

My cock just became a steel rod. I'm so hard there's now a

gap at the waist of my boxers, and I can see right into them.

Annie notices and peers over to look. "Impressive."

"I, um. Thank you." I gulp, and the room is so quiet I'm sure they heard it. I start to fidget, not knowing what to do with my hands. My instincts want me to mirror Blake's pose, but as they keep reminding me, I'm just the dog walker. I'm rescued from my awkwardness when she turns her attention back to Blake. Lifting her chin, she gives instructions.

"Go back downstairs to our guests, *Mijn Diamant.* We've been gone long enough. I have some paperwork for Cole to fill out." She kisses Blake's forehead, and she retreats out the door without a sound.

Annie turns back towards me, and her intense glare makes me want to shrink away. "Trust is key, Mr. McGrath. Are you a person I can trust?"

"Can you trust me? Of course."

"You see, you've crossed a line in the sand that very, very few people have ever done. I wasn't exaggerating when I said I keep my work and private life separate." She's pacing the room, only making her more intimidating. "As I'm sure you've witnessed tonight, this is my private life. You've put me in a very precarious situation, Mr. McGrath, and I'm not sure exactly how to proceed from here." I've never been so fucking turned on in my life, and from being chastised, no less.

"I'm so sorry, Danika." Fuck. I just used her full name, and the tilting of her lip lets me know she noticed it too. "I promise I won't ever speak of what I've seen her tonight. Please forgive me." Am I begging? What is this woman doing to me?

"Oh, I'm not worried about that." She slips a piece of paper on the desk next to me and takes a pen from a drawer. "I'll need you to look over and sign this NDA. Honestly, I'm not sure why I haven't had you sign one already since you've become Candy's permanent dog walker. I suppose since I was in need at the time and you're my hairdresser's brother, it slipped my mind. I'll rectify that and your background check tonight. "

Okay, an NDA. Reading over the paper, it seems pretty standard. Don't talk of anything or anyone I've seen here tonight. Reading over one particular line, I give Annie a questioning look.

"A million dollar minimum penalty for breach of the NDA?"

"You have to understand, Cole. Most of the people downstairs are in the 1 %. A million dollars isn't even a threat for them." Under my breath, I mumble, "What did I walk in on?" She hears me and replies, "More than you realize." I believe her.

"Now, how do you suppose we deal with the other situation?" I'm confused. I must be missing a piece of this puzzle.

"What other situation are you referring to?"

"BlakeLynn has seemed to have taken an interest in you. In the two years we've been together, I've never seen her so instantly infatuated with someone." *Oh.* I wasn't aware that Blake was a *situation.* I thought it was just harmless flirting.

"I swear I won't touch her. It's obvious she belongs to you and-" She puts her hand up to stop me from speaking any further.

"You misunderstand. She wants you. I want her to be happy. She gets what she wants, and I get what I want." *Shit, okay.* "We have a healthy sex life and have, on occasions, added a third person. Is that something you would be interested in?"

61

"I'm sorry. I'm a little confused about what you're asking me." She sighs and sits at her desk.

"Please sign the NDA." Okay? Is our conversation over? This is honestly the most bizarre situation I've ever been in. I put my signature on the line, and she signs under mine. "Thank you."

"Should I leave? I'm still unsure what's going on."

"To be honest, Cole, so am I. Let's table this conversation until after I can have a discussion with Blake." *Okay Cole. If there's ever a time to shoot your shot, this is it.*

"Can I say something before I go?"

"If you must." Fuck. This woman is so frustratingly sexy.

"I met you both individually and had an instant attraction. So, if whatever you're thinking involves sex, I'm in." She starts to laugh at me, and I give her a confused look.

"Cole, when we met, I was sweaty, disheveled, and practically naked. How was that attractive?"

I step up to her and lean over the chair. I let my lips brush the shell of her ear and whisper, "It's exactly how I imagine you'll look after I've fucked you." I give her earlobe a quick nip, stand, and head toward the door. "The party was amazing. I say keep the pole. I'll be here on Monday to take out Candy."

14

Blake

From across the room, I see Cole get dressed and leave. Several minutes pass, and Annie still hasn't come down.

Knocking on her office door, I listen for an acknowledgment before I walk in. I hear a faint "come in" and open the door.

Seeing her sitting in the chair, I asked, "Annie or Danika?"

"Annie, Darling. Come sit on my lap." She pats her legs, and I walk over and straddle her in the chair.

"Is everything okay, Baby? You've been up here by yourself. Come back and enjoy the rest of the party."

"I'm fine. Cole just shocked me a bit, and I'm not used to being caught off guard."

"I want to apologize-" Her hand covers my mouth.

"Shhh, Little One. There's nothing to be sorry for. I felt a bit out of sorts and needed to control the situation. Having Cole mixed between my two lives was startling."

"I am sorry, though. I was a little lust drunk and got carried away. You were right to correct me. I didn't have permission to touch. Those are the rules when we play with others. We have rules for a reason." Her hands are making lazy circles on my upper thighs, distracting me from my thoughts.

"We do, and I think we need to have a talk about Cole." I place my hands atop hers, stopping her movement.

"I hope you didn't fire him over me. Candy seems to love him." I'll feel terrible if I caused that.

"No, nothing like that," she reassured me. "I saw the way you were looking at him." I dip my chin, and she lifts it back up. "None of that." She knows me so well. I couldn't help flirting with Cole. It felt so natural I didn't even realize I was doing it until she called me out.

"*Mijn Diamant*, let's go to your favorite little coffee shop tomorrow and discuss things. The one with the s'mores dessert bar."

"Really? We can go to S'morgasm? Can we go shopping while we're there?" I give her a hopeful look. In the front, S'morgasm is a coffee shop with the cutest build-your-own s'mores table toppers, but in the back is a secret 18+ toy shop. We always spend too much when we go there, so Annie keeps me on a short leash. Figuratively speaking.

"Yes, Darling. I wouldn't tease you with a trip to S'morgasm and not let you shop. I'm not that cruel." She knows me so well.

"You really do love me, Annie." She kisses me several times on my neck.

"You know I do, and don't you ever forget it." I yip when she playfully pinches my nipple.

"Baby," I whine at her. "Don't start something you know we can't finish."

"Oh, are you giving orders now, little girl?" *Oh shit.* That was the wrong thing to say to her. She shifts in the chair and lifts me onto her desk. Moving the center piece of my dress aside, she pushes my legs apart and swirls her tongue around my clit. "Lay down. You'll give me two orgasms and make them quick. Our guests are waiting."

"Yes, Danika." Laying down on the desk, the wood is cool on my bare back, sending a shiver through my body. She wastes no time ramping me up for my first orgasm. Her skilled tongue knows the exact pressure and speed that I need. I want her finger inside me, but I know she'll save that for the second orgasm. She sucks my clit into her mouth and hums, and I almost buck off the desk with the intensity that crashes through me.

"Oh fuck, Annie. Fuck, fuck fuck." I'll pay later for that slip of her nickname, but fuck. My orgasm is still rolling through me when she finally slips two fingers inside. She continues to suck on my clit as she pumps in and out, brushing my G-spot every time. She wanted quick. My second orgasm is about to roll right over the end of my first, and I feel the intensity building inside me. The feeling that only means one thing, and I can't even breathe enough to warm her. I grab two handfuls of my own hair because my hands need something to do other than claw her desk. Her fingers stop pumping and directly massage me exactly where she knows I need it to squirt. She releases the suction on my clit just long enough to nip it, and my dam bursts.

"I love you. Oh god, I fucking love you! Fucking fuck, Danika." When she finally removes her head from my thighs, she offers me her hand to sit up. Her face is glistening, and I grab her cheeks and press a hard kiss to her lips.

"Fuck. I taste good on you."

"You were really pent up, weren't you, Little One? You squirted without much effort. What got you so worked up?" I've been salivating over her outfit all night, the Rope Dress, the pole dance, and the interaction here in the office. Maybe just Cole in general. I need to do some self-evaluation before we go to S'morgasm. She must see the expression on my face. "You're doing an awful lot of thinking for a simple question."

"I don't want to give the wrong answer."

"Honesty is never the wrong answer. It's just sometimes the hardest." She wraps her arms around me and softly kisses my lips. I love the way she tastes, and I'm sure I've made a mess of her desk. "It's okay to say it was Cole. He seems to have had the same effect on me, Darling."

15

Annie

The party was a success, as always. Blake and I finished the night learning some acrobatic skills from the silk dancer. We may need to look into taking some classes from her. The silks were fun and erotic.

After our run-in with Cole, neither of us felt like finding anyone to join us for the evening. It's interesting how he affected each of us differently. Blake was clearly intrigued by the new stranger. She never disobeys me. Seeing how she reacted to him, how she lost all of her inhibitions and wanted to take her own initiative, was a turn-on. We've never switched rolls in the bedroom. I'm always in charge. Even on the occasions she tries to be a brat, she always knows I'll take care of her, and her sass is purely to get a rise from me.

However, when Cole whispered in my ear and implied that he was going to fuck me, I had to bite the inside of my cheek to hide the instant physical reaction his words caused my body. I am a dominant woman in every aspect of my life. I have to be. The corporate world chews females up and spits them out. I have to assert my dominance before they even get a chance to think about it.

Warm petite hands wrap around my waist from behind as I stand at the blender. Blake nuzzles her nose into my neck and hums.

"I love the way you smell after you run." I'm standing in the kitchen making myself a smoothie after running 5 miles on the treadmill in my home gym. "Sorry, I missed it."

"Liar." I spin in her arms to face her and bury my hands in her hair. "You just like to see me in spandex while I'm running." She scrunches her nose and purses her lips because she knows I'm right. I kiss her adorable little nose. Her face relaxes, and her eyes close as I massage her scalp. She hums her appreciation and melts into me.

"*Mijn Diamont*, what time would you like to go to S'morgasm?"

"I have a few errands to run this morning. I have to meet with my landlord for the final walk-through of my apartment at 11. I have to stop at the dry cleaner and-"

"You know I have a service that does that for us? You only need to put your clothes in the dry cleaner bin." Some of the luxuries of having money are hard for Blake to adapt to. I have a house cleaner who comes twice a week, and the gardener and pool cleaner come weekly. On Sundays, Sarah, my home cook, comes and prepares meals for the entire week. She'll be by this afternoon and is excited to have Blake here now to expand my menu. That reminds me, "Don't forget that Sarah will be here around 4 to start the meal prep for the week. She'll need your list of likes and dislikes by noon so she can do her shopping. Her number is on the refrigerator, so you can text her all the information."

"I know, Baby. The dry cleaning is old. I got the reminder

text yesterday." A slight shiver runs up my spine as she glides her fingers across it. I'm wearing red biker shorts and a matching sports bra, leaving plenty of exposed skin for her to caress. "And I have my list ready for Sarah. I just need to send it to her. Are you sure she doesn't mind cooking for me, too? That's double the work."

Running my nose across the hollow of her neck, she smells like vanilla and the faintest hint of my fabric softener. I love knowing that when I crawled out of bed to work out this morning, she was sleeping soundly in *our* bed. She smells like *my* fabric softener because her clothes are being washed in *our* laundry room. My hands find the hem of her tiny sleep shorts and slip into them so I can feel her soft skin.

"Baby?"

"Little One?" She giggles as I nip at her ear.

"I asked you a question about Sarah." She did. I got so lost in the feeling of her that I forgot.

"Trust me, Sarah doesn't mind." I slide my hands lower into her shorts and gently massage her ass cheeks, thankful she doesn't wear panties to sleep. "I doubled her salary for double the work. She thanked me and said she could put her granddaughter through college with the increase."

"That sounds like a lot of money. I know you can afford it, but I don't mind cooking." Gliding my right hand across her hip, she gasps as my finger slides down to her pussy.

"Money is not anything you need to worry about anymore." Her eyes close, and her lips part as my fingers make quick circles over her clit. "If you want to cook for me, Little One, I'm happy to eat what you make." I slide a finger inside her and use the heel of my hand to continue to put pressure on her clit while pumping in and out. "Though my preference would be to eat you for dinner every night."

"Oh god, Annie." The walls of her pussy are already starting to tighten around my finger, and I know she's almost there.

"Are you going to come for me, Little One?" I bite her neck where it meets her shoulder, and when she mumbles a "fuck yes." I remove my hands from her shorts. "I'm going to jump in the shower. You can drink my smoothie if you'd like. It's peanut butter banana." I kiss her on the cheek and walk away with a big grin on my face.

Before I'm out of her sight, I look back over my shoulder at her. "Oh, and Blake, hands off. Next time, don't call me Annie when you know you shouldn't." I hear the shaky huff that escapes her lips. She'll hate me right now but love me for that edging later.

Walking into my bathroom, I turn on the shower then cross the hall to my office to check my email. When Cole mentioned he worked as a game tester, and Blake asked if he might work for me, I had to know. I emailed my lawyers about Cole's background check and the head of HR last night inquiring about his employment. I'm just waiting for a response, which hasn't come yet.

16

Blake

"Oh, and Blake," blah, blah, blah. "Hands off." Blah, blah, blah. "Don't call me, Annie…" Gah, it's so unfair. How did she turn the table on me? I walked into this kitchen, intending to seduce her. She really does smell amazing after a workout. It always reminds me of sex, and it turns me on. The spandex definitely helps.

I felt her get out of bed and quietly watched as she walked into her closet, *our* closet, naked, and came back out wearing my favorite color to see on her. Red looks so amazing on her pale skin. She walked into the bathroom, and when she came out, her hair was tied up in a high ponytail. Quietly, she came over to my side of the bed and kissed me on the cheek before she walked out of the room. The smell of cinnamon, her preferred toothpaste flavor, and vanilla, lingered in the air.

Now, I'm standing here alone in the kitchen, drinking her stupidly delicious smoothie, with weak knees dying to orgasm. But, no, I can't do that. She said "hands off" so I can't touch myself to take care of this ache. So frustrating. And seriously, what did she put in this smoothie? It's so good.

I want to join her in the shower, but knowing Annie as well as I do, she'll only continue the edging, and I'd rather not look like a frazzled ball of yarn when I meet with my landlord. Annie bought out the rest of my lease, so I didn't incur any penalties and hired someone to clean it after I moved everything out. Not to mention the movers she hired to pack everything for me.

A girl could get used to being spoiled. But that's the beautiful part about Annie. She makes everything feel so natural. She has endless money but lives in this modest house. She indulges in her luxuries but doesn't do anything over the top. Well, except for her parties. We love to throw big lavish parties like last night.

By the time I make it upstairs, Annie is already getting dressed, and I take a moment to admire her from the doorway. Her body is toned in all the right places. She loves her squats, and I love what those squats do for her firm round ass. Especially when she wears the cute boyshorts like she has on right now, matched with a sheer lacy bra, she's my own personal wet dream.

"Take a picture, *Mijn Diamant*. It lasts longer." *Oh, now that's an idea.*

"Can we?" She turns to me with a questioning look.

"Can we, what?"

"Take pictures. Can we do a boudoir photoshoot? Maybe you could tie me into the Rope Dress again, and we could get pictures of the process. It would be so sexy. Please, Baby." The images of what the pictures could look like are flashing through my head, and I love every one of them.

"Anything for you. I'd be more than happy to tie you up any

time." She starts to walk in my direction, and I quickly spin around her before she grabs me.

"I love you, but if you touch me right now after what you did to me downstairs, I might not survive."

"Little One, are you challenging me? Because you know you'll never win. I've made you pass out once already. I'd love to see if we could get you past 13." *Oh god. Proceed with caution, Blake. You're a mouse in the snake's pit right now.*

"I...I...need to shower." I beeline for the bathroom, but I'm not quick enough. She grabs my wrist and pulls me into her, lowering her lips to my ear.

"If you didn't have somewhere to be, I'd tie you to our bed, put on your favorite strap-on, and fuck you until you were unconscious. Now, go take your shower, and meet with your landlord. We can meet up after for a light lunch, and then we'll head over to S'morgasm. Does that sound good to you?" My chest is heaving and my nipples are hard from the image she just painted in my head. I can feel the wetness begin to pool in my panties. She's impatient with my delayed response, grabs a handful of hair at the back of my neck, and tugs until I'm staring at her. "Answer me, little girl, or I'll buy your entire old apartment building so you don't need to do your walk-through, and I'll keep you here all day and have my way with you."

"Yes, Danika. It sounds wonderful." She loosens her grip on my hair, and I miss the sting of the pain.

"Good girl," she purrs into my ear. "Now go get cleaned up, and I'll see you after your appointment." She removes her hand completely from my hair, and I stumble a little as I walk to the bathroom. She has me in a lust-drunk fog.

After my shower, I head into our large walk-in closet to find clothes. Annie's organizer is a miracle worker. You'd never know there is twice the amount of clothes now compared to two weeks ago. Everything is hung up on beautiful black velvet hangers. The drawers are filled with our lingerie organized by color. Our leggings are rolled into perfect spirals and laid out like a display at a department store. I may be three inches shorter than her, but our sizes are similar. I turn and stare at Annie's enormous shoe collection. Now this is my favorite size that we share. Running my fingers along a shelf with different styles of shoes, all in red, I try to remember when I've seen her wear each pair.

Turning to walk away, my finger catches on the heel of a red knee-high boot. When it hits the floor, a small black velvet box tumbles out. I freeze, staring at it. Very slowly, I bend down and pick it up, along with the boot. I feel like I'm holding a bomb; one wrong move, and it will explode.

Is this what I think it is? I can't be. Right? She told me yesterday she was planning to propose, but I assumed she meant in the future. What should I do? I really, really want to open it. She would know if I did. I can't. No. I have a better idea.

Hugging the boot to my chest I shuffle my feet to the table next to the bed. I pick up my phone and send Annie a text.

Me: I need you to come save me please <picture of ring box in my hand>
Annie: *Mijn Diamant*, don't move.

She doesn't have to worry. I have no plan of moving. To my luck, she is only in her office, and within a minute, she's standing in front of me.

"Little One, did you open it?" Will she believe that I didn't? Yes, I don't lie to her ever.

"No, but I wanted to, which is why I text you."

"How did you happen to find that? Were you snooping?" Her tone is accusatory, laced with humor.

My head is shaking vigorously while staring at it before I can even speak. "No, absolutely not. I was admiring your shoes. You know how much I love your collection. I accidentally knocked over the red knee-highs. It's so tall it just tipped over. I promis-" She places a finger over her lips.

"Shhh. It's okay. I appreciate your honesty." Her tone is soothing to my live wire nerves. "Do you have any idea what's in here?"

"I can guess. Not much comes in those small velvet boxes."

"Little One, can we put the boot down?" Her eyes widen in shock as she realizes she's still holding it.

"Oh my god, yes." I laugh as she drops the boot at our feet. "Would you like to see?"

"See what's in the box?" Why is she asking me that? Of course, I want to see, but I don't want to ruin anything.

"Um, you don't need to show me anything until you're ready." My heart feels like it's trying to gallop out of my chest. She carefully takes the box from my hand that's been outstretched the entire time between us.

"I think you'll be pleasantly surprised." Is she really going to open it? Is she just going to show me, or is she going to propose right now? I'm wearing a towel, and my hair is a mess. This isn't how I imagined a proposal would be. I run my hands through my hair in an attempt to look a little less like a drowned rat.

Torturously slowly, she opens the box, and I gasp.

"Oh my god, Annie. They're…oh my god." Nestled in the black velvet are two large yellow diamond stud earrings. "They're gorgeous." I release a shaky breath and graze my fingers across the stones.

"Were you expecting something else?" There's a hint of amusement in her tone, and I see the corner of her lip twitch up the slightest bit.

"Ummm. No. No. Not at all." Her head tilts in warning. I close my eyes and take a deep breath composing myself. *Answer honestly, Blake.* "Well, yes. I thought, maybe…"

"You thought it was your engagement ring?" *Your. Mine.* She takes each earring out of the box. "May I?" She gestures to her hand, silently asking if she could put them in my ears, and I nod. "I told you last night, *Mijn Diamant*, you will be mine." She clasps the earring back in my right ear and kisses my neck just below it. "I would never be so foolish as to leave something so important in a place you might accidentally find it." Securing the left earring, she kisses my neck again. I can feel the flush along my chest.

"What are these for?" I touch the cool stones and trace the square diamond in my ears.

"Do I need a reason?"

"No, of course not." Her hand comes up to caress my cheek. Her fingers trail over my jaw, and she grabs my earlobes admiring the earrings.

"When I was shopping for…other things, I saw them. They are my favorite color, as you know. I wanted to buy them for you so you would think about me whenever you looked in the mirror."

"Oh, Annie. I think about you all the time. You didn't have to buy me huge diamonds for that."

"Exactly. I didn't have to." Her hand moves back to my cheek, and she tilts her head to give me a gentle kiss. "I wanted to." *Kiss.* "So I did." *Kiss.* "Because I love you. And I can." Kissing my forehead, she places the empty box on the nightstand. "Now get dressed, or you'll be late.

"Thank you, Annie. I love you, and I love them."

17

Cole

Oh, man. The Bethel's weren't kidding when they said Mercy was a handful. I'm not sure how a 5 month old Golden Retriever can possibly have so much energy. Now I understand why they signed up for a two-hour session. I'm going to need a nap and a stiff drink after this.

We took a three-mile walk around the neighborhood, and I spent half of that trying to convince her she couldn't walk herself with the leash. Luckily Mrs. Bethel works from home and only needs me twice a week. I'm not sure I'd have the stamina for three mile walks five days a week along with my other clients. Today is a trial run, and if I take Mercy on, I won't need to be back until Wednesday.

I feed Mercy once we get back, and as we leave her apartment for her 30 minute walk after lunch, I hear a familiar giggle. The sound comes from around the corner, so I can't confirm whose voice it is until we get closer. I stop when I'm close enough to see them standing at the elevator.

"Thank you, Mr. Porter. It was a pleasure living here."

"It was wonderful having you, Ms. Rogers. You're going to be missed. Please thank Ms. Poulsen for getting the apartment cleaned. It looks wonderful."

"I will. Enjoy the rest of your day, and thank you again." Just then, the elevator dings, and Mercy yips at our lack of movement. Mr. Porter steps onto the elevator with a final goodbye.

"Cole?" *Crap.*

"Hey, Blake."

"What are you doing here?" Mercy takes that moment to run towards her. I'm caught off guard, and the leash slips from my fingers.

"No, Mercy." She reaches Blake and starts jumping at her legs. Her very long, toned legs under very short cut-offs. As Blake is trying to pet her, Mercy is trying to make a snack out of her fingers. "I'm so sorry. I think she was a raptor in another life. The world is her chew toy."

"That's okay." She takes a considerable risk by crouching down while vigorously petting Mercy's head. The little shit is loving it. She even rolls to her back and lets Blake rub her belly.

"Well, I'll be damned. Mercy has been a terror for me. An adorable terror but still one nonetheless." I have a fantastic view of Blake's ample cleavage from this angle. Her low-cut pink tank top shows off the round swells of her breasts. Last night I saw her practically naked, but I think I prefer this sweet innocent look better.

Seeing her down at my feet has my adrenaline pumping. When she looks at me through her dark lashes, my cock twitches as I imagine all the dirty things I want to do to her right here in this hallway.

79

"Down, boy."

"Mercy is a girl."

"I know. I was talking to you." I follow her line of sight and realize that my erection is very prominent and at her eye level. I turn around and adjust myself.

"Sorry," I mumble as I turn back toward her. She stands up and smiles at me.

"Don't be. I got a nice eyeful last night with fewer layers." Last night. When she tried to seduce me while I was in nothing but my boxers. How could I ever forget? "You never answered me about what you're doing here, but I have a feeling this pretty girl might have something to do with it." She bends over, petting Mercy again.

"She does. Mercy is a potential new client. Today is our trial run. She belongs to the Bethel's." I motion to the elevator where her landlord just left." I guess you're officially moved out?"

"Yep. Today was my walk-through, but Annie did everything to make sure the apartment looked better than when I moved in." She looks down at her hands and starts picking at her nails. "Listen, about last night. I wanted to apologize. I came on to you pretty strong."

"Blake, you have nothing to apologize for. I enjoyed being objectified by a gorgeous woman. Women." I flash my megawatt smile, and something changes in her eyes.

"Oh, Cole." She reaches up and grabs my chin, shocking me. I have almost a foot of height on her, but the attitude behind her words at the moment makes her seem ten feet tall. "Are you being a brat?" *Fuck. Me.* She tugs on my chin, and I lower my head to get closer to her level. In a husky whisper, she says, "I may be Danika's sub, but that doesn't mean I can't make you my good boy, Wine Guy." *Holy mother fucking fuck.*

She taps my pec twice in a dismissive gesture and walks away from me toward the stairs. I stand there stuttering to myself long after the door has shut. I don't move until the elevator doors open, and Mercy jumps up from the floor where she had apparently been lying.

18

Annie

"This is the weirdest part of being rich," Blake whispers to me in the back of the sedan.

"What is?" We're driving to S'morgasm after having sandwiches and salads at home.

"Being driven around. Having a driver." I see Josh's brown eyes flash to us from the rearview. I always have a driver to and from work since I don't particularly like driving in Chicago, and it allows me to still do work on the commute. Since we're going downtown now, I asked Josh to drive us.

"Josh has been driving me into the city longer than we've been together. And there's no need to whisper. Josh's NDA is as iron clad as it gets. He hears too many private work calls to not keep myself protected. Isn't that right, Josh?"

"You're correct, Ms. Poulsen." He looks at me in the rearview and nods.

"You're welcome to use him anytime, Little One. His on-call hours are 7 AM until 9 PM, but that doesn't mean he isn't available outside of those hours. I like to try and give him the courtesy of prior knowledge when it will be though."

"Anytime you need me, Ms. Rogers, just call."

"Thank you, Josh." He nods at her, and she turns in toward me and lowers her voice. "It's still weird, and he's a little handsome." I laugh and pull her hand into my lap.

"Get used to it, Darling." I look in the rearview again and see him watching our exchange with a slight smile. I don't generally look at the opposite sex, but I'm intrigued by her definition of handsome. Josh has robust features, a square jaw, brown eyes, and black hair. He wears a suit by my request and fills it out nicely. He's tall and broad in a muscular way, and I find his cologne a pleasant smell. I can understand her appeal.

10 minutes later, Josh drops us off at a corner near S'morgasm. We walk hand in hand until we reach the shop. Opening the door for Blake, we get hit with the sugary smell of chocolate and the bitter undertone of coffee. I almost run into her back as she stops short to take a big inhale.

"*Mijn Diamant,* I almost trampled you. Why did you stop?"

"I'm sorry. It always smells so amazing here." The inside of S'morgasm makes you feel like you've stepped inside a log cabin. All the tables, floors, and counters are made of a honey-colored wood. There is open shelving behind the register decorated with sacks of coffee tied at the top with twine. Around the room are several brown leather couches and chairs scattered for seating. Decorated along the walls are old window panes and rusted signs. All except for the one next to the register. The one you see when you look into the store's big front picture window. This particular wall is Blake's favorite.

The top half is a giant chalkboard skillfully decorated with their coffee menu and all the choices for your s'mores bar.

The bottom portion has several rows of hooks with coffee mugs hanging from them. Customers can purchase a mug, or bring in their own, then buy a coffee and hang it on one of the hooks. The coffee mug symbolizes that a cup has been purchased for someone else to drink. The mugs are specially marked and will be filled without question when brought to the register. All someone needs to do is look in the window, to see if any cups are hanging, and come in.

I've never told Blake, but after the first time we were here, I contacted the owner and put her in touch with my financial department. We set up an account specifically for S'morgasm. If the wall ever has less than 20 mugs, she charges it to the account, and my company covers it.

Chicago has extremely cold winters, and unfortunately, a large homeless population. This is one way I can give back to the community, without any over-the-top recognition.

When we reach the counter, we order our coffees, and a s'mores setup with Oreo's, chocolate chip cookies, and sprinkles. Blake also purchases 5 mugs for the wall. I happily swipe my card and take the tabletop card holder with our number on it. We find a seat on a sofa in a corner and make sure our number is visible on the coffee table in front of us.

I follow Blake's eyes and find them staring at the blue door at the back of the store that leads to their toy room. It's an impressive economic strategy, and you'd never know that the unsuspecting door leads to a den of sin.

"Focus, Little One. We have matters to discuss." Her eyes snap to mine, and she sits up straighter, pulling her knee up on the couch so she can face me.

"That reminds me. You'll never guess who I ran into this afternoon at my old apartment."

84

"Who?" I don't even have a guess.

"Cole. He was walking a new puppy for someone on my floor. She was the cutest little raptor."

"A what?" I never expected her to run into Cole, and what kind of dog was he walking this time?"

"I'm pretty sure it was a golden retriever. Her name was Mercy, and she was friendly, and fluffy, and full of nipping teeth."

"Ah, now I understand the raptor term. Did he have anything to say about last night?"

"We didn't do much talking, but it was definitely an interesting encounter?" Every encounter with Cole seems to be more interesting than the last.

"How so?"

"I accidentally turned him on when I was down on my knees, and I got an eyeful of his impressive bulge." I'm missing something.

"I need more information than that. Details, Darling." Why was she on her knees? I know what the sight of her on her knees does to me. I can only imagine what he was thinking to have that kind of reaction.

"I crouched down to pet the puppy. I told you how adorable she was. When we were talking, I didn't have a choice but to look up, and I'm sure he had an interesting view looking down." She looks down at her cleavage, which I've found my own eyes drifting to since lunch. I have a feeling I know exactly what made him hard. Blake is a wet dream with her ample chest and tiny waist. Oh, the shopping in the toy store is going to be expensive if I don't get myself under control.

Our s'mores bar is delivered, and we begin to make our little confections. In the middle is a small fondue pot filled with melted chocolate with a sterno under it to keep the chocolate warm. Around it, in individual compartments, are all the extras that we ordered, along with marshmallows and graham crackers. Blake likes to make s'moreos, as she calls them. She opens the cookie, dips her marshmallow in the chocolate, and then places it between the two halves. The treat is messy and adorable every time we are here. It's so much fun and I love it and her reaction to all the different flavors.

"Did Cole have anything else to say?" She pauses mid-dip of her marshmallow, and a sly smile forms on her face. "What did you do, Little One?" Her grin grows wider. She peeks at me through her thick black lashes. Yeah, I know precisely why Cole was turned on.

"I may have gone all baby Domme on him. I'm not sure what came over me." Her cheeks flush the sexiest shade of pink.

"Care to elaborate, or are you leaving me to use my imagination?"

"Umm…"

"Use your words, little girl. I'm intrigued to hear what you consider baby Domme actions." Her eyes fall to her lap.

"After he made a sassy comment…I may have told him that if he kept being a brat I'd…" I can tell she's unsure about her next words, and I never want her to worry about an adverse reaction from me. I caress her cheek until I feel her lean into the palm of my hand.

"Look at me." Her head slowly drifts up to meet my eyes. "What would you do if he kept being a brat?" She closes her eyes.

"I told him if he kept being a brat, I'd make him my good

boy." She snaps her eyes open to look for my reaction. The corner of my mouth slowly rises to a proud smile.

"Were you trying to top him from the bottom, Little One? He's very much an Alpha male. What was his reaction?"

"I didn't wait around to find out. I was so shocked at my boldness that I turned around and walked away. He didn't try to stop me, and I think I heard his sputtering, but I can't be sure."

"Interesting. And how did you feel after?" I can see in her eyes she's still unsure. She loved it and is afraid to tell me. "Is a role reversal something you'd like to try in our bedroom?"

"No!" Her statement has no hesitation. "I love what we have and would never want to change it. But I felt...powerful. I didn't even do anything but string a few words together, but damn, it felt good. Is that how you feel? Powerful?"

"Sometimes it's about power. Sometimes it's control. Sometimes it's a release. It all depends on where my head is."

This is an interesting turn of events. Blake radiates submissiveness. We met three years ago when her boss, Mr. Adelman, hired my company for a rather strange request. He was prosecuting someone who had used technology to hack into my competitor's gaming software and stole financial information. He wanted to know how it could be done, and I agreed to help him because I wanted to know how to make my software more secure.

Blake came with Mr. Adelman to most of the meetings. Ever the diligent secretary, always on his heels doing things before he could even ask. Occasionally I would catch her eyes lingering on me longer than needed. Crossing and uncrossing her legs when she knew I was looking.

It took me months of watching her before I made the

slightest move. She had come into my office late one evening, alone, to drop off paperwork. As she was walking out the door, I stopped her.

"BlakeLynn." She slowly turned around to face me.

"Yes, Ms. Poulsen?"

"You always do such a fine job. You're a good girl, BlakeLynn."

Something inside of her instinctually responded to those two words. I watched as her spine straightened, and she inhaled a sharp breath. Her eyes shot to the ground, and I could tell she wanted to respond but wasn't sure of the etiquette.

I took a business card from my desk, the one that few people get, with my personal cell number, and slowly walked up to her, stopping mere inches away. Lightly, I ran my finger up her forearm; she shivered, and her eyes closed. I leaned close to her ear. Our body heat mixed, and I heed her a warning.

"Did you like that, BlakeLynn? Being called a good girl. Before you answer, I want you to think about what that might entail. Take my card. Keep it safe. I only give my personal number to my inner circle." I slip the card into her hand and close her fist around it. "Enjoy the rest of your evening, Little One."

She called me two days later. S'morgasm was our first date. She had no idea that the back room here even existed. I've spent over two years opening her up to an entirely new world.

19

Blake

Talk about a whirlwind of a day. An edging, an almost engagement ring, a baby Domme moment with Cole, and now sitting here trying to figure all this out with Annie. Where was my head at when I said those things to him?

"Is it possible to like being submissive and also dominant? I've never thought of being anything or anyone else's but yours, Annie."

"Mijn Diamant, you can be anything you want to be. I'm happy to help you explore. Do you think you'd like to explore this with Cole since he seems to bring it out in you?" Cole. I guess he is the reason we are here.

"He brings out a lot in me. I don't know what it is about him." Maybe it's his striking eyes or his fucking delicious body. After seeing him dance on the pole, I can understand how he earned every ripple and ridge on him.

"We may have a slight problem down the road. I received an email earlier from the HR department. Cole McGrath does indeed work for a subsidiary of MAD Gaming Inc."

"Oh wow, I was only joking last night. What a crazy coincidence." Is this about to end before it starts?

"I don't believe in coincidences which is why I looked into it. He's obviously very far removed from me, but there is always the potential for complications."

"Oh." I feel slightly crushed. Maybe I'm more interested in Cole than I realize.

"Darling, it just means we must make sure we cross all of our T's and dot all of our I's. Company policy states that any fraternizing needs to be documented with HR. It's a simple form, but there's one stipulation. Having any type of romantic relationship with one of your superiors is frowned upon. As I'm the company's head, everyone is my subordinate."

"Okay, so what does that mean for us? This morning might have been a fleeting moment of insanity. I don't need to do anything about it." She stops me with a finger on my lips.

"Blake, please understand that, with me, you will want for nothing if it is within my power to give it to you. I will speak with HR and my lawyers and ensure we write up a new NDA, contract, or whatever I need to secure my safety. You, on the other hand, don't work for MAD Gaming Inc. I'm happy to watch as you dabble in your dominance. I just can't participate with him until I have all the details ironed out."

"But Annie, I would never do anything without you." My head is swimming, and I'm not sure if it's a sugar overload or the intensity of this conversation. I've mindlessly been eating all of the candy on my s'mores bar.

"You wouldn't be. You know my preference is not for men, and I know you've never been with another woman before me."

"Well, there were those few parties in college…"

"Don't be sassy, Little Girl." *Oh shit.* I'm tip-toeing on the line. "As I was saying. I can't join in with Cole. That doesn't mean I can't engage with you while you participate with him." Leaning close and lowering her voice, "I just have to watch where my hands roam."

"I think we could work that out, but how do we approach him about it? I can't imagine walking up to a man like Cole and just saying, 'Hi, wanna play sub to me while I experiment and decide if I like it?'" I left him speechless while I walked away. I have no idea what my words did to him. What if he says no? He's Candy's dog walker, and she loves him.

"Let me worry about that. If this is something you would like to pursue, I'll make it happen for you. Now, how about we go spend some money in the toy store?" Oh yay. Toys are my favorite.

"Yes, please."

"How about we pick out some accessories that *you* might like to use? You can look at things from the other side of the coin."

We clean up our table and get in line at the coffee counter. We have to show our IDs to get buzzed into the back room.

Once inside, we head straight for the back of the store. It's set up from the tamest toys and accessories in the front to the more risqué and skilled items in the back. I'd definitely like to pick out new rope for our boudoir photoshoot. Annie seems to have something in mind and heads toward the vibrators. Following her, I realized she wasn't looking at the vibrators, but the butt plugs. I wrap my arm around her waist, and she pulls me under her arm.

"We haven't used ours in a while. Do you think we need something new?"

"I think you might need something new for Cole. Maybe one that vibrates?" I like the way she's thinking. "I may not be involved, but I can at least enjoy what I watch."

We search the different options together until we come across a three-pack of black silicone rechargeable butt plugs. Each one is slightly bigger than the next. We have to be very careful with the toys we purchase because I have a latex allergy. Nothing kills the mood like a burning crotch, or in this case, a flaming asshole.

We finished our shopping trip with ropes in several colors, a new vibrator, the butt plugs, and nipple clamps. We've been playing more with pain stimulation, and I'm really enjoying it.

We exit out the back door. The store is one way in and one way out to keep it discreet. Annie must have texted Josh because he's waiting for us when we walk out.

20

Cole

I step out of my silver SUV and admire the shine after the much-needed car wash I just gave it. It doesn't look as out of place outside Annie's house now.

Ringing the doorbell, I wait to hear the lock click like usual, but instead, my phone rings, and I see Annie's name flashing on my screen. *Fuck. Am I fired after my little dance this weekend?*

"Hello." I hear the door lock disengage, and I breathe a sigh of relief.

"Yes, Cole. I need to speak to you in my office whenever you have time this week."

"Oh, um, I…Where is your office?" I have no idea where she works. There's a pause before she finally answers.

"It's the MAD Gaming Inc. building in downtown Chicago." *No fucking way.*

"Yeah, okay. I know that building." It's hard not to. It's one of the larger buildings. MAD Gaming Inc. owns and uses all of the floors. I have to meet there once a month for my game tester meetings.

"Good. When will you have some time to come by?" I

mentally go over my schedule. I have Lucy, then Titus in the mornings, Candy at noon, and I don't need to walk Mercy until Wednesday. Today and tomorrow are my soonest options.

"I can come today or tomorrow after Candy's walk."

"Excellent. Should I have my driver come by and pick you up in an hour?" Alright, I guess today it is.

"Thanks, but I can drive myself."

"I'll have him come by. If Josh picks you up, you won't have to worry about parking." Hmm, that's actually a convenient perk. Not that she's leaving me much of a choice.

"Okay. I didn't think about that. That's a good point. Yes, please send your driver."

"He's on his way. He'll be ready to bring you here whenever you're done with Candy."

The line goes silent, and I look at my phone. She hung up.

I step inside and put Candy on her leash to take her on her walk. As promised, when I return, there's a black sedan waiting for me. I make sure she's settled back inside before coming out and greeting the driver, who is now waiting for me outside of the car.

"Sir." He tips his head while opening the door.

"Hi, thanks. I'm Cole."

"Josh, Sir." He shuts the door and gets in the front seat. "The traffic is light this time of day. We should be there in 30 minutes." His tone is curt and formal.

"Um, thanks." I'm filled with nervous energy. My leg shakes involuntarily while I play on my phone, trying to entertain myself. Several times I catch Josh glancing at me through the rearview with suspicion in his eyes.

When we pull up to the building, he swipes a key card to

enter the private parking deck, pulls up to an elevator, and steps out of the car to open my door.

"Right this way." He gestures to the elevator, where he swipes the keycard again, and the doors open. He steps into the elevator, places a key into a lock on the button panel, and swipes his keycard one last time. Stepping out, he turns back to me. "Ms. Poulsen is waiting for you."

As the doors start to close, I realize he hasn't pushed any of the buttons to take me to a floor.

"Josh, what floor am I going to?"

"The top," he says as they finally close. The top? As in the top floor of the building? He couldn't really mean that could he? I look up and find a distorted reflection of myself looking back at me through the mirrored ceiling. That's how my nerves feel right now.

The top floor of any building always houses the highest executives. Blake joked about Annie having money, but if she's on the top floor, she has *money* money. It would explain the opulence behind the party they threw.

The doors open, and I'm blinded by the white marble floors. I take two tentative steps forward, barely making it out before the elevator doors close. I hear a pair of high heels echoing off the tall ceiling before I see who they belong to.

"Mr. McGrath?" A small sugary voice asks me. I must look like a complete idiot standing here, blinking my eyes rapidly, trying to regain my focus.

"Yes, sorry. I was blinded by the floors." She chuckles at my misfortune.

"It's alright. It happens to everyone the first time they come up here. You quickly learn the spots to look to avoid the glare. If you'll follow me, Ms. Poulsen is expecting you."

I follow the petite brunette down a long hall. She's wearing a dark green dress with a gold zipper down her back and matching gold heels that continue to click on the floor. I can't help but stare at her ass for a moment longer than appropriate. The base of the zipper swaying with her hips has mesmerized me, and I almost run into her when she stops abruptly in front of a floor-to-ceiling door. *Shit. I really need to get laid.*

She pushes the door open, and I walk into a modest-sized office. The floor in this room is covered with a large decorative area rug. The dark teal couches, matching chairs, and several bright green plants made the room feel cozy. Not at all what you would expect in an executive's office. Her desk is a solid piece of white marble held up by thin gold-colored legs, and behind the desk sits Annie, looking as stunning as ever.

She stands and gestures to the couch and I take a seat.

"Thank you for coming. Would you like a drink? I have the standard hard liquors, wine, and a few dark beer choices." I follow her gaze to a light wooden bar cart in the corner with a small refrigerator next to it.

"I'll take a beer since I'm not driving. Thanks." She walks over, takes two beers out, and opens the tops with a bottle opener attached to the side of the cart. As she walks back to me, I notice the distinct difference in the lack of clicking from her tall heels. Unlike the loud noise on the marble floors, the rug in this room allows her to walk around almost entirely silent.

Annie's outfit says she's ready to dominate a board room. Her black high-waisted skirt goes down to her knees and hugs every curve. Her burgundy silk blouse is tucked into her skirt, and a chunky black belt is around her waist. Her light pink heels make her legs look impossibly long, and I'm reminded just how much of those long legs I saw only a few nights ago.

"I'm sure you're wondering why I've asked you here." She hands me my beer and sits in a chair across from me.

"I am."

"Before we get into the 'why' of this situation, I need to disclose something to you."

"You mean besides the fact that you're clearly way more important than you present yourself to be? Fuck, Annie. You're in the head honcho's office."

"And therein lies part of our problem. The company you work for, PC Madness, is a subsidiary of MAD Gaming Inc. Officially, I'm your employer. My signature is at the bottom of your paychecks. All finances for my companies funnel through the same channels."

"Wow, it's a small world. But I'm still confused. Is that a problem because I walk Candy?" I'm not sure why it would matter that I work for a company that's probably a blip in her portfolio. She reaches for a folder on the table between us that I hadn't noticed. Inside are two pieces of paper and a pen.

"I'd like you to sign these before we proceed with this conversation." She must see the confusion on my face. Before I can ask any questions, she answers them. "This top one is a standard NDA for the employees at this level." She motions around the room. "I know you signed one when you started working for PC Madness, but this one is more detailed. The second piece of paper is an amendment to the NDA you signed at my house. I told you I keep my business and private life very separate. These amendments bridge the gap between my two lives and protect me as a whole."

I take a moment to read through the pages; they are exactly as she described them. Glancing up, I questioned her when I read the penalties. "No million-dollar clause?"

"You seemed unimpressed by that, so I had my lawyers change it to jail time for you specifically." Wow. She must really see me as some kind of a threat. What she's about to tell me must be major.

I sign the papers and place them back into the folder, closing it.

"Thank you. Now we may speak freely." Her tone went from stiff to almost *friendly.* I'm not sure I'd go as far as to use the "F" word, but it was a significant change.

"Blake and I had a discussion this weekend. It seems she may have said some interesting things to you when you ran into each other." I feel a slight heat on my cheeks when I think of her calling me a good boy. *Dammit.* I need to get that thought out of my head. If I show any weakness around Annie, I'll be eaten by the sharks. "Interesting. You liked it, didn't you?"

Well, I guess I failed at hiding that emotion. I look into Annie's eyes. She is a wonderfully professional businesswoman. Her face is neutral, not a hint of how she's feeling. She leans forward and places her beer bottle on the table between us. When she sits back in her seat, she crosses her legs. Although her skirt comes to her knees, the few inches that it creeps up her thighs when they cross has me shifting in my seat.

The slight tilt of her lip lets me know she sees my every twitch, and she's enjoying it. I need to take back some control of this conversation.

"I told you at the party that I find you both attractive.

98

Obviously my body would have a reaction to beautiful women."

"Cole, Blake and I are well aware we are attractive women. And you and I know that slight pink tint on your cheeks has nothing to do with our attractiveness and everything to do with her calling you a good boy."

Well, fuck me if she didn't just lay it all out on the table. I felt the flutter low in my stomach when she just said those words but not the same reaction when Blake did. When Blake called me a good boy, I wanted to drop to my knees at her feet. If she didn't turn and leave immediately after saying it, I very well might have.

"I can't get a good read on you, Cole. You perplex me. I'm watching this war play out on your face. I imagine it's a similar look to the one I had on mine when you dropped your bomb before leaving my home office." That makes two of us. I'm not quite sure how I'm feeling about any of this either. Is this why she called me here, to discuss my reaction to Blake's words?

"Annie, why am I here?" I can't decide if I'm embarrassed, turned on, or just plain confused. Probably all of the above.

"As I stated at the party, Blake wants you. It's also come to light that, technically, you and I can not fraternize. I'm already speaking with HR and my lawyers to change verbiage and protect us both."

"Protect us? What do we need protection from?"

"Each other." I'm utterly confused. Does she think I'm going to hurt her?

"Annie, I'm not a violent person. I'd neve-"

"Cole, I'm talking about entering into a sexual relationship." *Oh.* Why does this sound like a business transaction? She wants to "enter into" a sexual relationship? It sounds so romantic.

"Um, okay."

"Now, until we get things settled with the lawyers, there will be no direct contact between you and me in a sexual manner." What in the actual hell is going on here? "Since Blake has no affiliation to my company-"

"Y-your company? MAD Gaming Inc, is *your* company? When you said you signed my checks, I thought you meant you were the CFO or something."

"I am the CEO and the head of the board. Completely in charge for the last three years when my father handed it over to me." *Holy shit. She's LOADED, loaded.* How did I not know who she was? Her last name doesn't match.

"Your father is Markus Jorgenson? And you've been running the company for three years? How have you kept this out of the media?"

"Lots of NDAs and backroom contracts. It's easier for my father's name to still be the face of the company. I want to earn respect, not just have it given. The day will come when we need to make the announcement, but hopefully, that will be years in the future. Now, back to business."

"So this is a business transaction," I mumble to myself.

"No, Cole, This is a trial run."

"Jesus, Annie. Whatever happened to: Boy meets girl. Boy likes girl. Boy and girl have sex. The end. Why does this have to be transactional?" My tone is clipped. I'm still not sure exactly what she wants, but I'm starting to feel like a male escort.

"Please, Cole. There's no reason to get agitated." I scoff, and my anger starts to rise.

"I suggest you get to the point, Annie, because I'm still not sure what you're asking of me. I may have been a stripper on a pole, but I know my worth, and you're making me feel really cheap right now." She looks taken aback by my outburst. She uncrosses her legs and sits forward, rubbing her palms against her skirt before folding them in her lap.

"My apologies. You're right. I'm not presenting this well."

"That's the problem. You're trying to *present* something to me. Just spit it out. What do you want? What are you asking me?" She's staring at me with squinted eyes. I don't think she's used to someone talking to her like this. She may want to *earn* respect, but her position alone demands it. She stands up and walks over to the front of her desk, giving me her back. Closing her eyes, she leans over the desk, palms flat on top. I see her lips barely moving. I think she may be counting to herself.

Quietly placing my beer bottle on the coffee table, I stand and walk toward the door. It doesn't seem like I'm going to get any answers today. I'm about to place my hand on the knob when she calls my name and walks towards me. I stop to wait for her to approach. She places her hand on my upper right arm, and her touch burns its imprint into me.

"I'm sorry, Cole. I'm doing a terrible job at expressing myself right now." I don't understand why, of all things, this conversation has eluded her twice. I make a split-second decision and hope it works.

I grab her wrist that's on my arm and push her back the two steps to the wall next to the door. As her back hits the wall, so does her arm above her head, and I wrap my other hand around her neck. I look directly into her eyes for a reaction. Her pupils dilate, and I can feel her hard nipples through her silk blouse.

"Danika." My throat is thick with desire. "Tell me. What. You. Want. Use your words." Her eyes dart back and forth between mine, and I realize I may be missing something vital for her. "You have permission to speak, Kitten."

Her mouth opens and closes several times before she shuts her eyes and inhales a ragged breath. I gently squeeze her neck, and her eyes snap open, looking directly into mine.

"Cole." My name is said as a whisper from her lips, and I feel her swallow.

"Don't disobey me, Danika. I said, tell me what you want." I take a small step forward, eliminating any space left between our bodies, and she whimpers. Fucking whimpers. The sound goes directly to my cock, now straining against my pants. I squeeze her neck tighter, and her body melts into mine as she gives me her submission.

"I want...to watch."

"You want to watch Blake and me?"

"Yes," she breathes out. Her pulse is racing under my palm. Can she feel how hard my cock is right now?

"Do you want to join?"

"I can't." Her answer is quick and firm. I shift my hand, forcing her jaw up so she has to look at me.

"I didn't ask you if you could. I asked you if you wanted to." There's a war waging in her eyes.

"I...I..." Her eyes close again. "I can't." Leaning down, I place a long kiss on her forehead. Releasing her wrist, I trail the back of my knuckles down her arm, leaving goosebumps.

"Okay, Kitten. I'm going to let this one slide because I know and understand your reasoning. You can't give me a truthful answer. *Yet*, correct?"

"Correct, Cole." Her chest is heaving with the matched desire I'm feeling. I gently squeeze her neck, and her eyes snap open, looking directly into mine.

"When my hand is wrapped around your neck or commanding your body, you call me Coleman. Understood?"

"Understood..." She looks confidently into my eyes. "Coleman."

"Good girl." I brush my knuckles against her cheek before making my exit.

21

Annie

I stood frozen on the wall until my heart and breathing were under control. I've never felt anything like that before. So, out of control yet completely calm at the same time.

Me: *Mijn Diamant*, will you be home for dinner tonight?
  Blake: I should be home between 6:30 & 7, depending on the train.

The train. Although Blake and I both work in downtown Chicago, we ride separately most days. Despite all my efforts to convince her to commute together, she enjoys riding the train. On the mornings I'm able to distract her long enough to miss it, we ride together. She's caught on to my devious ways though, and it doesn't happen as often.

Me: How about Josh picks us both up, and we can have dinner out tonight?

The three bouncing dots appear and disappear multiple times. Several minutes later, my cell phone rings, and it's Blake calling.

"Darling, It's always a pleasure to hear from you during the day."

"Annie, is everything alright?" She sounds concerned.

"Yes, why wouldn't it be?" Did I give her any reason to worry? We only exchanged a few texts.

"You asked me to dinner." Do I not feed her enough? I don't understand.

"Yes, Darling. Is that strange? We often go out to dinner together."

"It's strange that you *asked.* You gave me an option to say no. Did something happen? Do you have some kind of bad news for me?" She's panicking. I suppose she's correct. I don't usually ask her to do things. I tell her what we are doing. It's how our relationship has always been, inside and outside the bedroom. She always knows she has the option to say no, but she also knows I'd never do anything to harm her mentally or physically.

"Little One, take a breath. There's no bad news. Everything is fine. I met with Cole today, and as all our meetings seem to go, he rattled me a bit. No, if I'm being honest, he rattled me a lot. "

"Oh. Is that why you want to go to dinner? To discuss your meeting? Annie, you have to give me something to work with."

"I want to discuss…you. I want to know how you feel when I dominate you in the bedroom." I'm not entirely sure I know how I'm feeling, but hopefully, she can shed some light on it.

"Did something happen? Did something happen with

Cole?"

"*Mijn Diamant*, please don't worry. Nothing happened per se. I'm fine. I want to take you to dinner and talk. Would you like to pick where we go?"

"I think you might have a fever, Baby. It's the fever talking, isn't it?" She's laughing at me now.

"Are you trying to be a brat, little girl?"

"No, Danika."

"Good girl. Now, Josh will pick you up from work. Just text him what time you need him. Okay, Blakey?"

"Can I still choose where we eat?" I smile and tell her yes, and I love her, and we end the call. I love that we have an unofficial stop scene-word. Calling her Blakey let her know she was free to be herself.

At 5:15, my secretary informs me Josh is here to pick me up, and I head down to my car. By 5:30, Blake is sliding into the back seat next to me.

"Hey, Baby. I've been thinking about you all day. Especially after your call." She gives me a quick kiss and buckles her seat belt.

"I'm always thinking about you. Where are we going for dinner?"

"Josh knows. And just remember, you told me I could choose, so you can't be mad." *Oh no.* Besides S'morgasm, there's only one other place in town that she really enjoys eating at. I look at Josh in the rearview, and see the apology in his eyes.

"Little One, must we?" I rub my temples with my thumb and forefinger. My day has been strange enough. I'm not sure I want to be degraded.

"I promise I won't tell them it's my birthday this time." I

groan at the memory. The last time we went to Debevics, she told our waiter, Scout, a guy wearing a green button-down shirt and a sash with badges, that it was her birthday. He brought a cupcake with a lit candle, and as the entire restaurant sang the happy birthday song, he yelled, "No one cares" at the top of his lungs. Then, before he handed her the cupcake, he blew out the candle and told her next year to "go somewhere else." She sat there with the biggest smile on her face the entire time.

Josh pulls up and quickly jumps out of the car to open our door. Stepping out, I stare up at the glass windows and see the debauchery going on inside. The restaurant has a 50's style design. In the middle is a raised catwalk the server/actors use to cause nonsense, with booths on either side. Blake always insists we wait for one of those booths because "you get the best show." I'll admit, the food is good, and I'll suffer through the evening because Blake loves it, but it's not my favorite place.

As we walk in, we're greeted, and I use that term loosely, by a nerdy-looking guy with a name tag that reads "Buzzy." He's wearing the classic suspenders, bowtie, and glasses with tape in the middle.

"Welcome to Debevics. We're not excited to see you," he says in a bored tone.

"Hi, can we sit in a middle booth?" Blake is practically bouncing.

"Do I look like I care where you sit? Find somewhere and hope a server greets you," Buzzy says. Blake grabs my hand and practically skips to a table. Several minutes after we sit, "Ziggy" comes over and greets us. He's dressed as a hippy with a colorful t-shirt under a brown suede vest with fringe and a headband across his forehead.

"Oh, joy. Another table here to waste my time. Are you ready to order? Because I need a nap break." He pulls out a notebook, ready to take our order. We know to have our selections ready, or they give you more grief. Blake orders first.

"I'll have a green mountain soda and Ed's Mom's Meatloaf." The hippy turns to me.

"I'd like a water and a chicken pot pie, and could we also order the spinach mozzarella sticks, please."

"Do I look like your mother? A 'please' does you no good here, sissy. Anyway, blah, blah. Yeah, fine, great. I'll be back eventually." He waves his hand in the air dismissively and makes his exit as Blake grabs my hands across the table.

"Baby, talk to me, please. What happened with Cole?" I'm honestly surprised she didn't bombard me with questions the minute she got into the car. I sigh, trying to figure out how to put into words what I felt in the office today.

"Let's start with you. Why do you like being my submissive? What do you get out of it?" Blake and I became this natural pairing after the incident in my office. *Huh, interesting.* I guess my office is a space for awakenings.

Before she can answer me, all the servers get up on the catwalk, the music volume increases, and they all sing and dance loudly to the *YMCA.* Blake is giddy, dancing in her seat, and I can't help but stare at this beautiful creature who allows me to call her mine. I need to figure out the perfect way to propose. She deserves the best.

When the song ends, she looks back at me with a contemplative look on her face.

"I never knew I was or even considered that I'd want to be a sub. I was never into women before you. Watching you work for all those months and the glances you would sneak made me curious. I knew I wanted more the day you called me a good girl and how my body instantly reacted to you. I wanted to explore that reaction." She removes her hands from mine and drops them onto her lap, along with her eyes.

"Mijn Diamant, what's wrong?" Her mood changed so quickly. She almost looks guilty.

"It's the same way I feel when I'm around Cole. I can sense something different, and I want more." She looks up at me with an expression of apology. "That makes me a terrible person, doesn't it? I shouldn't have those kinds of feelings for anyone but you, Annie."

It's my turn to look guilty. Is that what I'm feeling? Wonder and want? I don't think I've been attracted to the opposite sex since puberty, when I thought I was supposed to be. I knew from the start my interest in Blake was more than my want to have a submissive. She's the only person I've thought about for almost three years. What is it about Cole that has both of us twisted in different directions?

"Blake, I admit I'm feeling the same way about him."

"You think he could be another submissive for you?" I chuckle as the memory of his hand around my neck flashes through my mind.

"Not quite, Little One." Is this really how I'm feeling? It goes against everything I know about myself and my life.

Our hippy server arrives with our drinks and appetizer and drops them off without saying a word. Already knowing the outcome but wanting the laugh anyway, Blake stops him.

"Could we please have some napkins?" He stops and spins, reaches into his apron, grabs a handful of napkins, and throws them in our general direction. The napkins fall around us, and Blake giggles as they land on the floor, our table, and our laps.

"Tell me what you feel, Annie." I rub my hand back and forth across my forehead, trying to figure out the appropriate words.

"Blake, something *happened* today in my office." I lightly touch my neck at the memory of his hand wrapped around it. "He grabbed my neck and pushed me against the wall. He-he spoke to me in a dominant manner and called me a good girl after permitting me to speak. It was all the things that I do and love doing to you. And…" I pause because I'm about to say the words out loud, and that will make them real.

"And what, Baby?" I look into her eyes, gauging her reaction. There is nothing but curiosity on her face.

"And I liked it. I liked the adrenaline rush it gave me. I liked the feel of his hands on me possessively. When he left, I felt more relaxed than I have in a while." I close my eyes, and Blake reaches out and takes my hands. "You are my forever, *Mijn Diamant.*" I open my eyes and look deeply into hers. "I've never wanted anything more than I want you. I love only you. This is a strange experience for me."

"Annie, I love you, too. And I feel the same way. What do you think it is about Cole?" I shake my head because I have no answer, and neither does she. We eat our mozzarella sticks and our food arrives shortly after. We watched the servers sing and dance to a rendition of *Footloose* on the catwalk, and Blake insisted we order two of their famous desserts, the world's smallest sundae. It's about three bites of dessert, and then it's gone.

When we asked our server for our check, he took it out of

his book, crumpled it up, threw it on our table, and said, "Pay me and get out." I'll never know why Blake loves this place so much, but I'll continue to suffer through as many dinners as she wants to keep seeing that smile on her face.

"Little girl," I whisper into her ear as we walk out the doors. "You owe me when we get home for enduring this torture for you. I think it might be time to test out our new nipple clamps." She peeks over her shoulder at me and smiles the sweetest smile.

22

Blake

Annie and I are both intrigued about Cole and what he does to us. We've had men join us in the bedroom on occasion, but this is obviously different for her, and it's definitely different for me.

Picturing the image of her and Cole in the position she described, I know exactly what she was feeling. It's how I feel when she takes control of my body. It's freeing and relieving.

"Baby?"

"Yes, Little One?" She turns to look at me, and I lean in closer and lower my voice so Josh doesn't hear our conversation.

"Do you remember the other night, when you threatened to tie me to the bed and fuck me until I was unconscious?" She replies with an "mhmm" and a smirk as she holds my hand and draws circles on my palm with her thumb. "Maybe we can forgo the unconscious part, and you can just fuck me with my favorite strap-on? Or yours."

"I should chastise you for trying to make demands for the bedroom, but it's already late and we have to work tomorrow.

Since I want to try out the nipple clamps, we will use your favorite strap-on. That seems like a fair compromise. Do you agree?"

"Yes, Danika. It sounds wonderful."

Josh pulls in front of the house and opens the door to let us out. We walk upstairs together, and Annie kisses my cheek before turning towards her office. She'll give me a few minutes to prepare myself for her before coming in.

The brushing and braiding of my hair is my favorite part of our scenes. Of course, I love the orgasms, but the attention and care she goes through before we even get started is what made me fall in love with her.

Once my hair is braided and tied, she tells me to sit on the bed. She leaves me alone as she walks into the closet to grab the accessories we need. We keep our daily use toys in the nightstand, but our special toys are in the walk-in.

When she walks out, it's the most beautiful sight. She's wearing a leather harness around her waist with a flesh-colored dildo attached to it. This one curves slightly up at the tip and has veins along the shaft. It's about 7.5 inches long and has testicles attached. She looks so fucking sexy. I think it might be because this is the most realistic looking one we have, which makes me like it most.

"Move to the middle of the bed." I slide backward until I'm settled. She ties my hands to the headboard with the same silk we always use, then comes down and straddles my hips. She runs her finger ever so gently from my wrists, down my arm, across my collarbone, and lightly flicks my nipples when she reaches them. My back arches at the sensation.

"I want you to use your colors and check in with me. You have permission to voice all of your colors. Don't ever forget that. Do you understand?"

"Yes, Danika." She takes the nipple clamps we bought out of a velvet bag. We decided on a tweezer style since we're just learning. They look like the shape of a "V" with a small tension bar. You raise the little bar to tighten the clamps.

Leaning forward, she takes my right nipple into her mouth. Her hot tongue swirls and flicks until it's hard. She sits up, grabs a clamp, and places my nipple inside the "V." Slowly, she raises the bar until my breath hitches.

"Check in, Darling." I assess my body for a moment before responding.

"Yellow."

"Good girl. I'm going to move it a little more, and you let me know if that yellow changes to orange. Your nipple looks glorious being squeezed by the metal." She moves the bar a small amount, and the pain bites at me. My breath deepens as I try to calm myself from the pain. "Can you take just a little bit more, or should we stop here?" The only reason she's asking me if we should stop is because it's our first time trying out nipple clamps. Once she determines the level of pain I can handle, she won't ask again.

"Y-Yellow." The pain is already starting to subside, and I want to feel more of it. She slides it a tiny more upwards, and it's the perfect pressure. My clit starts throbbing with need.

"Orange, Darling?" I nod in response and watch her make a mental note of the position of the sliding bar.

Looking at her accomplishment and being satisfied, she switches nipples and begins the process again until my body is sparking like fireworks with sensation and need. I'm whimpering, needing to be filled, touched. She rolls my body over and my knees are pushed under me, ass in the air.

114

Reaching into the nightstand she pulls out a small bottle of lube. It's one of the flavored ones. Wildberry, if I can guess by the color. She pushes on my hips a little more until I prop up on my elbows so there isn't as much pressure on the clamps. She comes to kneel by my head and opens the top with a click, pours lube straight on the strap-on, and rubs it all over.

"Lick." Opening my mouth, I stick out my tongue, and she slides the dildo up and down. I was right. It's wildberry-flavored lube. Also one of my favorites. "Are you ready for me? I see the way you've been rubbing your thighs together." She sits back so my mouth is free, and I can answer.

"Yes, Danika." She rewards me with a smile, and she resituates herself behind me. The lube cap clicks again and I feel her slick fingers sliding around my entrance, then circling my clit and back again.

"You're already so wet we may not have even needed the lube. Did those nipple clamps excite you that much, little girl? We'll have to use them more often." Not a question for me. No response needed.

Her left hand grabs my hip while her right grabs the dildo, and she teases my entrance with the tip. I'm so ready to be filled. To feel the flesh of her thighs slapping against mine. Finally, she pushes in a few inches. I feel some release from the anxiety of the anticipation. Her right hand finds my hip, and she takes long thrusts until I feel her flesh on my flesh. When she is fully inside me with the strap-on, she pumps in and out of me for several minutes. We enjoy the feeling of being connected before she pulls out the little pink remote from a small pocket along the belt harness. This particular dildo also vibrates.

She clicks the button twice on the remote, and a low steady

vibration starts inside me. It only takes a few minutes before the reason this is my favorite presents itself. Not only am I on the cusp of my first orgasm, but so is she. The vibrating does as much for me as it does for her. Using this strap-on is the only time she lets herself go when we scene. Her thrusting becomes less fluid, and I can tell she's trying to hold her release back. I, on the other hand, can't, and I tip over the edge, bucking my hips back into hers. She clicks the button on the remote to prolong my orgasm, but she can no longer hold hers back, and she starts panting.

"Fuck, BlakeLynn. You're so fucking perfect. You're all mine. *Mijn Diamant.*" She starts to come with me. Her moans are music to my ears, and a second orgasm rips through me. When she can't take it anymore, she clicks the vibrator off and slows her pace to a lazy in-and-out pump so we can both catch our breath.

Her hand strokes my back, and I mewl at her touch. "Such a good girl. Was that two orgasms?"

"Yes. Yes, Danika." She rubs both of my ass cheeks in adoration.

"Your pussy looks so beautiful stretched around my cock, Little One." She removes herself from inside me, and I whimper, instantly hate the empty feeling. "Shh, calm down. I want to flip you over and remove the clamps. I'm sure your nipples are sore from the friction."

I hadn't even realized until she mentioned it, but she's right. They're throbbing in time with my heartbeat. She slowly turns me over and unties my wrists. She takes a moment to admire the clamps on my nipples before giving me instructions.

"I'm going to remove them quickly, one at a time. I'd like

your help this first time so we can get it done efficiently. You may not feel pain right now, but as soon as the clamp is removed, you'll feel a sharp sensation. It shouldn't last more than a minute, but you'll be hypersensitive for at least 30 minutes after. Now, take your thumb and your forefinger and pull your nipple taught. I'm going to hold the bottom of the clamp for stability and then pull the slider bar down. I'll count down from three."

I do as instructed, and when she counts to one, and the nipple clamp is removed, I'm flooded with the strangest feeling of pain and euphoria. I inhale a sharp breath and exhale a moan. She brushes light fingers around my breast but never touches my nipple. I don't think I could take it if she did.

We repeat the process on the other side, but this time, when it's removed, she pushes my knees up and buries herself into my pussy with the strap-on. Her finger rapidly flicks my clit while she pumps into me, and I'm so overly sensitive that I instantly orgasm. The type that takes your breath away. My body is convulsing under her, and the only sound coming from my mouth is squealing noises. It's so fucking intense. Then I feel the vibrator turn on inside me, and I scream. A scream that, at first, I'm not sure where it's coming from until I feel a hand caressing my cheek.

"Shh, Blakey. You're alright, Darling. I've got you." I reach my hand up to hers and realize it's wet. I'm crying, and I didn't even know. She leans over and kisses me tenderly. "I think you've had enough for tonight." Turning off the vibrator, she pulls out of me and I feel a sense of release. I've never come that hard before. "Let's get you cleaned up. I'll start the shower and be right back."

I watch her walk to the bathroom as I try to compose myself. She is a gorgeous sight to see. Reaching into the shower, she turns the water on to heat up, then takes off the strap-on and places it on the counter. She removes the dildo from the harness and sets it aside before returning to me.

"I'll clean those later. Right now, let me take care of you."

23

Cole

What the hell is going on with me? I think a dominatrix propositioned me to have sex with her submissive girlfriend while also being brought to my knees by said girlfriend while ALSO dominating the dominatrix. I'm just confused overall.

Those two women are all I could think about this morning while walking Lucy and then Titus. They are driving me crazy, horny, and confused–three very different emotions.

Walking up to Annie's house, I ring the bell like I do every day. The lock disengages and Candy isn't standing there to greet me when I open the door. Strange. She's always here.

"Candy, *Kommen.*" Still silent. I wander deeper into the house. I don't usually have to go any farther than the kitchen to make sure her water bowl is full. "*Kommen,*" I tried again. Maybe she's in the backyard. I check the backdoor and see that the doggie door is locked, but I look outside anyway.

Behind me, I hear the clicking of her nails coming down the stairs.

"There you are, Candy. Are you ready for your walk?" I

hear a muffled bark before she comes around the kitchen island into view.

"What the fuck! Candy, what are you doing? Put that down. Oh my god." I step closer to her, and she dips her front legs wanting to engage me in a game of tug-of-war.

"Abso-fucking-lutely not. Drop it. What's the damn German term for drop it." Taking my phone out of my pocket, I quickly search the internet for the translation.

"*Lass es fallen*, Candy. *Lass es fallen*. Dammit, drop the dildo." I slap my hand to my forehead. Chasing a dog with a dildo in its mouth was not on my bingo card for this year. Or ever.

I take a tentative step toward her, and she steps back. We do this dance for several more steps before she turns and runs back up the stairs.

Fuck, what do I do? I don't want to snoop in their house, but I can't exactly call Annie and explain this to her. Fuck. Wait, Nicole. She knows all about Candy. Maybe she will have some ideas.

I scroll through my contacts until I see my sister's name. It rings once, and she sends me to voicemail. I hit call again, and she sends me to voicemail again. I try one more time, and she finally picks up.

"Cole, I'm with a client."

"Candy has a dildo and I don't know what to do, Nicole." I hear a muffled "I'll be right back" on her end of the line, and then a door shuts.

"What the hell are you talking about?"

"I came to Annie's house to walk Candy, and she has a dildo in her mouth. She won't give it up. I don't know what the hell to do. She ran from me when I told her to 'drop it.'"

"A dildo. As in…"

"As in a dick, a cock. A flesh-colored appendage probably made of latex or silicone that you use for sex. Candy has a dildo in her mouth. God, this is mortifying." Candy comes trotting down the stairs, so fucking proud of herself.

"Candy, *lass es fallen*, pleeeeease." She ignores me and walks towards the living room.

"What the hell did you just say, Cole? What language was that?" I don't know why I called Nicole. It's not like she can do anything to help me. I guess I just needed moral support.

"It's German for 'drop it.' Candy knows German commands as well as English. Unfortunately, I don't think 'drop it' is one she knows." I know I sound insane, but I'm panicking. She sighs at me from the other end of the line.

"I have to get back to my client. What exactly do you want me to do?" She sounds exasperated.

"I have no fucking clue. What should I do?" Please give me any ideas.

"Cole, you need to call Annie. I don't know what else to tell you." Any idea but that.

"I can't call her. This is too embarrassing." I'm definitely losing my job today.

"I've got to go. Good luck, little brother."

"Wait, Nicole. Please don't tell anyone. Annie is really private. I shouldn't have called you. Please."

"I got you. Don't worry. I'll stay quiet. Byeeeee." Before she hangs up, I hear her laughing, and now I'm faced with a dog, a dildo, and a dilemma. Not the triple D's I associate with this house.

I try walking toward Candy, where she's taken up residence on the couch, the dildo between her paws, licking away at it. She's wagging her tail, and damn, that thing looks real. Balls and all. She picks it up with her teeth when she sees me, and I instinctually cringe and grab my crotch in sympathy.

"Candy, are you going to save me the mortification of having to call your mom and put down the dildo?" Fuck, I've never said the word dildo so many times in my life. This has to be a record.

Taking another tentative step toward her, she jumps off the couch, and I chase her around the living room a few times. I even dive over the couch in an attempt to cut her off, but she's just too quick for me.

"Fuck, fine. But, if I get fired, I hope your next dog walker is ugly." I back up to the closest wall and slide down until my butt hits the ground. I take a moment to stare at her number on my cell phone screen, trying to figure out what to say. Finally, I find the courage to hit the call button.

"Cole." Oh god, what now. I have to speak.

"Um, hi, Annie, Danika, Ms. Poulsen. Hello." Shit, I've forgotten how to speak.

"Cole, what's wrong with you? Is everything alright? Is something wrong with Candy?" Candy. Right. I look over, and she's back on the couch, licking the dildo.

"Candy is...fine. I have a bit of a situation here at your house, though." How do I even explain this?

"What sort of situation? Hold on." Once again, I hear a muffled "I'll be right back" before she comes back on the line.

"I'm so sorry, Annie. I didn't know what else to do but call." *Fuck, fuck.* I have to tell her.

"Cole, what is Candy chewing on?" *Oh shit.* I look up and around. Of course, someone in her position would have cameras in the house. "And why are you sitting on the floor over there?"

"Okay, so that's what I'm calling about. She has an um…
accessory in her mouth."

"A what? What kind of accessory?"

"The toy kind."

"I can't zoom in that close, and it doesn't look like any toy
I've bought her. What exactly is it that she has in her mouth,
and what's the problem?" Oh god she's going to make me say
it. *Shit, shit, shit.*

"She has a…um…dildo," I mumble the last word.

"A what? I couldn't hear you." I bang my head back against
the wall a few times. With all the courage I can muster up, I
speak again. The words hastily pouring out of my mouth.

"Annie, she has one of your dildos in her mouth, and she
won't put it down, and she runs off anytime I try to approach
her." The phrase "silence is deafening" has never been more
true. There is no sound from the other side. I look at my
screen, and the line is still connected. "Annie, I've tried. I
even looked up the German command for 'drop it,' and she
ignored me." The silence seems to stretch on forever.

"I'm 30 minutes away. Let me call Blake. She's out running
errands for her boss. She's probably closer. Hold on." The
line goes silent again.

It feels like forever before she speaks. I make another
attempt to get the dildo from Candy with no luck. I know
there's a good possibility that Annie could be watching, and I
don't want to embarrass myself any further.

"Blake will be there in 10 minutes."

"Okay. Thank you, Annie, and I'm sorry."

"No, this is my fault. I'm sorry." The line goes dead, and I'm
in shock. That was a genuine apology.

24

Blake

"Hey, Baby. I'm surprised to hear from you during the day. What's up?"

"We have a bit of a situation at home, Darling. Are you still with Josh? Cole needs some help. I hope you're closer to home than I am." Situation? What could possibly be going on at our house that he needs my help?

"I am. I'm about 10 minutes away. What's going on?"

"After our shower last night, we went straight to bed, and I forgot to clean up the toys."

"Oh, no." My hand comes up to cover my mouth. "Josh, head home, please."

"Oh, yes. We are going to need to replace your favorite dildo. Evidently, Candy has a hold of it, and she won't let Cole take it from her." I close my eyes and shake my head, snickering. I'm imagining Candy with our dildo in her mouth in front of Cole.

"It was the wildberry lube, wasn't it?" I can't help laughing when I meet Josh's eyes in the rearview. How does he keep such a straight face?

"That would be my guess. You know she's a sugar fiend." I can hear in her voice she's trying not to laugh.

"Baby, it's funny. You can laugh." I hope I can contain my laughter when I see Cole.

"Cole is embarrassed. He called me Danika and Ms. Poulsen. I may need to give him a raise or a bonus."

"Or *we* could give him a bonus." I can feel Josh's eyes on me again. I really hope Annie's NDA is as airtight as she says. This man hears far too much.

"Little One, why don't you see if Cole has some free time this weekend, and we can make plans." *Holy shit.* I was joking, but I'm absolutely down for that.

"Can we go line dancing?" I love line dancing. Annie says it's not her favorite, but damn, does she look sexy out on the dance floor. I hear her heavy sigh on the phone.

"Go rescue our dildo, see if Cole is available, and if you're a good girl, we can go country line dancing. I love you." *Squeee.* I'm bouncing in my seat with excitement, and I see Josh wince at my outburst. I mouth "sorry" to him.

"I love you, too, Annie. I'll go rescue our dildo." I see Josh biting the inside of his cheek, trying not to laugh as Annie hangs up.

"It's okay to laugh, Josh. It's funny." He smiles, and a small chuckle escapes him.

A few minutes later, we arrived at the house. I walk in the door and don't immediately see anyone.

"Cole? Cole, are you still here?" I see a figure rise from behind the sofa, and I jump grabbing my chest.

"Shit, Cole, you scared me. Why were you on the floor?"

"I was wallowing in embarrassment. Candy ran back upstairs when she heard you pull up." I peer up the stairs before turning back to him.

"I'm so sorry, Cole. I can't even imagine what you've been going through. Let me go take care of her, and I'll be right back."

"I'll be right here, mourning my ego once again." I give him a confused look and head upstairs. Candy is in her dog bed in our bedroom, happily chewing on my favorite dildo.

"Oh, Candy. Why this one, you sugar whore?" I approach her and easily remove it from her mouth. She rests her head on her paws in apology.

Sighing, I walk back downstairs. When Cole sees what's in my hand, he turns in the opposite direction. Waving the dildo in the air, I walk towards him so he can see me.

"Cole, does this embarrass you? Toys are an essential part of our bedroom life. If you can't put on your big boy panties and look at a little dildo, you can't hang out with the girls."

"Blake, I have no problem with dildos, vibrators, ropes, or anything you want to play with. But only if I'm invited to play with them. Walking in and seeing *that* in Candy's mouth was not something I was invited to. That is part of your private sex life with Annie. I also didn't want to walk down the street with that thing hanging out of Candy's mouth." I can't help but laugh at that thought. It would definitely be a sight to see. "And there's nothing little about that thing. Also, why does it look so real?"

I hold the dildo up in front of me and start to stroke it. "Are you intimidated by its size? Afraid you won't compare?" I see the heat flash in his eyes. I've struck a nerve, and I like it. Does he like degradation?

"I know what I'm working with. That *thing* doesn't compare. Trust me, I'm not worried." Hmm, he sounds confident. I remember the outline in his boxer briefs at the party. He has a reason to brag. "My eyes are up here, Blake."

"But the view is so nice down there." I catch myself biting my lip and release it.

"Blake." My name is a warning. I don't think I like him using that tone with me.

"Cole," I say with a little clip to my tone. I see his jaw tense. That's the reaction I was looking for.

Slowly I stalk towards him, dildo still in hand. He's watching my every move. When I'm only a foot away, I slam the dildo on the kitchen counter, the suction cup on the base firmly holding it in place.

"I want you to show me." His brows pinch, not quite understanding what I'm asking. "I want you to show me how you pleasure yourself. You say you can hang with the girls. I want a demonstration."

He stands there and stares at me. No movement towards the dildo, no objection, just frozen, staring. I take a few steps around him and hop up on the counter so I'm sitting with his back to me. Leaning over, I speak directly into his ear.

"I'm going to tell you about our safewords, Cole. You always have the option of saying no." I graze the shell of his ear lightly with my nose. He groans and closes his eyes. "Yellow is Annie's favorite color. It means everything is good, keep going. Orange is my favorite color. It means you need a moment, you're unsure about the situation or activity. Red means stop." I reach over his shoulder and grab his chin to look at me. "Do you understand, Pup?" He looks me directly in the eyes. His crystal blues are so full of wonder and eagerness.

"Yes, ma'am." Oh no, that won't do.

"BlakeLynn." It takes him a moment to understand, and I see the spark in his eyes when he does.

"Yes, BlakeLynn. I understand." I slide my hand from his chin and cup his cheek.

"That's my good boy," I purr. The hairs on the back of his neck stand up, and he shivers. "Now, I told you to do something before you were properly educated on your options. That won't happen again. I apologize. What I told you to do was show me on this very realistic dildo how you pleasure yourself. If you aren't comfortable with that, tell me your color or start stroking now."

I can feel the heat as it begins to radiate off his body. I remove my hand from his face. I want him to feel like he can make his choice without me touching him. I lean back, placing my hands on the counter to support me, and cross my legs, waiting for his choice.

"Cole, color?" He looks at me over his shoulder. "If you're waiting for me to permit you to speak, don't. The colors, you're safewords, never need permission. And, if those don't work for you as safewords, we can find something that does. We have to trust each other. I have to be able to trust that you'll use your safeword if you need them, and you have to trust that I'll respect them and hopefully never put you in a position to need to say red." Maybe I'm taking too much of a risk. I really have no idea what I'm doing. His breathing is rapid, and I can see his broad chest heaving. "Cole, color?"

He gives me a long searing look as he lifts his hand. "Yellow, BlakeLynn." *Oh fuck, we're doing this.* He grips the dildo, and squeezes the base tightly. I'm mesmerized as his hand strokes up and down a few times.

I realize he probably needs some kind of lubrication.

Looking around, I see the glass bottle of olive oil on the counter, grab it, and flip the lid. I hold it a few inches above the tip of the dildo. We both watch as it slowly drips out and slides down the sides of the silicone shaft. His hand starts to slide more effortlessly, and a moan escapes my lips at the erotic image in front of me.

I hear the clinking of his belt buckle and look down to see him undoing his pants with his spare hand.

"I didn't say you could touch yourself, Pup." He pulls down his zipper and breathes a sigh of relief, then wiggles his fingers in the air to show he isn't going any farther. Peering over his shoulder, I realize he was trying to give himself some room for the raging erection he has.

His pumping is increasing, and so is his breathing. I notice his hips rocking slightly in rhythm with his hand. I hear my cell phone ding in my purse, notifying me of a text message. *Shit, I'm supposed to be working. I need to check that.* Cole hears it and slows his hand.

"I didn't tell you to stop." Hopping off the counter, I walk over to the entryway table where I dropped my purse and keys when I came in.

Annie: Help him with that problem in his pants, little girl.

I smile a Cheshire cat smile and look up to where I know the cameras are. She's watching. She's giving me permission to touch Cole. She said she wanted to watch.

Me: Yes, Danika. Any requests?
Annie: He's using his hands. Help him with yours. The first time you swallow his cock, I want to be there to see it, so stay

129

off your knees but give me a good show.

Just as I put my phone down, one more text comes through. I watch Cole for a moment, hunger in my eyes, before looking back at my phone.

Annie: And, little girl, if you kiss him without me there, there will be punishment.

Fuck. Do I want punishment? The thought of her watching me being directly disobedient gets me even more excited. But I never disobey Danika. The fucking decision.

I walk back to Cole and can tell he's wondering what just happened.

"It seems we have an audience." I motion at the two cameras that are angled toward the kitchen. "Danika would like a show. She thinks you might need a little…help." My eyes drift to the protruding bulge in his pants, and he smirks.

I see his mouth open to respond and place a red-painted finger over his lips. "I haven't given you permission to speak, Pup. You may only answer direct questions, and the only words you can say without permission are your colors. Do you understand the rules?"

"Yes, BlakeLynn." My name sounds as sweet as honey coming from his mouth. I run my hand over his chest and feel the firmness.

"Do you want to give Danika a show?" His eyes raise to the cameras, and he nods, then looks back at me.

"Yes, BlakeLynn." I raise my hand and caress his cheek.

"That's my good boy. The instructions given to me are hands only and no kissing. Although, I haven't decided yet if

I want to follow the second rule. That will depend on how well you please me and if I'm willing to take a punishment for my insubordination. Now, stroke that dildo while I stroke your cock."

I trail my thumbs under the waistband of his jeans and push them until they drop to the floor. I do the same with his boxer briefs and almost drool when I look down.

His very erect, very long cock is standing at attention, pointing up at his stomach. I drop to my knees and examine the sight in front of me. He grunts, not knowing my intentions.

I run my fingers up the bottom of his shaft, and he inhales sharply as I count. "Three, four, five...six. Six? Fuck me, Pup." I stand and see him biting the inside of his cheeks. His smug smile is trying not to burst out. Grabbing a handful of his dick, I squeeze, and his smile falls as he gasps. "I may find your Jacob's Ladder piercings interesting, but you need to stay respectful to me."

Fuck me. Those are more than interesting. Those six black barbells are crazy fucking sexy. I can't wait until I get to feel them sliding in and out of my pussy. Or better, watching them disappear in and out of Annie's. Involuntarily I moan, thinking of those images.

I lift my hand and hold it, palm up, to Cole's face. "Lick" He starts at the base of my palm and licks all the way to the tips of my fingers, looking into my eyes as he goes. Wrapping my hand around his long shaft I stroke from base to tip. He hisses but holds in any other noise. "You're allowed to make as much noise as you'd like. I love a vocal partner. Please don't hold back."

It seems that's all the permission he needed. As we find

a rhythm of stroking the dildo and his cock, he moans and grunts. When I use my other hand to cup his balls and run my thumb along the seam, he growls. I very much enjoyed that noise and made a mental note to take him do it again.

I suddenly realized that Annie hadn't said if I was allowed to come or not. *Dammit.* My clit is throbbing, and there's probably a puddle in my panties. The feel of the barbells of his Jacob's ladder shifting through my fingers is intoxicating. Bump, bump, bump. Over and over. Six bumps each time. The slower I stroke, the more drawn out his moans are. The faster I pump, the quicker his breathing gets.

"You're so responsive, Pup. I can't wait to get you inside me. To feel your piercings rub all the sweet spots in my pussy." He closes his eyes and bites his lip. I know he's thinking about how it will feel too.

"You can stop stroking the dildo. You did such a good job. Do you want to come?"

"Y-yes, BlakeLynn. Please." I push on his shoulder so he's leaning back against the counter. I step closer to him, stroking his cock between our bodies. I want so badly to drop to my knees and swallow him.

"Say it again. Beg me to let you come, Pup."

"Fuck. Please, BlakeLynn. Please let me come. I'll be your good boy. Please." His hands are gripping the counter, and the veins on his neck are bulging. I swirl my thumb along his tip where pre-cum has pooled. He bites his lip, and a long moan escapes him. He mouths, "Please."

"I'm going to take mercy on you and allow you to come. You've been a very good boy obeying all the rules. Come for me, Cole."

His head rolls back, and he roars as hot ropes of come spill over us. He lunges forward and threads his fingers through my hair. His head dips to my neck, and he grabs a hunk of my flesh between his teeth, sucking it. I'm momentarily lost in the feel of his tongue on my skin when reality snaps back.

"Cole. Tsk, tsk. Bad boys don't get rewards." I try to step back, but he growls a feral sound while gripping my hair tighter in his hands and sinking his teeth deeper into my neck. His tongue swirls a few times over the piece of flesh in his mouth before releasing me.

I'm in a lust-filled daze and don't even realize my hands wrapping around his neck and pulling him in for a kiss until it's already happening. I bypassed his lips completely and thrust my tongue into his mouth, needing to taste him. The feeling of our tongues tangled together makes me moan. It's not long before I come to my senses and pull away. He presses his forehead to mine.

"Color, Pup?" He smiles a bright, heartfelt smile.

"As yellow as the sun, Princess." His fingers move deeper into my hair. "You weren't supposed to kiss me." He's massaging my scalp, and I melt into his chest.

"No, I wasn't." I shake my head against his chest and laugh.

"What's so funny?" I take a small step back and look down between our bodies.

"I'm supposed to go back to work, and you've made a mess of us."

"Technically, I'm at work right now." He shrugs and laughs at himself. "Hey, Princess, how much trouble are you going to be in with Annie?" I look up at the cameras before answering.

"Hard to tell." It's my turn to shrug. "I've never disobeyed her before."

"Never?" I can hear the disbelief in his tone without even

looking up.

"No. I'm not a bratty sub. I enjoy the multitude of orgasms she gives me and have never felt the need to be disobedient… until you." I'm not entirely sure what's going on, but I can feel a shift in dynamics.

"I should probably get cleaned up and take Candy for her walk. That *is* what I get paid to do, after all." He winks and smirks at me. I take a step back so he can pull his pants up from the floor and give his body one last quick perusal. His thighs are massive, probably from pole dancing. Annie and I have been with a few men over the years, but none that I've ever appreciated this much.

"You're drooling." I wipe my mouth with the back of my hand and hear his chuckle. He's making fun of me.

"It's hard not to. You're so pretty." I start to unbutton my blouse and walk away to change. "Oh, Cole, are you free this weekend? Annie and I would like to take you out."

"Out?"

"Yes, out. You know, someplace that requires clothes, unlike the last time the three of us were together." He's staring at me with a heated look, and I realize it's not because of my comment. I'm standing at the bottom of the stairs with my blouse completely unbuttoned and my white lacy bra on full display. I let the fabric fall off my shoulder to give him a better view.

"If you like what you see, come out with us this weekend, and maybe you'll get a better view." I don't wait for a response and head up the stairs. "You'll come out with us on Saturday to Midnight Moonshine, Pup. I promise it will be fun."

25

Annie

She's in so much trouble, and I'm going to enjoy it. I watched them from the privacy of my office. When I saw her drop to her knees, my stomach flipped. I had given her specific instructions. Lucky for her, she appeared just to be looking at his penis.

Watching the two of them together was beautiful. I had to push the button in my desk drawer, locking my office door, to ensure I wasn't disturbed. I touched myself while I watched the erotic scene play out in front of me.

Despite directly disobeying an order, I came on my fingers when she kissed him. I had to cover my mouth with my hand to stifle the moans escaping me. I've never considered myself a voyeur, but I'd happily watch Blake and Cole together again.

She seemed to come to her senses quickly while kissing him, but she did it, and it can't be taken back. Then I watched her tease Cole by taking her shirt off. I kept the entire interaction on mute because I wasn't sure what might happen, and I didn't want anyone else to potentially hear anything.

·ᴗᴗ˙ᴗᴗ·

I peer across the dining room table where Blake and I are having dinner. I can tell there's a slight tenseness to her. She's wondering when I'm going to bring up her indiscretion. Her motions are stiff as she twirls her pasta around her fork.

"Thank you for rescuing Cole today. And I apologize for not putting the strap-on away. I've already ordered another dildo to replace it. We can't have you going without your favorite one."

"Thank you, Baby. It wasn't your fault. No need to apologize." She continues to nervously eat her food.

"I enjoyed the show." Her eyes meet mine, full of anxiety, and she freezes, hand mid air.

"I, um…" She dips her head back down and takes a large mouthful of garlic bread. I'll put her out of her misery in a moment, but her unease is entertaining. Reaching across the table, I grab her hand, and it startles her. She chokes on her bread before composing herself.

"Little One, relax." Her eyes are as wide as saucers as she searches my face for a reaction.

"But, Danika. I…"

"You disobeyed me." Her eyes drop to the table, and she releases my hand, clasping them in her lap–a submissive pose. I don't want her to feel shame for what she did. I instigated them both.

"Blakey, look at me." Instantly her demeanor changes. She sighs, and the tension releases from her shoulders.

"I'm so sorry, Annie. I got caught up in the moment. He bit me, and my mind short-circuited." She reaches up and brushes her finger along a spot on the top of her shoulder. I notice a faint purple mark, and I suddenly feel very possessive. I want to crawl across the table and replace his mark with one of my own. "Annie? Your eyes just went wild. Is everything okay?"

Calm down, Danika. She belongs to you and isn't going anywhere.

"Yes, Darling. The mark caught me a little off guard. I saw him bury his face into your neck, but I didn't realize that had happened. I felt possessive just now when I saw it. It's not a feeling I've ever had before." She pushes her chair back and stands, walking around the table to me. I lean back, and she climbs onto the chair, straddling me.

I love the differences between us. Blake's dark, slightly wavy hair to my straight blonde. Our eyes are both brown but opposites of the spectrum. Her angelic face has a smattering of light freckles across her nose and cheeks that she covers up with makeup. My skin is clear of any markings.

"You know I love you, right, Baby?"

"Of course I do. Why would you ask that?" Am I showing some insecurities that I'm not aware of?

"I don't want you to ever doubt that. There's no reason to feel possessive. I belong to you." She lifts my wrist with hers, displaying our matching bracelets. "Permanently."

"I love you too, *Mijn Diamant.*" I think about how to express my feelings. "I've never had to share you before." I brush her hair aside and run my fingers along the purple bruise. "He marked you. He marked what's mine. I feel this primal need to mark you as my own, too. To stake a claim. You were mine first."

"First? Are you thinking Cole is the second?"

"How about we just take this one step at a time? Did you ask him to go out this weekend?" She has an adorable expression on her face. I kiss her on the nose because I can't help myself. "What did you do?"

"I didn't quite ask. I kind of *told* him he was."

"Told? What exactly did you tell him?" I like this new side of her. She seems to have more confidence. Despite our roles in our relationship, she knows she's always in charge. But to see her actually take control is a turn-on.

"Something along the lines of, 'You'll come out with us on Saturday to Midnight Moonshine, Pup. I promise it will be fun.'" I'm so proud of her. I pull her closer to kiss her.

"Good girl using your words. Was this before or after you shocked him by removing your blouse?" I watch as the blush trickles up her neck towards her cheeks. "Yes, I watched it all. You did nothing wrong." Except for that kiss. I still need to tell her what her punishment will be.

"I told him after." Her smile is wide and devious.

"Little one, you know you have a punishment coming for that kiss." I see her chin about to dip, and I stop it before it does. "None of that. You have to face the consequences of your actions. I have something special in store for Saturday. It's nothing to worry about now. I just wanted you to know I haven't forgotten, and it isn't being ignored."

"Okay, I understand."

"Was your little Pup informed of the rules before he engaged in any activities?" She nods. "Do you feel like he needs a punishment as well? He did kiss you back without trying to stop it." I see her eyes sparkle at the idea.

"I think he does."

"Alright, Darling. How about you leave it up to me, and I'll have a punishment prepared for the both of you on Saturday?"

"I think I'm too excited for it." Oh, she has no idea what's in store for them.

"Me too, Little One, me too."

26

Cole

When I walked into Annie's house yesterday, there was a note waiting for me on the kitchen counter.

Cole,
Please arrive here tomorrow at 7 PM.
Josh will drive us, and we will have dinner and drinks at
Midnight Moonshine. Plan to dance and dress accordingly.
~Blake and Annie

Looking down at my outfit, I hope I'm dressed appropriately. I'm wearing a lot more clothing than I'm used to dancing in. I made sure to iron my pale blue button-up shirt that I have cuffed to my elbows, and I wore my favorite pair of dark-wash jeans. I don't own a cowboy hat or boots, but I wore black dress shoes. I'm comfortable enough to dance in my entire outfit, and it sounds like that's the plan.

I have no idea what to expect tonight. I looked up Midnight Moonshine before coming over. They have a large dance floor, several bars, a full restaurant, and a mechanical bull. The club that I worked at before moving here had a mechanical bull. I'm excited to ride it and wonder if I can get either of the girls to do it with me.

Pulling into their driveway, I see Josh and the sedan waiting for us. He watches me intently as I approach the front door. I knock, and when it opens, my jaw drops.

"BlakeLynn, you look...fucking edible." Patting my cheek, she rolls her eyes at me.

"Don't start now, Pup. There will be plenty of time for that later." She spins on her heels and skips away. Fuck me. Can she even leave the house like that? She is every cowboy's wet dream right now in super short daisy duke shorts and a red flannel top tied just under her tits. I've never had a desire to motorboat anyone before right now. The front of her shirt is barely buttoned, leaving the tops of her breast completely exposed in her black bra.

I follow the skipping little pixie into the kitchen when I'm floored once again.

"Fuck, Kitten. Goddamn, you look sexy." I trail my eyes from her silver cowboy boots up her black pants that look painted on to a black and silver bodice tied up the front with a two-inch gap all the way up. I want to unwrap her like a present and expose her breasts that are barely contained. Her blonde hair is wavy, and she has a black suede hat on her head.

Blake moves to stand next to Annie, and the sight of these two gorgeous women before me could make me come in my pants with a single smile. My dick is already twitching, wanting to be released.

"There's no way I can go out with you two tonight. I'll spend the entire time beating the men off you. How is it legal to look that fucking sexy?" Blake walks up to me and puts her arms around my neck as best she can. Without her high heels, there's a significant height difference between us. She tickles the hairs on the base of my neck, teasing me. I bend down, grab the back of her thighs and lift her up, wrapping her legs around my hips. Blake squeals and giggles.

"Hey, Kitten, how much trouble would I get into if I kissed your girl right now?" I look over my shoulder to see a smile on her face.

"You're both already in trouble tonight. I guess it depends on how deep you want to dig your hole."

"I can't get any deeper than six feet under, so I think I'll take my chance." Looking back into Blake's bright brown doe eyes, I lean in and gently caress her lips with mine. The kiss we shared earlier in the week was desperate and frantic in the moment of passion. This one is much more relaxed and sensual.

She tastes fruity. I noticed some cans of alcoholic seltzer on the counter when I came in. The girls must have been pregaming.

I pull away before I try to carry her upstairs and find a bedroom. Annie still has a huge smile on her face as Blake and I catch our breaths.

"Are you ready for your punishments?" Annie seems far too excited about whatever is about to come. She picks up two boxes from another counter and hands us each one. My eyes pop open, looking at the picture on the box.

"What is this?" I look between my box and Blake's.

"They are both vibrators attached to an app in my phone that you'll be wearing tonight while we're out. Cole, yours is a cock ring with two attached silicone rings. One goes around your cock, and the other your balls, and the little cylindrical piece will sit on top of your penis, and vibrate. Blake has seen hers before." I peer at her's and see a purple vibrator that's shaped like a 7 or an L depending on your angle. "It will get inserted inside her pretty little pussy and the shorter end will sit on top of her clit for double stimulation. They're both attached to an app on my phone." Is she kidding me? Am I supposed to wear this all night?

"But why me? Blake broke the rules." Blake moves to stand in front of me and toys with the highest button on my shirt. She pops it open, exposing more of my chest.

"Oh, Pup. You broke the rules, too. You knew I wasn't allowed to kiss you, and you didn't stop me. So, tonight you're going to be a good boy and take your punishment just like I am. I hope you wore waterproof underwear because tonight will probably be messy." I can't blame anyone but myself for what's going to happen. She's right, I broke the rules just like she had, but I don't regret a single moment of that kiss.

"Okay, I'll take my punishment. How long do I have to wear it?"

"All night," they say simultaneously and start laughing. I take in the sight of them. I've never seen Annie more relaxed than at this moment. It's a beautiful sight. I put the box on the counter and step closer to her so we're almost chest-to-chest. I thread my fingers into the hair at the back of her neck and tug lightly until she's looking at me.

"Please tell me you've heard from the lawyers and gotten everything sorted out because I really want to fucking kiss you right now." She looks and feels incredible in my hands, bending to my will. Her lips part, and her eyes stare at me as if she's in a trance. When she doesn't respond, I tighten my grip on her hair and give her a little shake.

"Danika, I asked you a question. Answer me." She rapidly blinks a few times before composing herself.

"Unfortunately, no. Their opinion is I should fire you, and they wouldn't have to worry about dealing with it." I can't help the growl that escapes me. I wrap my other arm around her waist and pull her flush to me. I hear a giggle behind me and find Blake biting her lip, watching our interaction.

"And what did you say to them about that, Kitten?"

"I told them I'm paying them to figure it out, and that's what they need to do."

Unclenching my hand in her hair, I gave her neck a gentle massage. I drop my mouth almost to her lips, before whispering, "Good girl," and planting a soft kiss at the corner of her mouth. I release her completely, stepping back, and watch her come out of her daze. I love a non-composed Annie.

"Are we ready to face our punishments? We need to put these on." Blake hands me my box with the black silicone cock ring. I read the description as I open it.

"They've already been cleaned, ready to use. Cole, let me know if you need any help."

"I think I can figure it out, Kitten, but I'll let you know if I need a hand." I wink at her, and she turns away from me.

Blake and I take turns in the bathroom attaching our vibrators. This isn't the most comfortable thing in the world, and I have no idea how I'm going to wear it all night. It was a little scary when I opened the box and saw how small the rings were, but they stretched around my piercings, and when I pulled the outer ring around my balls, I lurched forward at the sensation. I'm not entirely confident that I'll survive this punishment.

Walking out of the bathroom, Blake presents me with a black suede cowboy hat. "This is for you." I take it from her and see she's wearing a white one.

"Are we ready? Josh is waiting," Annie asks.

"After you, ladies."

27

Annie

Midnight Moonshine is everything that Blake loves. It's loud and flashy. She gets to dance and drink, and I get to watch her enjoy every minute of it. Seeing her happy is all I want for her in life, and the sight I'm seeing right now is about to make her giddy.

Blake decided, since Cole had never been here before, he needed the official welcome to Midnight Moonshine. She's sitting on the sticky bartop with him standing between her legs, waiting for her supplies. She ordered him the Kickin' Cowboy shot. Typically this is done by the bartender, but I paid to let Blake do the honors.

The bartender sets a shot glass and a cup of water beside Blake. She's caressing Cole, talking to him sweetly. He has no idea what's coming, and I can't keep the smile off my face. She mentioned to me that she thought he might like a little degradation, and we're about to find out if she's right.

Stepping closer, I lean against the bar, just far enough to stay out of the splash zone but close enough to get a good view of his face. Blake hands Cole the small cup of clear liquor and tells him to drink. She picks up the cup of water next to her, and when he chugs the shot, she throws the water in his face and slaps him across the cheek.

He stands there for a moment, processing what just happened as a perfect imprint of her hand blooms on his cheek. I can see the mix of emotions flashing through his eyes. Finally, he reaches up and places a hand on each of her exposed thighs, squeezing. Gazing into her eyes, he speaks through gritted teeth.

"Fucking. Do it. Again, BlakeLynn." It seems her little pup does like degradation. I motion for the bartender to bring us another round. "Make it two more," he calls out, eyes still locked with Blake.

I turn to him with a questioning look. Is he really going to let Blake slap him two more times? "One is for you, Kitten. I want to be branded with your handprint tonight, too." *Oh.* He wants me to slap him. Glancing at the grin on Blake's face, I can tell she loves the idea.

"That's not usually something I engage in, Cole." Breaking his hold with Blake's eyes, he leans into my ear to keep our conversation more private. When he speaks, there's a huskiness to his voice.

"You can call me Coleman when you speak to me, Kitten. I know the safewords. I'm telling you that I want you to throw a cup of water in my face and slap me. So you tell me. What color, Kitten?" He leans back and looks into my eyes, impatiently waiting for my response.

My instincts want me to slap him simply for daring to speak to me like that, but my body has other thoughts. My body wants to obey the request that was just presented to me. No, not a request, a demand. I still hold the power of the decision.

Rationally, I know this doesn't break any boundaries I've set for myself until we can get the legal matters situated. Glancing over at Blake, she nods at me, smiling. I turn back and look him in the eyes.

"Yellow, Coleman." He steps over and lifts me onto the bar next to Blake, eyes locked with mine. Blake hands me the cup of water and gives him the shot. Without looking away, he downs the shot and waits. I hesitate, and he squints his eyes in warning. I pick up the cup of water, throw it in his face and smack him.

My hand stings, and my clit pulses. That was incredible. I watch his jaw tick, and his pupils dilate. He places his hand on my collarbone, just below my neck–an acceptable placement for a public display of dominance.

"If I could kiss you right now, I'd make you come without even touching your pussy." My heart is galloping as Blake grabs my upper arm and pulls me in for a kiss. I return it, silently thanking her for rescuing me from making an extremely irrational decision and letting him kiss me. The cat calls around us cause our kiss to end. I almost forgot we were in a public place.

Blake and Cole take their last Kickin' Cowboy shot, and she leans in and kisses him, wrapping her arms around his wet body.

As they get lost in each other, I pull my phone out of my pocket and pull up the app connected to their vibrators. I turn them on simultaneously to a low vibration and watch as they separate, and both constrict forward, shocked by the sensation.

"Fuck, Kitten. That's cruel." Blake buries her face into Cole's neck as her hips start to pulse on the bar. I turn them off, and they sigh in relief.

"That was on low," I warn them. "Let's go have dinner, and then we can dance."

·ᘉᘉ·ᘉᘉ·

Midnight Moonshine was Blake's favorite place before we started dating. She knows all of the dances and looks sexy doing them. Watching her hips sway and her ass shake to the rhythm seems to capture Cole's attention as much as mine.

After dinner, Cole and I chose to sit at a high-top bar table on the edge of the dance floor and watch Blake dance for a while.

"This place is awesome," he says over the music. From the outside, you'd have no idea what's happening in here. When you walk in the front door, it looks like a ticket booth for an old movie theater. Once you pay and walk through the inside doors, your senses are bombarded. The dance floor is in front of you, lit up by dancing strobe lights. The music is a mix between country and pop, but every song they play has a coordinated dance. There's a bar on the left and right sides of the large dance floor, and off to your right is a set of double doors that lead to the restaurant area and another open room with the mechanical bull. Cole has already advised us that he plans to ride the bull.

"Oh, hell no." I look at Cole and follow his gaze to where Blake is dancing. Someone has walked up behind her and is attempting to put his hands on her. Cole moves to stand up, and I place my hand on his chest.

"I'll take care of it. It happens all the time." I walk over to

Blake on the dance floor, and she's politely trying to let the guy know she isn't interested. I pull her into my side by the waist and look up at the tall half-drunk guy.

"She's taken, and you're not her type." The guy looks between us and runs a hand down his unruly, long beard. I see something in his eyes that I don't like. As I open my mouth to speak again, I feel an arm wrap around my shoulder. I look up to see Cole embracing both Blake and me.

"They are with me. Back off, dude." Cole's tone is firm and confident. The guy chuckles and looks between the three of us.

"That's not what she just said. This little blonde bimbo just told me men weren't their type." He sneers at me, and I feel a growl rumble in Cole's chest on my back.

"No, man," Cole starts as he looks the guy up and down. "She means little bitches like *you* aren't their type. Now, I suggest you walk away before I release the little blonde kitten on you. She has sharp claws and knows how to use them." I confirm his words with a sweet smile to the rude asshole.

"Everything okay over here?" We all turn to see a tall, built gentleman with a beard and cowboy hat assessing our interaction.

"Yeah," Cole tells him. "Our friend was just leaving."

Our attention turns back to the drunk guy. He takes one last sweep of the three of us, throws his hands in the air dismissively, and mumbles "whatever" as he walks away.

Cole turns to our new arrival. "Thanks for that."

"No, I'm sorry you had to deal with him. Security is taking care of it." He extends his hand to Cole, who accepts it. "My name is Tucker. I'm the owner. Please let me know if you have any more trouble."

I hear Blake squeal and turn to her. She has enormous puppy dog eyes. Grabbing my arm she whispers shouts, "He's the owner. I'm totally fangirling."

"Do you know how adorable you are, Little One?" I pull her into me for a kiss as Cole and Tucker finish their conversation.

Cole says his goodbyes and turns toward us. Blake breaks our kiss and bounces over to him, throwing her arms around his neck.

"That was amazing, Pup. You can come to my rescue any time you like." She rewards him with a kiss, and he soaks up every second of it. "Let's dance. We'll teach you."

We spend time dancing and laughing. Cole picks up all the dances easily, and the night goes by quickly. After a while, a slow dance comes on. I excuse myself to get us water, and they stay on the floor to dance. I decide to take this opportunity to give them the full effect of their punishment.

I purchase three water bottles, sit at a table, and pull up the app on my phone again. Deciding to choose a pulse setting instead of a steady vibration, I watch as they freeze in the middle of the dance floor, making me smile. Cole bites his lip, and Blake's mouth drops open. They look around for me, but I've chosen a table behind a pole, so I'm not easily visible.

My smile widens as I increase the intensity of the vibrations. I can see the bulge in Cole's pants as his erection grows. He pulls Blake in close to his chest to try and hide it. Her eyes are closed, and I can see her chest heaving. The dance floor is still crowded, and their actions aren't drawing any attention.

The song is about halfway over, and I need to speed this up if I don't want them to get noticed. Increasing the intensity, I switch to a steady vibration. A laugh escapes me as I see Blake's knees buckle, and Cole tightens his grip around her waist.

I see the moment she orgasms. Her hands grip his shirt into tight fists, and she buries her face into his chest, her shoulders heaving. It's a beautiful sight to see. I see their relief when I turn off both vibrators. I don't know how close Cole was, but whether he came or not, isn't the point. This is a punishment for them both. I put my phone away, grab the bottles of water, and walk close to the edge of the dance floor, so I'm in view. They walk towards me. Cole has lust in his eyes and a prominent bulge in his pants that he's trying to hide by walking behind Blake. I see her cheeks are flushed, and her eyes are glassy.

"Did you have a nice dance?" I can't help the devious smile that's taking over my face. Blake knows better than to question my intentions, but that's not the dynamic I have with Cole.

He grabs me by the arm and spins me around so my back is to his chest. He grinds his pelvis into me.

"Do you feel how much I liked that dance, Kitten? My cock is so fucking hard right now, but the ring around my balls kept my orgasm at the very precipice. Not that I want to come in my pants but, fuck, if that wasn't the most torturous edging I've ever had."

"I'm glad the vibrator did its job." I grind back into him before I can stop myself.

"You're a feisty kitten, aren't you? Behave before I do something about that." He steps back and swats my butt. "Let's get back out there and dance and keep you occupied from using that app again."

We spend the rest of the night out on the dance floor. Just before last call, Cole makes an announcement.

"It's time to ride the bull. Who's coming?" Blake enthusiastically leads him towards the bull ring. I follow because I have no choice. It's not my favorite thing to do. I don't continue to do something I'm not successful at, and, despite several attempts at trying, I fall off quickly every time.

"Who's first?" Cole asks, looking between the two of us.

"Definitely me!" I'm glad I convinced Blake to wear the short shorts instead of the short skirt. She would have ridden the bull either way giving everyone more of a show.

I watch as she walks over to the ride attendant and has a quick conversation with Dale, the gentleman she's known from her years of coming here.

"Annie, Dale said he will go easy on you if you want to ride," she tells me when she returns.

"I think I'll sit out this time." I'd rather not embarrass myself. Cole leans over and whispers into Blake's ear, and her eyes light up. She bounces back over to Dale, and I see him nodding and looking in our direction. I look around us and see the room is mostly empty. The restaurant closed at midnight, and this section is only open for the bull riders, but almost everyone has left or is still on the dance floor. Dale smiles and nods at Blake, and she sashays back to us.

"I'll go first." With grace and agility, she swings her leg over the bull, and the mechanical beast starts teetering up and down. Her body looks sensual as she fluidly rocks against the harness. Dale knows her and knows what she can handle. Eventually, she falls off, giggling.

She comes over to us and grabs my hand. "Your turn!"

"No, I'm okay, Darling." Cole grabs my other hand and leans down into my ear.

"Let's go, Kitten. It's our turn." He takes my purse and

hands it to Blake.

"What?" What on earth is going on? *Our* turn? We walk over to the bull, and Cole helps lift me up. Then he climbs onto the bull, too. He's facing me with his back to the bull's head, straddling his legs over mine.

"What are you doing? You can't be on here with me." Can he? Is this what Blake and Dale were talking about? Was this Cole's idea? He places his hands on my hips, and the mechanical bull starts rocking slowly. Dale knows I can't handle too much and always starts slow for me.

Cole's hands slide up from my hips and travel along the sides of my bodice, over the tops of the exposed swells of my breast, and then down my arms. Our bodies move back and forth in opposition to the bull's movements. I grab his hips for some stability, and I hear him swear.

"Fuck, fuck fuck. Goddammit. Annie, where's your phone?"

"You handed it to Blake before you tossed me up here. It was in my purse." I glance over at her and see a smirk on her face. Looking back at Cole, I see the tortured look in his eyes. "Did she...?"

"Yes. She turned on the fucking vibrator," he answers me through gritted teeth. His hips start to pump against my stomach, searching for friction that has nothing to do with being on the bull. We're still being pushed back and forth with the motion of the animal beneath us. Cole pushes me down onto the bull until I'm lying under him. He stands above me, and when the bull tips up, he tips down. Cole's sliding up and down my body in what I can only imagine looks like he's dry-humping me. He's moaning and grunting, but the music is so loud I don't think anyone else can hear him but me.

"I need to come so fucking bad, Kitten. I feel like I'm going

154

to explode." God, I know the feeling. There may be layers of clothes between us, but my pussy is pulsing like he's inside me. Dale turns the bull off, and Blake must turn off the vibrator because Cole lets out a long shaky breath. "Thank fuck. Can we please get out of here?"

"Oh, Coleman. That's what happens when you manhandle a woman without her permission." His eyes flash to mine, and he growls again. I never thought I'd like that sound as much as I do. We dismount from the bull, and Cole stalks over to Blake. Her eyes widen as he gets closer, and she squeals when he grabs the phone and throws her over his shoulder.

"What are you doing, Pup?"

"Getting us out of here before I come so hard I cause an earthquake. Do you have a problem with that, Princess?"

"Nope." She pops the P as she giggles.

28

Cole

My dick is trying its hardest to burst out of my pants as we leave Midnight Moonshine. The energy in the car is electric, and it feels like, at any moment, one of us is going to break. Josh must also be able to feel it because he keeps looking back at us.

"I think we need a bigger vehicle. I'll go shopping this week." What? Is she really thinking about cars right now? I'm trying not to strip these gorgeous women naked with an audience, and she's thinking about cars.

"That sounds wonderful, Ms. Poulsen." Josh gives her a bright smile through the rearview.

"Cole, should we discuss the expectations for when we get home?"

"Um, sure." I look at Josh, who seems to be ignoring the conversation now that it's not directed at him, although his jaw looks tense.

"I've already looked at your medical records and seen that your last check-up was a few months before you moved here. You were checked for STDs and came back clean."

"You've looked at my medical records? How?"

"Do you forget who I am? There isn't much that I can't acquire if I ask the right person." Okay, she has a point. But why? "Have you been with anyone since being here that we would need to worry about?" Okay, so now we're getting personal.

"Um, no. I haven't been with anyone." Blake puts her hand on my knee, that I hadn't noticed was bouncing. She sat in the middle with Annie and me on either side of her.

"Good because Blake has a latex allergy, and if we needed to stop for more contraceptives, we would have." Contraceptives? Now we're talking about birth control. This goes both ways.

"What about you ladies?"

"Blake and I get tested after every partner we add in the bedroom. You can never be too careful." Well, good. It seems we're all clean. Wait, "every partner."

"How often do you have other partners in your bedroom?" I'm beginning to wonder if she'll have another contract waiting for me when we get to their house.

"Not often, Pup." Blake squeezes my knee. She's been silent until now. I wonder if she heard the uneasiness in my voice. I like these women. I'd like to have more than a quick fuck.

"We have on occasion invited another person, men, and women, into our bedroom. It typically occurs during one of our parties. As you've seen, they tend to get very sexual." I did notice that. There were all kinds of activities going on at the party that I accidentally crashed.

"You should also know that we are both on birth control, so it seems we're all covered in the contraceptive area." Annie is definitely covering all of her bases. *Wait a minute.*

"Hold on. You said, 'If we need to stop.' Does that mean you have non-latex condoms at your house or...?"

"It means, since we are all clean, there's no reason for the three of us to use them at all."

"No condoms *at all*? You want me to go bare?" I must be hallucinating.

"Correct, Cole. Is that a problem?" I know Annie is waiting for a response, but I'm currently wading through the mush that my brain has become because there's no way she's giving me the option of taking Blake raw. "Cole, is that a problem?"

"N-nope. No problem at all. It's just not something I've ever experienced before." I can see the question in Annie's eyes. *Oh my god. Does she think I'm talking about sex?* "Bare. Raw. No condom. I've never had sex without a condom before."

"Oh, well then, I suppose you'd be in for a treat. Now, regarding sexual activity tonight and going forward in the foreseeable future, I will stay out of the equation. Until my lawyers stop dragging their feet, I can't take any chances being involved." Alright, I guess we're just glossing over my confession.

"Baby," Blake whines. "That's no fun." Annie strokes Blake's cheek.

"Little One, I can play with you. I just can't play with Cole yet. You can have all the fun you want, and I'll enjoy watching." *Yet.* I like the sound of that. While I wish I could indulge in them both tonight, I understand Annie's reservations, and I'll have to continue fantasizing about the day her "yet" becomes a "yes."

"Okay, I guess." Blake sticks out her bottom lip in a pout and I want to bite it. Annie sees the same opportunity, and she takes it. She sucks Blake's lip into her mouth, and they both moan.

Blake's hand slips up my leg getting closer to my still hard and desperate cock. It won't take much for me to come once I remove this cock ring. Especially without a condom.

This evening has been erotically torturous. Having Blake orgasm in my arms, even if I didn't do it myself, was fucking phenomenal. She contained her moans as best as she could, but I could still hear her and feel her body vibrate in my arms.

"Neither of you are allowed to take your vibrators off until I say." Does she think she's in charge?

"Kitten, I don't think I like that idea."

"But I do, Pup." *Okay, well shit.* She can be in charge.

"Yes, BlakeLynn." She kisses me on the cheek and whispers, "Good boy." My eager cock twitches in my pants.

The rest of the ride is silent as we consider the events that are hopefully about to occur. I wonder how far Annie will let things go between Blake and me. She talked about contraceptives, so there's the assumption of sex, but I don't want to actually assume anything. Being shared by these two women is a wet dream come true.

Josh drops us off at the house, and I'm appreciative of the ride, despite the intense glares he gave me. We all drank a fair amount tonight, and driving wouldn't have been safe.

Blake catches me off guard and jumps on my back when we exit the car. "Piggyback ride, Pup! Take me inside and ravish me."

"At your request, Princess." Annie unlocks the front door, and we head into the kitchen. I deposit Blake on the counter, and try to walk away but she doesn't unlock her legs from my hips. Her arms snake around my front and slowly unbutton my shirt until she reaches the bottom. She removes the fabric

159

from my shoulders and lets it fall to the floor.

"Much better. As much as I enjoyed the wet t-shirt contest you gave us earlier, I prefer you au naturel." I close my eyes and just feel as she rubs her hands all over my upper body, front and back. Her touch switches from gentle fingers to full hands, and I love each touch better than the last.

I spin around in her legs, grab the knot at her cleavage and untie it. The black bra that had been teasing me all night is now on full display. I bite my lip as my eyes roam over her mouth watering tits.

"Kitten, I need to know my boundaries. I need to know exactly what the expectations are for tonight because my dick is aching to be inside something. You got me so worked up with this fucking vibrator all night that I'm dying." I look back over my shoulder at Annie, and Blake latches onto my neck. Her tongue swirls, and her mouth sucks as I attempt to focus on Annie and get my questions answered.

"Tonight, she's in charge of you, so you need to ask her." *Fuck.* I'm having trouble concentrating with Blake's mouth all over me.

"Princess, can I have a minute so I can talk to Danika?" She shakes her head against my neck. "Please, BlakeLynn?" She reluctantly releases me, and I walk over to Annie, embracing her in my arms.

"Kitten, I need to know you're comfortable. I may not be able to touch you right now, but I want you to enjoy yourself. You can play with Blake while I indulge in her. If we get too close to your boundaries, use your safewords. How does that sound?"

"It sounds good, Coleman." I brush her hair aside and place a chaste kiss on the side of her neck.

"Good girl using your words. Now why don't you lead us up to your bedroom." She nods, and I step back into Blake's legs. She jumps on my back again, and I reach my hand out for Annie. She takes it and leads us upstairs.

By the time we reach the bedroom, Blake has removed her shirt and bra and unbuttoned her shorts. I drop her onto the bed and watch as her perky tits bounce from the motion. I help her out of her boots, and she scoots to the middle of the bed in only a tiny pair of black panties. I turn to Annie.

"Kitten, will you *please* let me untie you from this bodice? I've wanted to unwrap this present all night. I promise to look and not touch." She looks at Blake, and I can tell she's still conflicted with the change in dynamics. She's used to being in charge and giving the orders. I'm politely asking her for something. I could demand it, and she would allow it, but I don't want to. I don't want to take advantage of something she can't control at the moment.

"Yes, Coleman. Please." My name sounds so sexy on her lips. I trace my fingers along the ribbons of the bodice until I reach the bottom, where the tie is. Slowly I pull out the string until the bow disappears. I pull each side of the ribbon out of its grommet. She takes deep inhales and exhales, clearly as affected by our closeness as I am. Blake has crawled back over to the edge of the bed to watch the show.

When I get to the last few grommets, her breasts begin to spill out. My resolve is tested when I remove the remainder of the ribbon, and the bodice falls to the floor. I have to bite my knuckles to keep my hands from reaching out and touching her.

"Isn't she a fucking wet dream?" Blake steps between us and palms Annie's breasts. I'm mesmerized by her fingers as she kneads them. "Place your hands over mine, Pup. Help me." I cautiously move my hands over Blake's, allowing Annie the chance to stop me, but she doesn't. Together we massage her breasts and pinch her nipples. It's erotic and just on the edge of her no-touch boundaries. It makes it an even bigger turn-on. Both women are moaning, and I'm not sure how much more I can take.

"Annie, can I please take this cock ring off? I'm so hard."

"What do you think, *Mijn Diamant*? It's your punishment."

"Please, BlakeLynn. Please, I need to come." I'm not above begging, and I know how much she likes it. She removes our hands from Annie and turns around to face me.

"Annie, why don't you have a seat and enjoy the show." Annie sits, and Blake smiles sweetly at me as her hands make work of my belt. Thank god. I'm finally going to get some relief. My pants hit the floor and she reaches for the waistband of my boxer briefs. I think she's going to remove them, but instead, she slides her hand on top over my erection. I groan both at the feeling of her hand and the loss of what I thought she would do.

"Annie hasn't seen what you're hiding in here yet. I think she will be pleasantly surprised." She drops to her knees, and if I wasn't wearing this cock ring, I would have come right then. The sight of her at my feet, looking up at me through her thick dark lashes with her plump lips so close to my cock is everything I've been dreaming about since I saw her ass hanging out of her trunk.

She pulls down my boxers slowly, and my cock pops out, hitting my stomach and giving Annie a perfect view of my piercings. I see her lick her lips, and her pupils dilate.

"Like what you see, Kitten? Does this give you more reason

to get on those lawyers' asses to make things right?"

"I wouldn't tease her, Pup. She still holds the remote to your cock ring." I look down into her big brown eyes.

"I thought you were removing it?" Isn't that why she's down there?

"Oh, not yet. I plan to use it to my advantage first." *Oh god.* What is she talking about? "Sit down on the bed next to Annie. I want her to have a front-row view." I do as I'm told and sit. Blake shifts to kneel between my legs, and she grabs my cock. The sensation feels like fireworks in my stomach. Her hands are soft and tiny. Her fingers don't touch, wrapped around my shaft. She looks to Annie with questions in her eyes.

"Danika?"

"Go ahead, little girl." There's permission in her tone that I don't understand until I feel Blake's warm mouth surround the head of my cock. She was asking for permission to give me a blowjob. Ever a submissive, even when she's dominating with my cock in her mouth, and fuck does it feel incredible. She pushes my dick against my stomach, flattens her tongue, and slowly licks a long stroke from the base over every barbell.

I feel the bed shift beside me and then hear a soft hum. Blake gasps as she swallows half of me in her mouth. I grunt, realizing what the humming is as Annie turns my vibrator on as well. My hips start to thrust involuntarily, and Blake takes every inch of me I give her. I already need to come, but I still can't because of the cock ring around my balls.

"Please take the ring off my balls. Fuck. I need to come. Please. Fucking goddammit, I need to come so fucking bad." I'm begging the room. I don't care who does it as long as someone lets me come. Blake sucks on the head of my cock, and I feel both of her hands move up my thighs. *Fuck yes.* She's going to remove this shit.

Annie turns up the intensity on our vibrators, and Blake releases me and drapes herself over my thigh as she orgasms. I didn't get to see the one earlier. I could only feel it as she was buried in my chest on the dance floor.

Her mouth parts as she continues to moan. There's a little crease between her eyes as she squeezes them shut from the intensity. It's stunning to watch.

Annie turns off our vibrators and leans between Blake's legs to remove hers.

"Good girl, *Mijn Diamant.* Now, finish your little pup so I can eat this pussy and make you come again."

"Yes, Danika." That's so fucking hot. My dick is 9 and a half inches of steel pipe sticking straight out of my body right now. Blake swallows as much as she can and uses one hand to pump the rest. I'm a panting, sweaty mess. Her other hand slides across the seam of my balls, and I think she's going to remove the ring again, but instead, she slides past it and massages a spot just behind them that has my toes curling.

"What the actual fuck are you doing right now, Princess? Fucking fuck, BlakeLynn." She releases the hand pumping my cock and removes the ring from my balls. She cups them firmly and tugs while her other hand strokes the spot behind them. My vision starts to tunnel, and the entire room spins as the most intense orgasm I've ever had in my life rips through my body. Every nerve inside me explodes. Time stands still. I forget my name. Black dots spot what little vision I have left. I'm coming so hard I'm worried how she's taking it all, but I can't do anything about it. I'm in pure ecstasy. My body becomes so hyper-sensitive that I need her to stop. I can't take it anymore.

"Stopstopstopstop." I'm chanting and begging as the words pour out of my mouth, and I'm curling into myself. I've done a lot of begging tonight, and I don't even care. Blake releases me, and I fall back onto the bed. The room is still spinning, and I'm breathing like I just ran a marathon. I hear the girls laughing, and it's probably about me, but I can't even care right now. I drape my arm across my eyes and try to feel my body again. "That was..."

"Mind-blowing?"

"Intense?"

"Earth-shattering?"

"Other worldly?"

They're taking turns throwing out different suggestions. "Yes to them all."

Annie pulls Blake on top of her next to me on the bed. She dives into Blake's mouth and moans. I know she's tasting me, and somehow my abused dick twitches at the thought.

"I see you enjoyed a little perineal massage, Cole." Annie continues to giggle, and it's beautiful and frustrating at the same time. I can't function right now. How the hell did Blake know how to do that?

"I warned you that you'd need to put on your big boy panties to play with the girls, Pup. Do you get it now?"

"You've ruined me, Princess. Kitten, how do you handle her?"

"Now you understand why I'm in charge. Isn't that right, little girl?"

"Yes, Danika." I love their relationship. How easily they slip in and out of their roles. It's so seamless.

"Are you ready to sit on my face while Cole's body comes

back to him?"

"Yes, Danika." Oh, this is a sight I need to see.

They stand and remove the clothing they still have on before moving to the middle of the bed, lying parallel to the headboard. I roll to my side to get a good view of them. Blake crawls up Annie's body before settling right on top of her face.

She wasn't kidding when she told Blake that's what she wanted her to do. Annie relentlessly laps at Blake's pussy, neither caring that I'm here and watching. Blake leans back, rubbing her hands down Annie's stomach, and her fingers disappear between her legs. Annie's thighs part to give Blake more room, and I prop up on my elbow to get a better view.

Blake's fingers fluidly circle Annie's glistening clit as they moan in pleasure. I would give anything to dive in and taste her pussy right now. I roll closer and grab Blake's wrist, startling her. She makes eye contact with me as I pull her hand from Annie and direct it toward my mouth. I need to know what that sweet pussy tastes like, and if licking it off Blake's finger is the closest I can get right now, I'm going to take it. I hear a pop of suction, and Blake's body jolts.

"Everything alright, Little One?" Annie's voice is muffled and husky. Blake watches as I get my first taste of Annie's arousal. I close my eyes at the incredible taste as I swirl my tongue between her fingers.

"I'm f-fine. It seems my impatient pup needed to know what you t-tasted like." Annie must have gone back to licking Blake because her eyes roll, and her head drops between her shoulder blades. "Sh-shall we give him a better sh-show, Danika?" A better show? This one is fucking incredible. I'm not sure how it could get better.

I'm proven wrong as Blake lifts from Annie's face and spins around before sitting back down. She leans over and captures Annie's pussy in her lips, and my jaw drops at the sight of them sixty-nining. I reach out and rub my hand over the globes of Blake's ass cheeks. My traitorous cock is somehow hard again and I stroke it while I watch them bring each other closer to orgasm. I want in on this so bad. I sit up on my knees, having an idea.

"Princess, Kitten, I have an idea. Do you trust me to try something?"

"What are you thinking, Pup?" What am I thinking? Will this even work?

"BlakeLynn, I want to fuck you just like you are right now. I want you to continue eating each other out while I fuck your sweet pussy." She shifts her hips to give Annie room to talk to us.

"Danika, what do you think? Can you handle him so close to you?"

"If you need to safeword me because it becomes too much, I'll pull out and go back to watching. It's just such a beautiful thing to see that I really want to join in if I can. And technically, Kitten, I won't be touching you." I'll be so close to her face but inside Blake's pussy. No rules will be broken if she agrees.

"Give me a pillow," Annie says. I grab one from the head of the bed, and she props it under her neck and pulls back on Blake's hips. The position change causes Blake's back to arch and her ass to stick out, giving me better access to her pussy. Annie starts sucking on Blake's clit again, and I take that as my permission.

I kneel behind Blake, over Annie's head, and line up with

her entrance. The next moment is about to change things between us. All the flirting and innuendos are about to come to fruition. I slide my hand down Blake's back before wrapping my hand around her hip. With my other hand, I grab my shaft and guide it into her dripping pussy. She's so wet from Annie's licking and her previous orgasm that my dick slides in easily, despite how tight she is. I feel each barbell as they disappear, one by one. The feeling of being inside her for the first time is intense enough, but paired with having no barrier between us, I have to close my eyes and breathe. The silkiness of her inner walls, the heat radiating between us, it's almost all too much.

"Pup? Are you alright?" I hear the humor in her question. She knows exactly why I haven't moved yet. She may not have said anything, but she listened to the conversation in the car earlier. You don't have to have a penis to understand there's a difference between a condom and raw.

I take another deep breath before I respond between clenched teeth.

"All good, Princess. I just needed a minute to feel nirvana." Her hips shift to encourage me to move. I set a slow, steady pace, trying not to jostle Blake too much and disturb Annie's rhythm. Blake's moans become loud and long, and I can tell she's enjoying the sensations my barbells are causing. Her molten pussy feels like heaven wrapped around my cock.

I'm enjoying the sight and feel of her when there's another warm sensation at the base of my shaft. I look down to see Annie's head dip back slightly from Blake's clit and lick a small trail on my cock as I pump into Blake. It happens several more times, and I realize she's doing it intentionally. I lower my hand and stroke her hair.

"I see my Kitten's being naughty. Daddy Coleman likes that." *Fuck.* Did I just refer to myself as Daddy? Why did I like that so much? Based on the fact that Annie seems to have found a rhythm of licking Blake and me, I think she liked it, too.

"Fuck, Pup, your piercings are rubbing right over my G-spot. Go harder and make me come. Annie can take it."

"At your request, BlakeLynn." I increase my pace, rocking both girls onto each other. Despite my life-altering orgasm not long ago, I can feel my balls starting to draw up. I watch as Blake sinks her finger into Annie's pussy, and fuck if it isn't almost my undoing.

"Are my gorgeous girls going to come for me? I want to fill up this pussy while you flood each other's mouths." Their moans are all the responses I need. Thrusting deeper into Blake, I feel her walls flutter around me. I'm close to coming when I feel my balls being squeezed.

"Fuck, Kitten. Fuck. You both better come right fucking now." My command is a growl as I bury myself deep in Blake and explode into her with a roar. Blake screams into Annie's pussy as she orgasms from my cock and her mouth. Annie is the last to tip over, and her moans are long and high-pitched as she comes.

We roll off of Annie and all attempt to catch our breath.

"Color check in?" Blake breathlessly asks.

"Yellow," we all say. I bob my head around, looking at us. We're a pile of sweaty, sated, messy limbs.

"I'll grab a warm cloth to clean us up. Be right back, ladies." Standing in the bathroom, waiting for the water to turn hot, I think I hear the soft sounds of Blake moaning. I must be imagining it because there's no way any of us could go another round so quickly. Right?

I wet the towels for us, and I almost lose my footing when I walk back into the bedroom. I was wrong. So very, very wrong. I take a step back and lean against the wall, taking in the sight on the bed.

Sprawled out between Blake's legs, I see Annie's head slowly bobbing. Blake's eyes are closed, hands laced through Annie's hair, and both women are now moaning. She's devouring Blake's pussy like it's her next meal. The pussy that I just came in, that I know is still dripping with my come.

"Jesus fuck." I must have said that out loud because Blake's eyes open, and a knowing smirk crosses her lips.

"Hey, Pup. Our Annie decided she needed to know what... ooooh god right there...what we tasted like togeth..." Her eyes roll back into her head, and she moans as her orgasm steals her words.

"Fuck me. I'm fucking ruined."

29

Annie

I need to bring Blake's ring to the jeweler one last time to ensure everything is perfect. First, I have to get through this meeting. I can't help but think of Cole as they drone on about all the testing done for the latest version of our game console. I wonder if he tested it.

I crossed my own boundaries the other night. I can't blame anyone but myself. Cole kept up with his part. He didn't touch me, but I couldn't help myself. Seeing his barbells sink in and out of Blake's pussy right in my face had me throwing away all my inhibitions. I had to feel him.

Then, when he left the room and Blake lay there on the bed, glistening with their releases, I became consumed with the need to taste him. Tasting their arousals mixed together was as delectable as I imagined.

"We are all set for our projected launch date, Ms. Poulsen." *What?* Launch date. Game console. Right.

"Wonderful. How does marketing look?" It's always the same. I don't know why we even have these meetings.

I glance at the clock and see it's almost noon. I asked Cole to take Candy out early, and meet me for lunch. I finally heard back from the lawyers, and we have some paperwork to sign. I had my secretary order food to be waiting in my office. As soon as we sign the papers, there will be no boundaries between us. My stomach has butterflies thinking about being alone with him in my office and nervousness about the loophole I allowed them to create.

Sunday morning, after Cole left, Blake and I had a long talk about what had occurred the night before. She was as surprised as I was at my loss of control. Cole seems to bring out sides of ourselves that neither of us knew existed.

We discussed where we saw our potential future with Cole and how he would fit in. Ever the sentimental optimist, Blake asked about "collaring" Cole. This is a new journey that she's starting with him, and she's still learning.

We reminisced about choosing our bracelets together, and she decided she wanted to order him a leather cuff for him to wear on his wrist with our initials on it.

"Do you think he would wear it if I bought it for him?" Her *nervousness is adorable.*

"Darling, I think that man would wear an actual collar if you bought him one. I don't think you have anything to worry about. A cuff sounds wonderful."

"Would you want your initials on it as well?" That's an *interesting question. I hadn't thought about it. Blake starts to giggle, and it turns into a full laugh before I can ask what she finds so amusing.*

"Our initials..." She's almost in hysterics.

"What about our initials, Little One?"

"All of our initials together are A,B,C. Or B,C,D if you want to

172

be technical. I'm doing it. I'm going to have a cuff made with our initials unless you have a genuine objection to it. Do you?"

BEEP. "Ms. Poulsen, your 12 o'clock appointment is here." The interruption I've been waiting for. I've never been so happy to hear the intercom.

"Alright, gentlemen. Keep up the good work. Enjoy the rest of your day." I leave the conference room and enter my office. Cole is sitting on the couch, peeking into the bag of burgers and fries I ordered.

"Kitten, I didn't take you for a greasy fast food kind of girl." He's gorgeous sitting there on my couch. His navy blue v-neck shirt is snug on him, accentuating the ripples of his arms and his broad chest. I want to run my fingers through his dark hair and get lost in his crystal blue eyes. *Get yourself together. Sign the papers.*

"Thank you for coming to meet me." He pauses from digging in the bag and looks at me.

"Okay, Danika. You have your business tone on. What's going on?" He leans back in his seat and crosses his arms waiting for me to respond. I walk over to my desk, pick up the manila folder, and sit beside him on the couch. My bare knee brushes the rough denim of his jeans as I sit, and it sends a jolt of lightning straight to my panties. *Down, girl.*

"The lawyers have redrawn the fraternization policy for me, for us. By signing this document-"

"Pen?"

"Cole, you don't even know what you're signing."

"Does it mean we get to repeat this past weekend without you carrying around any guilt?" I have been carrying around guilt which is ridiculous because this is my company.

173

"It does."

"Do I get to keep my job? With Candy and PC Madness?" I love that he thought of my dog in this discussion.

"You do."

"Okay, then I need a pen, Annie."

"Cole, you need to know what this paperwork says." His face has changed from playful to concerned. "The lawyers presented me with their two options for allowing us to have any kind of sexual relationship, and I chose the one I thought was the easiest to uphold.

"Okay. First, tell me the one you didn't choose." I'm not sure he's going to like this one.

"The first choice was to get married. There would be no reason to do any paperwork if you and I were to wed."

"Well, that's a crazy idea. What was the option that you did choose?"

"Sperm donor."

"I'm sorry, what?" He moves away from me on the couch to get a better view, and I miss the contact.

"This in no way implies you are required to impregnate me. My lawyers know I'm in a committed same-sex relationship. When Blake and I decide we want to have children, we will need to seek outside resources. My lawyers suggested by writing you in as an 'outside resource' it would mean that you and I could have a sexual relationship and stay within company policy."

"So their solution was to write me in as your what? You're sex slave?" *Oh god.* How could he think that? He's clearly getting upset.

"Please don't think that way. It has perks. You'll be entitled to the company's executive health benefits. You will receive a monthly stipend as well as your regular salary. An access card to the company gym and pool. And, in the event that a baby is conceived, you will get a sizable bonus." He stands and starts pacing the room.

"Stipends and bonuses? Access cards? Fuck. Do you really think I want any of that? Jesus, Annie. I don't want your money or your privilege. I wanted you. You and Blake." *He said wanted.* I stand up and walk toward him, but he walks in the other direction.

"Cole, Coleman."

"Danika." There's no emotion behind my name.

"Please don't look at it like that. It's to protect us."

"You've said that before. Protect us. Protect us from what? You own the entire goddamn company. I've signed every NDA that you've put in front of me. I'd rather be your dirty little secret than the CEO's manwhore."

"Coleman."

"Danika, don't." He stalks towards me, and I don't flinch. I'm not afraid he'll hurt me. Instead, he wraps an arm around my waist and threads his other hand through the hair at the back of my neck. Pulling me flush with his body, he uses his grip on my hair to tilt my head back, lowering his lips to mine in a slow, sensual kiss. This is what my body has been craving. My arms wrap around his neck, and my lips part to allow his tongue entrance. Our mouths fuse, and the kiss is filled with passion and desire and almost a bit of sadness.

When he pulls away, he rests his forehead on mine as we catch our breath. He kisses my forehead, and I smile.

"I can't sign your contract, Annie. I can't reduce the feelings I'm developing for you and Blake to an 'outside resource.' You can consider that kiss on the house. No need for a bonus."

He steps away from me and walks towards the door. I want to chase after him, but I'm frozen in place. When he reaches the door, he pauses, and I think he's changed his mind.

"Thank you for the ride here, but you can let Josh know I'll take the train home. Goodbye, Annie." He walks out and closes the door behind him.

The audible click of the door closing feels like a weight on my heart.

30

Blake

Annie asked me if I was going to be home for dinner
tonight. She sounded off. Earlier, she texted me
saying she had good news, but the later text sounded
ominous.

Annie: I'd like to talk to you tonight. Will you be home in
time for dinner?
Me: Yeah, Baby. I should be home around 6:30. We have a
late client. Everything okay?
Annie: Yes, Darling. Just a rough day.

Annie greets me at the door when I get home.

"*Mijn Diamant*, I've missed you today." She embraces me in
a hug, squeezing tighter than usual.

"Baby, something happened. Tell me. Whatever it is, we
can figure it out together." There's a tortured look in her eyes,
and it almost breaks my heart. She always looks so confident
and put together, even when she's in lounge clothes. But right
now, in her black leggings and oversized t-shirt, with her hair

piled on top of her head, she looks beautifully defeated.

"I've made a mistake, Little One, and I'm not sure how to fix it."

"What did you do?"

"I insulted Cole. He came to my office today because the lawyers created a loophole in our fraternization policy." This must have been the good news she told me she had this morning.

"How did you insult him?" Her eyes dip to the floor. Whatever she said must be bad for her to have such an extreme reaction.

"The lawyers basically wrote him off as a piece of meat. At least that's how he felt before he walked out on me." He walked out?

"Annie, I need all of the details. I don't understand what could have upset Cole so much he would walk out." For the next several minutes, she explains the conversation in her office as we sit down to eat dinner.

"He called himself the CEO's manwhore? Oh, my poor Pup. How could you think that was a good idea, Annie?" She looks so guilty. I know this is tearing her apart inside.

"The only other viable options they came up with was termination or marriage. That one sounded like the easiest choice."

"You thought asking the man we are newly entering into a sexual relationship with if he would agree to be our sperm donor? Does it sound as terrible to you out loud as it does to me?"

"It does, Little One. It does." Her hands begin to wring the napkin in her lap. She's barely eaten anything. "I just wanted to protect us."

178

I reach across the table and grab her upper arm. I slide my hand down her until it reaches the napkin she's holding.

"What are you trying to protect us from, Baby?" She removes my hand and stands, moving behind her chair, trying to put distance between us.

"Protect us from me, my father, my past."

"Annie, what are you talking about?" What has she done in her past that warrants this kind of behavior?

"Have I ever told you what the company name means?"

"No, I don't think so." She's never spoken much about her company or family other than the basics.

"MAD Gaming Inc. is named after my father and...my birth mother." My brows pinch because she said, birth mother. "Markus and Danique. M. A. D."

"I thought your mother's name was Sofi?"

"Sofi was the name of the woman who raised me. The woman who I knew as my mother for the first six years of my life before she passed. The woman who was married to my father for twelve years. But she was not the woman who gave birth to me."

"Annie, I had no idea." Why has she been hiding this from me?

"No one does, and I only found out a few years ago when I took over the company. They made sure of it. My father and Danique had an affair for several years while he was married to Sofi, before I was conceived. My father's family has always been rich and powerful in Denmark, and there was no way they could allow a bastard child to be born. But my mother could not conceive, and my father's family felt this was the perfect opportunity.

"When I was born, my mother, Sofi, assumed me as her own

179

child. That was the year that my father's company, Jorgenson Enterprise, turned into MAD Gaming Inc. They paid off Danique for her child by giving her half the company. Her only stipulation was my name, Danika. She insisted that it be my first name because it was so close to hers, and she didn't want Sofi to ever forget who I truly belonged to. For her silence, Sofi insisted that I take her last name, Poulsen. My parents moved us to the States as an opportunity for their business as well as anonymity.

"It was hard at 30, finding out that the woman you knew as your mother your entire life, isn't. The lawyers disclosed the information when we started the process of turning over the company to me."

"Annie, I'm so sorry this all happened to you, but Baby, what does this have to do with Cole?" I still don't understand.

"Danique took advantage of my father. He suspects that she got pregnant on purpose after watching my parents try for years. He thought they were in love and would have left Sofi if she didn't insist she wanted nothing to do with me. She just wanted money. My father stayed with her until I was born, and then they left once the ink was dry on all the paperwork." I walk around the table and take her hands in mine, showing her support.

"Do you think Cole would try and take advantage of you?"

"I can't ever be too sure. It's always in the back of my mind that everyone wants something from me. That's why I have my policy in place for my company. My father was Danique's supervisor. Despite their extensive relationship, when everything happened, he was worried she would use that against him and he could lose everything.

"He only lost half of the company, and little did Danique

realize, but everything reverted back to my father upon her death. She passed away five years ago, which is why four years ago, he started turning the company over to me. That's when it was revealed to me the truth of my maternity."

"Were you ever worried about me taking advantage of you?" She looks deeply into my eyes before answering.

"When our relationship started, we had a very different type of contract. I'm sure you remember sitting down with my lawyers. When we crossed from Domme/sub into a true relationship, I sat down with them again, and we decided everything was covered well enough in the original contract."

"Okay, good. I would never do anything like that to you. I think I can understand your apprehension now with Cole. After hearing the three options presented to you, if those were the *only* options, your choice was the best one."

"I almost didn't tell him. He was ready to sign, no questions asked. But, Blakey, we do want children someday, don't we? We haven't officially talked about it, but I've always gotten the impression that you did."

Wow. I wasn't prepared for the topic to change this quickly. I've always wanted to be a mother but hadn't thought much about it since getting together with Annie.

"I do. Do you?"

"Yes, absolutely. I want to have children with you, Blake. We don't have to decide right now but have you ever thought about how and which of us might carry a baby if it *was* one of us? Obviously, money isn't an issue, so the possibilities are endless."

"I guess I haven't put much thought into it. It sounds like you might have, though."

"Since the moment our relationship changed. In my ideal

world, we would have one donor, and both carry babies together." She places her hands on my lower stomach. "I'd love to see your belly grow with our baby." She's painting such a beautiful picture.

"Would you only want the two?" She shakes her head.

"I only want to carry one, but if you want one or two or twelve, I'll happily raise them all with you."

"Baby, are we really planning a family?"

"I believe we are, *Mijn Diamant*." I brush my lips against her and smile at the thought of our babies running around this house.

"But, Annie, what was the issue with Cole?" She sighs and leans her head on my shoulder.

"The way he affects both of us. What if he belongs to us, too? I didn't want to coerce him into something without his knowledge. Even if it was just a loophole and wouldn't change anything."

"Baby, I think we need to talk to Cole."

"Blake, he kissed me and left me. It was a goodbye kiss. I insulted everything that we were building. I threw money at him. I showed him all of the worst parts of me." I take a step back and take her cheeks in my hands.

"Danika, if he can't love you at your worst, then he doesn't deserve to love you at your best."

31

Cole

It's been over a week since I walked out of Annie's office. The only time I spoke to her was via text the day after, when I confirmed I would still be coming by to walk Candy. Keeping both of my jobs, ironically with Annie, is important to me.

Blake and I have exchanged a few friendly texts but nothing more than a check in.

As I walk down the tree lined street with Candy, my phone vibrates in my pocket. Pulling it out, I see Nicole's name on the screen.

"Hey, big sis. How's it going?"

"Hey, little brother. It's going. How about you?"

"I'm just out walking Candy. Is this a social call because you usually only call me when you want something." I hear her huff of exasperation.

"Okay, fine. I'll just cut to the chase. I had a client this morning that's a party planner. Her customer rented out the restaurant at Midnight Moonshine this coming weekend and hired a male dancer, if you know what I mean." Nicole knows that I was a dancer in a strip club and believes it brought in good money. She isn't aware of my skills on the pole that, in actuality, made me the money that put her through school.

"Yes, Nicole, I know what you mean. What does this have to do with me?"

"Well, the dancer called while she was in my chair and canceled. He slipped off a stage and broke his foot." *Fuck*. I have a terrible feeling I know where this is going.

"And?"

"And I may have mentioned that I know an excellent dancer who is very talented and good-looking." Oh course she did.

"Nicole." *Please, no.*

"Coleman."

"You didn't." I already know she did or she wouldn't be calling. I sigh, running a hand down my face in frustration.

"I did. It pays really well, and I know you're eager to get out of my apartment. And just think of the tips. They rented the entire restaurant out for their private event." I stop walking and pinch the bridge of my nose. While the situation isn't ideal, she's probably right about the money. "There's one more thing."

"More than stripping for a bunch of horny women? Or are you going to tell me I'm stripping for men?" It wouldn't be the first time, unfortunately.

"No, it's definitely women. I think she said it was an engagement party or something. But anyway. She mentioned that if you're willing to do some kick, kicker, kicking something, she will pay you extra."

"Kickin' Cowboy?"

"That's it! Do you know what that is? I've never been there before. Country isn't my cup of tea." Closing my eyes, I let out another big sigh and groan.

"Yes, Nicole. I know what a Kickin' Cowboy is. Let's just say it's wet and slightly painful."

"Um, I don't think I want to know how that goes along with stripping."

"And don't forget a mechanical bull."

"A what?"

"There's a mechanical bull inside the restaurant. Anyway, I'm assuming you gave her my number, and I should be expecting a call or text."

"Correct, little bro. I really should start charging a finder's fee for all the business I send your way."

"Nicole, are you offering to be my pimp?" I laugh, and she gasps at the realization she's done exactly that by setting me up for this party.

"Goodbye, Coleman."

"Bye, big sis. Love you."

"Yeah, yeah, Love you, too."

"Well, Candy, it looks like I need to hit the gym hard before this weekend."

The text with the party information came a few hours later, and I had enough time to order a cowboy costume online before the weekend.

She emailed me the contract with the pay details and stipulations. Because this is a public venue, I can't get any more naked than a thong. Since I'll be the only dancer, all tips are mine to keep. And the pay...there were four zeros after the one. I confirmed with the party planner that there wasn't a mistake, and she assured me that was the correct amount. I agreed to the Kickin' Cowboys, and the bonus was added to the total.

~~··~~

As I stand in the staff bathroom of Midnight Moonshine, securing my assless chaps and straightening my cowboy hat, I'm trying not to remember the last time I was here. I still have 30 minutes before I'm supposed to make my appearance. I found out the engagement will actually be taking place here, and this is a party to celebrate. Someone is pretty confident that their partner will say yes.

Before I came in to change, I checked out the setup in the restaurant. Tables and chairs have been decorated in navy and silver accents and rearranged for a dance floor. All around the room are fancy serving stations for food. In the corner, next to the mechanical bull, there's a stage with a single chair set up for me to dance on. These people went all out. There were already some guests starting to arrive so I quickly made my way in here.

I can hear the commotion start outside the staff lounge, where I've been waiting for the party planner to come and get me. Suddenly I hear screaming and cheering and clapping. I guess the question was popped, and their confidence paid off. I can't imagine I'd be hearing that kind of reaction if the answer was no.

Shortly after, the party planner comes in and tells me it's my time. My top is just a vest, and I reach into my bag and grab a cotton pad and a bottle of baby oil, and spray glitter. Pouring some baby oil on the cotton, I wipe it all over my chest and upper arms, then spray myself with the glitter. Women love a sparkly man, apparently. The amount of times I've heard someone yell, "Oh, my god! It's Edward," is too many to count. But the tips always seem to be better when I sparkle, so I go with it.

Walking out into the restaurant, I'm briefly blinded by the colorful strobe lights I hadn't expected. It wasn't flashy in this room last time, so I was unprepared. The lights have been dimmed, and the music playing loudly is bass heavy. I guess they really are ready for me.

As I approach the stage, I notice something that wasn't there before. A pole has been secured to the front. The party planner mentioned they had one for me, but it wasn't there when I looked earlier. This just made my night a whole lot more fun.

When I reach it, I grab the pole and give it a quick spin, testing the stability and type. It's surprisingly secure, and it spins. It's going to be a great night. The tips triple when the women can put them in my thong from upside down. I begin dancing with some basic moves on the pole. The party planner said I'm mostly here for background entertainment unless the engaged couple has any requests.

As I'm slowly spinning down the pole, I hear someone yell my name. But it's not just any someone. It's my someone. I look out into the strobe-filled crowd and see a bouncing brunette heading my way. She looks gorgeous in a bright blue sleeveless dress. The top of the dress is mesh showing off miles of cleavage, and the bottom is full and fluffy.

"Princess?" When she reaches me, she jumps into my arms and climbs my body like a tree. "What are you doing here?"

"Pup, oh my Pup. I've missed you." She's planting sloppy kisses all over my face. "What are you doing here? You look fucking sexy. Are these assless chaps?" She leans over my shoulder to check and hums in appreciation when she sees they are.

187

"Uh, my sister got me this gig. She knew the party planner and gave her my information." She's moved to giving my neck and upper chest kisses. It's been two weeks since I've seen her and the feel of her skin on mine, my hands holding her bare thighs, is giving me goosebumps.

"What are you doing here, Princess? Do you know the engaged couple?" Her cheeks blush so red I see it in the dim strobe-filled light. She pulls her left arm from around my back and puts it in front of her chest, wiggling her fingers. An extremely large yellow center stone with orange and white diamonds on an infinity band sits on her ring finger. *No.* "No fucking way?"

"Yes, way. Isn't it gorgeous! OMG, Pup, it's so wild you're here." Wild isn't the word I would use. If Nicole knew this was Annie's party, I might need to find a new sister.

"So, you and Annie are engaged now? I'm happy for you two." And I am, but I can't help being slightly disappointed. I was still holding out hope that maybe the three of us could work something out. I try to set her down, but she clings to me like a koala.

"What's wrong, Pup?" I don't want to ruin her exciting evening.

"I should get back to work. Annie is paying me an obscene amount of money to dance on stage and get slapped."

"You're doing Kickin' Cowboys? Let's go." She jumps off me and grabs my hand to follow her, but I don't move.

"Blake, I don't think that's a good idea." She stops and spins back around to face me. Her playful face is gone, and BlakeLynn is here.

"What do you mean you don't think it's a good idea? It wasn't a suggestion, Pup. I said, let's go." Every cell in my body wants me to follow her order. To obey her. But I don't belong to her. I can't. She's engaged to Annie, and Annie and I can't have a relationship without loopholes.

"Blake, please." I dropped her hand. I didn't realize my voice would sound so tortured when I spoke. I just want to hold her in my arms again.

"Cole, I'm not sure what's going on right now. Is it the thing with Annie?" The *thing* with Annie is more than just a thing. I wonder how much she knows. I'm sure Annie told her everything. They have that kind of open relationship.

"Blake, this night is about you, not me. You should go find your fiancée and celebrate."

"Oh, okay. That's what this is about. Nope. Let's go. We need to fix this. It's gone on long enough." She takes my hand again and tugs it forcefully. I guess I'm following her.

32

Annie

Where did my gorgeous fiancée run off to? I can't believe she's one step closer to officially being mine. The night has been perfect. I chose Midnight Moonshine to propose because I know how much she loves it. We have nothing but good memories here, and tonight we made another one.

The morning started with breakfast in bed. Chocolate chip pancakes and strawberries. Two of her favorites. After breakfast, I made sure she had a few orgasms before we showered and headed to the spa for a couples massage. We picked at a charcuterie board while getting manicures and pedicures, and I surprised her with her new dress.

She was excited when I told her we were coming here for dinner. What she didn't know was that I planned to propose. I blindfolded her in the parking lot, wanting everything to be a surprise. I brought her into the restaurant with all our friends and got down on one knee before telling her to remove the blindfold.

"BlakeLynn Elise Rogers, from the moment you walked into my office, I've been captivated by you. Your free spirit, your sweet nature, the way you see the beauty in every situation. But most of all, I fell in love with your kind heart.

"You've changed me in so many ways for the better. You give me something to look forward to every evening. Just seeing you smile at me is the highlight of my day.

"We've made plans for our future together, and I can't wait to start those plans.

"BlakeLynn, Mijn Diamant, will you continue to make every day the happiest day of my life? Marry me."

She dropped to her knees and cried into my shoulder, chanting yes. I thought she was going to faint when she finally looked at the ring.

The yellow diamond matches the earrings that she found in our closet. My original plan was to give them to her on the day I chose to propose, but she found them first. I made sure she wore them today, though. They perfectly complement the dress I bought her.

Finally spotting the blue dress walking toward me, a big smile blooms on my face, but it's short-lived.

Walking next to her is a confused-looking Cole. I imagine my face looks much the same right now. I haven't seen or spoken to him since he kissed me. A searing kiss that I haven't been able to get out of my head.

Without stopping, she grabs my hand and keeps walking us through the restaurant. We walk towards the bathrooms but stop in front of a door that says "Staff Only."

"We all need to talk. Right now." My immediate instinct is to chastise her for her tone towards me, but I know she's right. We do need to talk.

"This is the staff lounge. My stuff is in there." Cole opens the door, and we step in. His stuff? I finally look at Cole and see what he's wearing. Realization dawns on me when I see the glitter sparkling on his chest.

"Are you our dancer tonight? Is that how you ended up here, Cole?"

"Yeah, you can thank Nicole for that. I guess you and your party planner have the same hairdresser.

"Who's Nicole?" Blake asks.

"My sister."

"My hairdresser." Cole and I say in unison. Blake bursts out into hysterical laughter, and I look at her as if she's lost her mind.

"Darling, what's so funny?" She holds up one finger asking me to give her a minute. She almost doubled over on herself. She's laughing so hard.

"His...his...sister...Nicole."

"Yes, Nicole is his sister and my hairdresser." She's still laughing, attempting to take big gulps of air to calm herself down.

"Nicole." She puffs in another big breath. "Cole." I hear Cole groan, obviously understanding her reaction before me.

"It's Coleman." I look over and see him pinching the bridge of his nose. I grab Blake's shoulders, trying to help calm her down.

"What am I missing here? I'm failing to see the humor."

"She's laughing at my parent's lack of imagination when it came to naming their children." I think about their names. Nicole. Coleman. Cole. Ni-Cole. I start to chuckle when I finally realize it myself.

"Enjoy your laughs. It's something we've lived with our entire lives." I rub my hands up and down Blake's arms trying to calm her and soothe myself at the same time. This isn't why we came in here. Turning towards Cole, he's standing in the middle of the room, staring at the floor.

"Hello, Cole. It's good to see you." He barely looks up at me.

"It's good to see you, too, Annie. I hear congratulations are in order."

"Yes, thank y-"

"Cut the shit." Blake's tone is stern. "We don't need the pleasantry, bull shit. Cole is hurting, and whether you want to admit it or not, so are you, Annie. Fix this."

"It doesn't matter." Cole's voice is low.

"The fuck, it doesn't matter. How could you say that?" Blake isn't usually one to get angry unless she's really passionate about something. It seems she's passionate about fixing things between the three of us.

"Blake." Cole's tone sounds defeated.

"No, stop that 'Blake' shit. I'm your Princess, and you're my Pup, and Annie is your Kitten. Or you can call us BlakeLynn or Danika."

"You belong to each other now. It's evident by the massive rock on your finger." He gestures to her ring and his shoulders knot with tension. "Annie couldn't figure out a way for us to be together without firing me or making me her fucking sperm donor. We tried. I don't know what more there is to do." It seems Blake's temper may be rubbing off on Cole. He runs his hands through his hair, tugging at the ends.

"Cole, you know I tried to find a way." I threatened to fire the lawyers, but they still kept presenting me with the same

193

three options: marry him, fire him, or list him as a potential sperm donor.

"Did you? It's your company. Write a new fucking policy yourself. I thought what we were starting was amazing. The things I was feeling. *Fuck.*" He turns towards the door, giving us his back. "I need to get back out there. You're paying me to entertain."

"Pup, you don't have to. It's okay if you want to leave." He turns and directs his answer to me.

"No, I signed a contract, and I'll fulfill what I signed. I know my role here. Strip, dance, get slapped. You're paying me for three hours of work, and that's what I'll do." He starts to leave, but stops at Blake, and wraps his hand around the back of her neck. "Congratulations. I'm happy for you, Blake." He kisses her forehead and leaves.

She turns to me with tears in her eyes. I close the distance between us and try to pull her into my arms, but she pushes me away.

"No, Annie. You need to fix this. Unless…unless you don't think there's room for him in our lives. If that's the case, we need to let him go." I pull her back into me.

"I'll fix this. I promise."

We walk back into the restaurant, and find Cole on the stage, entertaining like he said he was going to. Groveling isn't something I do, but right now, I'm willing to do whatever it takes for Blake. And for me, if I'm being honest.

Blake goes off to talk with friends, and I approach the stage. He's ignoring my presence, and I can't blame him for it. Blake was right. We're both hurting, and I'm the only one who can fix it. I try calling his name a few times with no response. I close my eyes and take a deep breath. I know what I have to

194

do.

"Coleman." His name is quick and sharp off my tongue. As I predicted, his attention turns to me. He stops dancing and stalks over, kneels, and lowers his cheek to mine.

"So, you've come to play, Kitten? Okay, let's play." He picks me up and throws me over his shoulder.

"What are you doing? Put me down." He sets me down on the chair in the middle of the stage. Placing a hand next to each of my thighs on the outside of the chair, he leans close to me and growls.

"You don't get to make demands when you call me 'Coleman.' You made your choice when you summoned me, Kitten. Now, stop being a brat, and deal with your consequences like the good girl I know you are."

Cole stands in front of me, and his body moves as if it's a wave in the ocean as he sharply takes off his vest. Barechested, he moves to the back of my chair. He grabs my wrists and pulls them up over my head, placing my palms on his firm chest. His fingers trail a line from my wrists to my elbows, skimming the sides of my breasts. When they reach my hips, they head inward until his hands circle my thighs, and he pulls my legs apart.

He drops to his knees and spins a 360 around the chair, stopping between my legs. He locks eyes with me before lifting my skirt and burying his head underneath it. I feel his hot tongue trail a line up my inner thigh. It's taking every ounce of willpower to stay composed and not shove his head where I desperately want it.

He pops up and closes my legs before straddling me on the chair. Encircling my wrists, he places my hands on his ass, then snatches a handful of hair at the back of my neck, thrusting my head to the side. He's fucking me over my clothes, hips moving back and forth, driving me mad. Leaning into my neck, he pulls a chunk of skin into his mouth, sucking hard before popping off and bending closer to my ear.

"I should fuck you right here on this stage and show you exactly what I think of your contract. Be your manwhore, Kitten. Bend you over this chair and sink so deep into you that you feel me in your throat."

"Coleman." His name is a breathless whisper on my lips. He grabs my cheeks with one hand, squeezing hard, making my lips pucker.

"This pretty little mouth is going to be a very addicting problem, Danika." He roughly rubs his thumb over my lips, smearing my lipstick.

Standing over me, still straddling the chair, he grabs me around the waist. Looking me in the eyes, he says, "Trust me. I've got you." Before I can even consider what he means, the chair is being pulled out from under me by his other hand. Guiding my body to the ground, he lays me on my back, nestling himself between my legs.

He sensually fucks me again over my clothes before he sits up on his knees between my legs. Every nerve in my body is buzzing like a live wire. In a move that seems more appropriate for the Cirque du Soleil, Cole spins around with his back facing me. He falls forward onto his hands and hooks his knees behind mine, interlocking our legs.

As quick as the blink of an eye, we barrel-rolled together until I'm on my stomach, arms sprawled out in front of me. He whips around, and I feel the weight of his entire body pressed on top of mine. His hand flies up my body, grabbing a fistful of my hair. Lowering his mouth to my neck, he bites me, while letting out a feral growl. He's marking me like he did to Blake.

"You belong to me, Kitten, and don't you fucking forget that." He rolls off of me and stands. Extending his hand, he pulls me into his chest, and wraps me in his possessive hold.

"Fuck the lawyers and fuck the loophole contract. You have two choices. Marry me or fire me, Danika. The choice is yours. But I'm not giving either of you up. And when I put a baby in you, I'm going to be a willing fucking participant. Not because some dickless assholes with too much money tell me I have to."

33

Blake

They looked so fucking hot on that stage. Watching Cole take control of Annie took all my willpower not to join them up there. They needed their moment to work things out between them. While we still have many unanswered questions, it feels like we're heading in the right direction.

"What are you going to do?" Annie told me about Cole's ultimatum after we left the restaurant. She lifts my left hand and kisses my ring, then lowers and kisses my bracelet.

"Of those two options, only one is feasible, Darling. *You* will be my wife."

"So you're going to fire him? He loves his job. That doesn't seem fair." Resting my head on her shoulder, I watch the lights of the sleepy city pass by us through the car window.

"I know he does. It feels like I've gone over every other option." Three best and worst possible ideas: Marriage, jobless, sperm donor. What if…?

"Annie?" She isn't going to like my idea.

"Yes, Little One." Here it goes.

198

"Do it." Brushing my hair behind my ear she gently kisses my forehead.

"Do what?"

"Marry him. Or have a baby with him. Pick one of the other options." She's silently ingesting my words. Shaking her head, she looks into my eyes.

"While I wish it were that simple, the ramifications of either of those options are huge. I can't marry Cole because you are the love of my life Blake. I'm going to marry you and only you."

"Our signatures on a piece of paper won't make me any more or less your wife, Annie. You ARE my wife. You are my future, forever and always. I love you, Annie, and I don't need a signature to prove that to the world."

"*Mijn Diamant*, did you have too much to drink tonight? I can't marry Cole."

"Okay, then, let's have a baby. He rejected that contract because it was a ridiculous idea at the time, but is it really that ridiculous? We can provide everything that a baby could want or need. You said you want to carry a baby. We want to have a family. Why not just do it?"

"You're painting a lovely fairy tale picture, Little One, but I'm not sure either idea is an option. We don't know him well enough."

"Tell me you don't feel it, Baby? I knew there was something special about you the moment we met. I felt you in my soul like a moth being pulled toward a flame. Cole feels…he feels like another flame." Maybe she doesn't feel it. Maybe I'm just being selfish. She sighs and toys with the ring on my finger.

"I don't think I've ever felt anything for the other gender my entire life. But you were right when you said I've been miserable without him." A flash of guilt washes over her face. "I've been watching him come and go on the cameras every day when he comes to take Candy for her walk."

"So what are you saying? Are you considering the other options?"

"I'm saying we invite Cole over for dinner, and we all have a discussion."

"I love the sound of that. Let's decide together." I cuddle further into her and imagine little blonde hair blue eyed babies.

34

Cole

I wanted to say no. I should have said no. On Monday, Annie asked me to have dinner with them Wednesday night. I gave her an ultimatum, and there's been no response.

Every night, for the past three nights, when I've logged into the gaming platform, I've expected to get a notification that my access had been denied, but it hasn't happened. Unless she's decided that she, they, want nothing to do with me at all.

Fuck. If that's why they invited me over tonight, to tell me it's been nice, but they're done, well, I'm not entirely sure how I'll feel. Each of these women bring out something different within me. I never saw myself as being submissive, especially not to a woman. But, god, when Blake calls me Pup, I'm ready to drop to my knees and worship at her feet.

My Kitten, my Danika. I've seen her dominance over Blake. It's beautiful to watch Blake submit to her. The trust they have with each other is unmatched by anything I've ever seen before. When Annie submits to me, when she gives that same trust over to me, I feel like I could conquer the world. Like *we* could conquer the world.

There was never an option for me to say no to this dinner, despite how badly I wanted to prolong the potential negativity that could come from it. We need to figure out how to proceed with whatever dynamic we choose.

Ringing the doorbell, a cheerful Blake and Candy greet me when the door opens. She looks so casual and comfortable in spandex shorts and a tank top and I give her a warm smile.

"Hey, Princess. You look beautiful." Her smile widens when she hears me call her Princess. Jumping up, she throws her arms around my neck, and I dip slightly, wrapping her thighs around my waist.

"Hey, Pup." Soft lips graze my jaw until they find mine. I soak in her warmth and the gentle caress of her tongue as it asks for entry. Parting my lips, I deepen the kiss. I love her petite body wrapped around me. She pulls away, still smiling.

"Dinner is almost done. Sarah made us something special for tonight." Closing the door behind us, I carry Blake in the direction of the kitchen.

"Who's Sarah? It smells amazing in here."

"She's our cook." I look past Blake and see Annie pulling a dish out of the oven.

"Hi, Kitten." I set Blake down on the counter next to Annie and turned to embrace her. There's a moment of hesitation before she steps into me. I dip and grab the back of her thighs to pick her up as I had just done with Blake.

My hand laces through her golden hair, inhaling her vanilla scent. It smells like comfort and home.

"You smell just as amazing as the food, Kitten." I pull back and look into her eyes. I can't tell how she's feeling, so I ask.

"Can I kiss you?"

"Yes, please, Coleman." *Well fuck.* I wasn't expecting a yes. That's all the permission I need and all the reassurance I've been waiting for. I sit her on the counter next to Blake, trail my hand up between her breasts and wrap it around her neck. I feel her swallow as her pupils dilate.

"Have you been a good girl? Do you deserve a kiss?" I can see in her eyes the moment her mind lets go, but she doesn't answer me. "What's wrong, Kitten? You don't think you deserve to be kissed?" Her eyes close, and she shakes her head. "Shall we ask your sub what she thinks?" Eyes still closed, she nods.

"Princess, has Danika been good to you?"

"Always, Pup." She caresses my arm that's wrapped around Annie's neck. "This is so fucking hot."

"Do you need a hand necklace, too, Princess?" The thought of having both of them under my control has my dick trying to break through my pants.

"Tempting, but not right now. What I need right now is to watch you make Danika happy. She's missed you. We both have, Pup. Kiss her, and then we'll eat dinner. We have things to discuss, and maybe we can have some playtime after." Because I can't help myself once I get the image in my head, I grab Blake's neck with my opposite hand and pull her in for a kiss.

The kiss is desperate and needy. It's been too long since I've tasted her. She pushes at my chest to release her and smacks me across the face. My dick jumps. I feel like a caged animal. My lust is consuming me from her slap. I want her to do it again. She grabs my wrist, and I jerk back, removing my hand. Sticking her finger in my chest, she chastises me.

"Bad boys don't get rewards, Pup. You were told to make Danika happy. Now, kiss her." My hand, still wrapped around Annie's neck, pulses a few times in anticipation of her mouth on mine. I take a split second to decide whether to make the kiss soft and tender or devour her.

Blake's hand rubs over my straining erection, and she whispers "Kiss her" into my ear. I launch myself at Annie like a slingshot. She moans into my mouth, and her hands grab my hips. Ideas of taking her right here on this kitchen counter float through my mind when I hear "Enough" next to me.

I step back from Annie, and she whimpers. I know exactly how she's feeling. I give them a hand to help them off the counter. For that one moment, they were both mine, and no matter what happens next, I'll remember the feel of their necks beneath my hands.

"Let's eat before the food gets cold. Sarah won't appreciate her ribs going to waste." Annie hands me a plate, and we all help ourselves before sitting at the dining room table. We quietly eat for several minutes before Blake seems to be bursting at the seems to speak.

"We want you to choose, Pup."

"Little One." Annie's tone sends a warning.

"Choose what, Princess."

"Get married, get fired, or get pregnant." I choke on the meat I'm chewing. She can't be serious. Firing me is the only reasonable option of the three.

"You're joking, right?" Neither of them look like they're joking. "You want me to choose my own fate? I've been waiting every day to get fired. Every evening when I log in, I'm both shocked and thankful that I'm not locked out of the system." I look at Annie. "What is this all about?"

"Just as she said, Cole. You were presented with three options. Blake and I discussed it and have decided that any of them work for us, so the decision is yours to make."

"Kitten, I want to talk to Annie, not Danika. I need to understand this. I need to know how you're actually feeling. You'd marry me? The two of you just got engaged. Why not just fire me?"

"Because you love your job. How could I take that away from you?"

"How could you take..." I wipe my hand down my face because I can't believe what they are saying to me. "No. I can't marry you, Annie. I can't take that away from you and Blake. I'll quit. I'll give my two weeks tomor-"

"Make a baby with me." *What?* Okay, I must have heard her wrong.

"Annie, we've gone over this. I won't be some potential sperm donor on paper to give us free rein to fuck." Sighing, I sit back in my chair. I've lost my appetite.

Blake stands from her seat and approaches me. Lifting her leg, she straddles my lap, and I grab her hips, flexing my hands. She cups my cheeks and stares into my eyes.

"Pup, Cole, we aren't asking you on paper. We want a baby." She turns to look at Annie. "We want a baby. With you." It's my turn to look at Annie.

"Is this really what you want?" She nods and stands, walking over to a drawer in the kitchen. Opening it, she pulls out a manila folder before returning to sit at the table and sliding it toward me.

"The contract my lawyers drew up already covered everything. You still need to be protected, and the details in here outline everything. Of course, we can negotiate anything more to your liking." I reach over and grab her jaw. I want all of her attention.

"Kitten, I've already told you I don't want anything from you. I don't want anything BUT you. And if I have the privilege of making a baby with you, that's all the bonus I need."

"So that's a yes to a baby?" Blake is bouncing in my lap, and there's no way she isn't feeling the effect it's having on me.

"That's a yes. But what about you, Princess? Do you want a baby?"

"Yes, but Annie first."

"Okay, if that's how you want it. I need a pen so I can sign this contract and start practicing."

Annie walks from the room and comes back with a pen. Handing it to me, she looks unsure. I take the pen and pull her into me by the side.

"Kitten, I wouldn't be signing this if I didn't want to. You know that because of the last time you presented it to me. I'm falling for both of you, hard. This relationship is more than just sex for me which is why I wouldn't sign it in your office that day."

"You're sure?" Grabbing a handful of her shirt, I pull her to me so we're face to face.

"Danika, I'm sure I want to be with you and create a life with you." I close the gap between us in a searing kiss. Blake's excitement has her bouncing in my lap again, and I groan.

"Princess, if you're going to continue to ride my cock, I'd prefer it if there were a lot less clothing between us." She giggles at me and peels her tank top off, revealing her naked tits directly in my face. "Fuck, alrighty then."

I take a handful of one of her supple breasts and suck her nipple into my mouth. Her back arches as I swirl my tongue, making her nipple harden. I peer up to Annie.

"Care to join me for dessert?" Her smile is radiant.

"Don't mind if I do." She leans down and mimics my movements on Blake's other nipple. Blake leans back in my lap and places her elbows on the table. I release her nipple and turn to Annie. With perfect precision, I aim at the spot on her shirt that I know is right over her nipple, and she hisses when I clamp down. Such a beautiful sound, and it turns into a moan.

"Off, Kitten." I tug at her shirt. She removes it, and I take in her creamy skin wrapped in a sheer blue bra. I reach behind her and unclip the bra with one hand, and her breasts spill out as the blue scrap of fabric hits the floor.

"God, fucking dammit. You're both absolutely stunning. I'm the luckiest man in the fucking world because I get to call you mine." Palming a breast on each of them, I swipe my thumbs over their hard nipples, and they moan and mewl at my touch.

"I want you, *Mijn Vrede*. I've been waiting to have you, and I don't want to wait anymore. Please sign the papers. Please." She strips off the rest of her clothes as she confesses this to me. She's so gorgeous. My eyes take in her smooth pale skin, and her curvy hips that I know will only look more incredible once her belly swells with my baby.

"It never gets old." I look towards a smiling Blake, who's biting her lip while also taking in Annie's figure in all of her naked glory. Blake climbs out of my lap and embraces Annie in a deep passionate kiss. I'm constantly in awe of seeing them together. I take the opportunity to strip from my clothes, and when I'm naked, I crouch behind Blake and slowly remove her spandex shorts and panties.

"Much better." I stand next to them and rub my hands down their spines, causing their bodies to shiver with goosebumps and quiet moans to form in their throats. "You're both so beautiful. I don't even know where to begin to worship you."

"Let's go to the couch, Pup." I quickly sign the contract, and she takes my hand and guides Annie and me to sit, with each one on either side of me. Blake's hands are soft and gentle as she traces the tattoos on my left arm. Her light touch almost tickles as she outlines the constellations and red roses. The dragon with green eyes mixed around tribal artwork.

"These are gorgeous."

"Not as gorgeous as either of you." I capture her lips in mine and show her with my tongue just how much I appreciate her beauty. Annie moves next to me, and I hear a drawer open. A piece of silk wraps around my eyes, and I realize Annie is blindfolding me.

"What are you up to, Kitten?"

"Just a little sensory play. Being blindfolded is one of Blake's favorite things. I thought she might enjoy being on the other end of it for once."

"Do you like that idea, Princess? Do you want to take advantage of me?" The thought of being at her mercy is enticing.

"I want you to talk to us. I want you to explain to us everything you're feeling, Pup?" She wants me to give them details of what I'm feeling while blindfolded. I think I can play their game.

"Ok, Princess. Kitten. I'll play." I sit back and rest my arms on top of the couch. Long seconds stretch without them touching me, and my nerves start to ignite with anticipation.

A fingernail trails along the ridges of my abs, and they constrict from the sudden sensation.

"What do you feel?" Annie purrs in my ear. "Explain it to us."

"I feel your hot breath on the shell of my ear. A sharp nail is tracing my abs, that's leaving a tingling feeling behind. Mmm. Someone's hot tongue is licking my pec, and it feels...oooh. I had no idea my nipples could be so sensitive. Shit." My body convulses inward as someone bites my nipple.

"Describe it, Pup." It must be Blake's mouth on me because my nipple gets bitten again.

"I feel the sharp pinch and it gives me a wave of pleasure as you drag your tongue across the bite."

"Keep talking." Annie whispers in my ear.

"Light feathery kisses across my collarbone feels like a butterfly dancing on me. Oh god. Something just brushed against my inner thigh." My cock twitched at the sensation. "I feel like I'm on fire with the anticipation of the first touch of my dick."

"You're doing so well, Pup." My dick twitches again at her praise. Based on the sound, she's the one between my legs. I want to beg her to take my cock in her mouth, but I have a feeling that will only prolong her actually doing it. *Uugggh.*

"Someone's sharp teeth are sinking into my neck, now licking. Your tongue is warm and wet, and I want to feel it all over my body. Oh, fucking fuck me. That's...that feels..."

"Describe it for us, Cole. Tell my Little One what her mouth feels like wrapped around your cock." I'm having trouble forming words. "Let me tell you what I see. I see a gorgeous brunette on her knees. Her head is slowly dipping back and forth. Your thick veiny cock disappearing and reappearing through her full, luscious lips. I see her hand stroking the length she can't fit in her mouth because you're so big. Now, tell me what you feel." Words. I have to form words.

"I feel..." Reaching down, I grab a fistful of Blake's hair. "I feel her silky strands under my fingers. I feel the heat from her tongue gliding up and down my rock-hard cock. Periodically her...ooooh...her teeth barely scrape across the top while her tongue plays with my barbells. Oh fuck. The back of her throat. I just felt the back of her throat on the head of my cock. Her t-tongue, her skilled fucking tongue is driving me mad swirling around the tip. Goddammit, mother fucker."

"What did she do? Tell me." Annie sounds as excited to hear as I am to feel.

"Sh-she squeezed my balls while sucking on my tip and stuck her tongue in my slit. P-P-Princess. Fuck I'm getting close already. Fuck no. Come back." She popped off when I said I was getting close. I just fucking whimpered. I whimpered because she stopped going down on me. Who am I?

I hear Annie giggle in my ear. I reach up and grab her neck, and the giggling stops.

"I feel your throat as you swallow and your pulse beating rapidly under my fingers. I feel your shallow breathing as your arousal increases. And in a moment, when I flip you over and put myself between your legs, I'm going to finally taste your pussy. I'm going to feel your clit under my tongue while I flick and nip it. I'm going to hear you moan my name, and I'm going to feel your pussy convulse when I make you come on my tongue."

"Coleman."

"Yes, Kitten."

"Do it. Now." Ripping off the blindfold, I quickly take note of where Blake is so I don't accidentally hit her. She's moved away enough that when I push Annie's back against the couch and drop to my knees as promised, she has a nice view of Annie's spread legs.

"Look at our pretty pussy, Princess. How did we get so lucky?" She sticks out her bottom lip and pouts.

"She doesn't let me enjoy her as much as I'd like to."

"Well, we can't have that, can we? Come over here and help me." Pushing Annie's legs up towards her chest, I move over to make room for Blake.

I take the first lick and drag the flat of my tongue from her entrance to her clit and listen to the delicious sound she makes as I devour her pussy. I let Blake have a turn, and it's obvious she knows Annie's body well.

"Do you have any idea how fucking gorgeous the two of you are together?" Blake slips a finger inside Annie's pussy, and she lets out a guttural moan. I need to join her. I need to be the one that causes those sounds.

The two of us lick, suck and nip at Annie. We take turns pumping inside of her with our fingers, working her up until she can't take another moment of our teasing. When she orgasms, her screams echo off the vaulted ceiling, and it's an incredible sound–our own personal symphony.

I crawl up her body and take her lips in mine. "That was fucking beautiful, Kitten." I nuzzle into her neck and breathe in her vanilla scent. Their vanilla scent.

"So, Pup, do we get to practice baby-making now?" Blake moves to sit next to Annie and me on the couch. Her excitement is palpable, the smile on her face wide. I reach out and glide my finger over her collarbone.

"How do I decide when I have two deliciously fuckable options?" A mischievous grin spread over her face.

"*Mijn Diamant*, what's going through that pretty head?"

"Okay, so I watched this video recently-"

"Was it porn, Princess? Are you about to make a suggestion from a porno you watched?" There isn't an ounce of shame on her face when she responds.

"Hey, your girl has a healthy appetite, and sometimes I have needs, and no one is around." *Your girl.* I love the sound of that.

"I'm here to fulfill all of your needs, for both of you. Day or night. I'm always willing to lend a helping hand, finger, or tongue."

"Or penis?"

"Princess, my cock doesn't help. It commands and dominates. Now, let's hear your crazy porno idea." She tells us about the video she saw, and I'm so fucking down with it.

·ᴗᴗ··ᴗᴗ·

"Baby, are you sure you're okay with it? I don't want to smush you." These two are adorable.

"Am I sure that I want your entire body laying on mine while Cole takes turns fucking each of us? Darling, is that really a question you're asking?"

"Okay, I get it. I'm not used to being in the position to make suggestions."

"Well, Princess, how about you get in the position to have my cock pumping in and out of you. You'll forget about having to make any decisions except how many orgasms you can handle."

"Oh, that's an easy one," Annie's tone is so nonchalant. "The answer is thirteen." My jaw drops. That's a lot of orgasms.

"Holy shit. You handled thirteen orgasms, Princess?"

"Well, technically, I passed out during the thirteenth one." She shrugs like it's no big deal.

"I'm a pleasure Domme. You haven't scened with us yet. You'll learn." She winks and lays face down on the chaise end of the couch. "Like this, Little One?"

"Hmmm, exactly like that. Let me join you." Annie is slightly bent, hanging off the end of the chaise lying on her stomach. Blake walks up behind her and climbs on top, straddling Annie's hips. Then she lays down, her stomach on Annie's back. Both women lay in full display before me, asses in the air. "Take your pick, big boy."

"It's a pussy pile, and it's all mine. Mmmm. Kitten, be sure to check in if you need to."

"Less talking, more fucking." I crouch next to her and grab her chin, forcing her to look at me.

"You aren't in charge anymore. I suggest you remember that, Danika."

"Yes, Coleman." *Fuck*. This woman is incredible.

"Good Girl. Now, you check in and use your safewords. Do you understand?"

"Yes, Coleman." I stroke her hair in approval and move to stand behind them. Not just one, but two glistening pussies await me. "Danika, remind me of your safewords."

"Yellow, good. Orange, think. Red, stop."

"Excellent. Princess, we are definitely watching porn together if you come up with ideas like this." I rub my fingers on their clits and listen to them moan. Using my hand to line my cock up to Annie's entrance, I line my fingers up to Blake's and enter them both slowly at the same time.

All three of us moan as the feeling of pleasure washes over us. I can feel every barbel as it enters Annie. I already know they are going to drive her crazy. I choose a steady pace to not rock Blake around too much. She has her arms wrapped around Annie's breast, playing with her nipples that are squished into the couch.

I pull out of Annie and switch my hand with my cock. My thick fingers push back into Annie while my cock enters Blake.

"Good girls take turns."

35

Annie

The pressure of Blake on my back while Cole fucks me is incredible. It feels like I'm in a blanket of pleasure. Blake's hands roughly pinch my nipples, adding to the already overwhelming sensations. His barbells line the entire length of his cock and run across my wanting g-spot, driving me mad.

I'm about to ask him to go faster when he pulls out and replaces his cock with his fingers.

"Good girls take turns."

Blake's breathing increases as he thrusts in and out of her. He seems to wait until she gets close and then switches again. Her moan as he pulls out is so sexy. He's being a tease. Eventually, he starts rotating back and forth between us with his cock, giving each of us a few thrusts before switching to the other. It's driving us fucking wild.

Cole finally shows us mercy, and we both get to come, his name spilling out of our mouths, but he's not done yet.

"Princess, on your back. Kitten, show me how good your mouth is and make her come again. I'm not done with your pussy yet." His filthy mouth is so damn sexy.

Blake rolls off me and crawls further up the couch. I happily crawl between her thighs, leaving my ass in the air for Cole to take. Now that he doesn't have to worry about Blake falling off when he sinks into me, he doesn't hold back. His thrusts are deep and carnal. His movements are dictating how I'm eating out, Blake. Her moans of pleasure tell me she's enjoying it as much as I am.

"How are we doing, ladies? I'm getting close, and I want both of you to have another orgasm. Can you be my good girls and come for me again?"

"Yes, Coleman."

"God yes, Pup." Cole reaches around and rubs my clit in quick circles, and I insert a finger in Blake's pussy. I find her sweet spot and rub. Cole adjusts his angle, and my hips buck back at him when my orgasm hits.

"Fuck, Annie. Oh fuck, Kitten."

"Oh my god, Annie." We all come together, yelling, moaning, screaming.

Suddenly, Candy comes bounding into the room, barking. We must have finally scared her with our noises. She jumps on the couch and licks us to ensure we're all okay. Blake and I are squealing, and Cole is cupping his dick, trying to prevent her from licking him there.

We collapse into a heap of laughter on the couch, and I feel lighter than I can ever remember. Surrounded by the woman I love, who will be my wife, my crazy dog, and a man who is rapidly stealing a piece of my heart, I feel like I'm home.

"How about we take this upstairs to bed? Would you like to stay the night, Cole?"

"I'd love nothing more, Kitten."

·ᴖᴖ·ᴖᴖ·

Waking up the next morning, I'm laying here trying to figure out how I'm covered in limbs. Somehow I'm between Blake and Cole, but Blake was in the middle when we fell asleep. Carefully peeling away their layers, I make it to the bathroom to shower before work. As I'm brushing my teeth, Blake walks in, looking adorably messy.

"Good morning, *Mijn Diamant.* Did you sleep well?" She sits on the counter next to me and grabs her toothbrush.

"I did. How about you, Baby? You're up earlier than usual." I hand her the mint toothpaste and replace the cap on my cinnamon. We may agree on body wash and shampoos, but we differ in toothpaste flavors.

"I woke up in the middle of a pile of people. It was a bit hot but also nice. And I'm up early because I have a lot on my mind."

"Anything I can help you with?" She finishes brushing her teeth and hands me her toothbrush to replace. I step to the side to stand between her legs and wrap my arms around her waist.

"No, Little One. I can handle everything. I need to get the signed contract to the lawyers. I need to call my doctor to make an appointment to have my IUD removed. I still need to go SUV shopping with Josh. I have a meeting this afternoon-"

"Hold on. You can't just gloss over the removal of an IUD like it's a cup of coffee. I know we talked about it, but there was never really a timeline discussed. You want to do this now?" Oh no, I assumed we were on the same page. Am I rushing this?

"Would you prefer to wait? I'm not getting any younger,

217

and they'll already consider me a geriatric pregnancy in a few months. I assumed we wanted to start now."

"We do. We do want to start now. I thought you'd want to wait, but I'm excited!" I place a tender kiss on her forehead.

"Good, Little One. I'm excited, too. I need to finish getting ready for work, and so do you. Would you like to ride with me?" I ask her the same question almost every morning. I'm about to walk away expecting her usual answer of, "No, thank you," when she surprises me.

"I'd love to." My finger traces the bottom lip of her smile, and I can't help but kiss her nose at her adorableness.

"Do you have any idea how much I love you? How happy you make me? You're my red rose in a field of weeds. My rainbow after a storm."

"If you're trying to get in my pants, I'm not wearing any." She winks at me, and I roll my eyes. "I love you, too. And don't let Cole see you do that. You might get punished for that sass."

"Don't let Cole see what?" Blake jumps in my arms, and I can't help but chuckle to myself. He startled her.

"Your Kitten is being a brat this morning and rolled her eyes at me." She grabs a hand towel from the hook and tosses it at him. "Cover that thing up. There's no time to play this morning." He drops the towel and crosses his arms, leaning against the doorframe in all his naked glory.

"There's always time to play, Princess. Are you challenging me? I only need ten minutes, and I can give you both orgasms." Blake jumps down from the counter, and I see the challenge written all over her face. Hands on her hips, she looks directly into his eyes.

"Prove it."

"You asked for it, Princess." He pushes her up against the closet door and drops to his knees. One of her legs comes up over his shoulder, and he buries his head between her thighs. Her moans are instant, and I see him lick two fingers and then slip them inside her. I recognize the motions of his hand and know he's going to keep his promise. It only takes two minutes on his knees before she's pulling at his hair, trying not to collapse as her knees go weak from her orgasm.

He helps her get steady before standing and looking at me. With a glistening chin and hunger in his eyes, he lifts me onto the counter.

"Hey, I never agreed to this challenge." His hands spread my thighs.

"Too bad no one asked you, Kitten." His mouth captures mine as he grabs my hips and thrusts his cock into me. I gasp at the intrusion, then moan as he slowly pulls out, and I feel each barbell. He slams back in and sets a punishing pace. With one hand on my hip, he uses his other to find my clit and matches his fingers with the motion of his hips. I wrap my arms around his neck for leverage and hang on for the ride.

I barely have time to take in everything happening when I feel my orgasm building.

"Holy shit."

"What's the matter, Kitten? I can tell you're already close. So am I. Did you doubt my skills?"

"I did," Blake chimes in from next to us. Cole leans down and kisses her, and the beautiful site of them together detonates my orgasm. My nails dig into his back as he pumps harder and starts moaning my name as his orgasm takes him, too.

"Fuck, Kitten." He buries his face into my hair and inhales. "Next time, Princess, you won't doubt me. I like a challenge." He looks down at his watch. "An entire minute to spare. Now get ready for work. Who's going to let me use their toothbrush?" The three of us laugh as I open a drawer and pull out a new toothbrush for him.

"Mint or cinnamon toothpaste?" I hold up both tubes as I see Blake turn on the shower.

"Who uses cinnamon toothpaste?" His nose scrunches in mild disgust.

"I do. Don't worry. Blake has the same reaction." I see him watching in the mirror as she gets in the shower. "Before you ask, playboy, no, you can't join. There absolutely isn't enough time now." I hand him the two toothpastes and join Blake in the shower. I hear him growl.

"This is completely unfair, just for the record, ladies."

"Enjoy the show, Pup. Maybe if you're good I'll show you the butt plugs I bought for you." Blake teases him and pulls me in for a kiss to be a brat. He stands for a moment, staring at us in shock and confusion. As he's leaving the bathroom I hear him muttering to himself. "Butt plugs? As in plural?" I can't help but chuckle.

"I love you, *Mijn Diamant.*"

"Love you too, Baby."

36

Annie

I love mornings. Waking up to Blake every day is a dream come true. I made us my favorite peanut butter banana smoothie, and she happily drank it while singing my praises on the way to work. I've been able to convince her to commute together more frequently.

"Baby, how good is Josh's NDA?" Such a random question. "The best."

"Is he due for a bonus anytime soon?" Why is she asking me this?

"Little One, what's going through your head?" I feel her hand brush over my knee and toy with the hem of my skirt.

"I know you're planning to go car shopping today. You looked online all weekend, and I'm sure you know exactly what you're buying. We never got to christen this one, so maybe it needs a farewell instead." Her hand slips under my skirt and brushes my inner thighs. She's become braver with her sexuality since Cole came into our lives. I love how submissive she's always been for me, but she's been taking more initiative lately, and I am very much enjoying it.

I glance up to the front seat and see Josh has headphones in and isn't paying attention to us. I scoot down in the seat and spread my legs as wide as my skirt allows. Her hand reaches the top of my thigh, and she toys with the edge of my panties.

"Take these off," she whispers in my ear. I give her a stern look. "Please, Danika." I stroke her cheek with my knuckles.

"Only because you asked so nicely." Very strategically, I slide down my yellow thong. She grabs them from my hand and stuffs them in her bra.

"Mine now." She swallows my objection with her lips. I would protest if I didn't keep spare clothes in my office. I can't go all day bare.

Her body is half on top of mine, shielding her actions from the front seat. Her fingers are cool as she rubs up and down my wet slit. The idea that Josh could be watching is exciting.

I do my best to contain my moans as she massages my clit, concentrating on my breathing to not tip off Josh. When she slips a finger inside me, an involuntary groan slips out before Blake can contain it with her mouth. It feels so good I don't even care if he hears anymore. Blake's right. He's due for a bonus.

She adds another finger and uses her thumb to continue massaging my clit.

"*Mijn Diamant*, I'm so close. Please don't stop." The pressure increases from her thumb, and her fingers inside me curl up. Josh is about to get a show because there's no way I can be quiet.

Threading my hand through Blake's hair, I pull her in closer as my orgasm crests. I try and drown my moaning into her mouth, but there's no use. My hips are bucking as she thrusts deeper into me.

"Oh fuck, Blake. I fucking love you, Little One." She kisses me until I come down. I can feel the heat on my cheeks as I lock eyes with Josh in the rearview mirror. He clears his throat and adjusts in his seat before looking away.

I look at Blake and see she's licking her fingers with a smug smile on her face. I realize the show Josh just got and feel a slight ping of embarrassment.

"Cole's cuff comes in the mail today. It's being delivered to my office. I can't wait to give it to him."

"That's wonderful, Darling. Any idea how you plan to present it?"

"Oh, Josh. I love this song. Can you turn it up?" Josh increases the volume from the steering wheel controls, and I listen as Blake sings and hums the lyrics, our previous conversation lost to the music.

"I will send out an army to find you...You're not defenseless, I'll be your shelter...In the middle of the hardest fight, I will rescue you."

A few minutes later, we dropped Blake off at her office. I promise her she can take a test drive in our new SUV tonight after work. When Josh drops me off at the elevator, his face is still a little flushed. I remind him I need to be picked up at 1 o'clock for my doctor's appointment, and then we will go to the dealership.

For only working half a day, its stretched on. I replaced my panties as soon as I got into my office and sent Blake a flirty picture. I weighed my options and sent it to Cole as well. He texted me back, letting me know he planned to christen the new SUV tonight, without Josh watching. Apparently, Blake had told him about our car ride this morning.

At 1 o'clock, Josh is waiting to take me to my doctor's appointment. As he drops me off, I ask him to run to the florist while I'm inside and pick up two dozen red roses to give Blake tonight.

My appointment goes well, and my IUD is successfully removed. We discussed my future of carrying children, and she has a positive outlook. It's a fulfilling appointment, and I have high hopes for the future and having a baby.

When I return to the car, Josh's demeanor seems off. He opens the door for me but doesn't say a word. I see he's picked up the roses I've requested, and I thank him as I move them over to make room to sit. He seems tense as he gets in the driver's seat.

"Josh, is everything alright?" He ignores me for a moment as he leaves the parking deck in the direction of the car dealership. His jaw ticks, and I can see him grinding his teeth. His short hair is out of sorts, as if he's been tugging at it. "Do you have something you need to say?"

"May I speak freely, Ms. Poulsen?" There's a slight shake to his voice. Almost as if he's nervous.

"You may."

"I've been your driver for four years. I've watched your relationship bloom with Ms. Rogers, and I couldn't be happier for the both of you." Is he going to say something about what happened this morning?

"Thank you, Josh." There's more. I can tell by his stiff posture.

"I've always respected you and your decisions, but Annie, you brought this guy into your life recently and…"

"And what, *Josh*?" He's never called me Annie before, always Ms. Poulsen, despite me trying to be less formal when he first

224

became my driver.

"And you've changed. You just had your IUD removed to have a baby with a man you haven't known that long. You're a very intelligent, powerful woman, and it seems… irresponsible." How dare he.

"Josh, I know I gave you permission to speak freely, but I don't think my sex life is any of your business."

"You sure made it my business this morning." My jaw drops. I can't believe he has the audacity to say something like that to me. Before I can respond to him, my phone rings, and it's Blake's ringtone.

"Darling, this isn't the best time."

"Is everything okay, Baby? Did something go wrong at your appointment?"

"No, everything went well at my appointment. I'm just having a little…business issue." Josh's eyes flash to mine, and I see his hand move to the radio. He raises the volume, and my blood boils. Michael Jackson's *Smooth Criminal* is playing. This song is the bane of my existence, and everyone close to me in my life, including Josh, knows how much I loathe it.

"Josh, please turn it down." His hand reaches up again, and the volume increases. He's making a show of turning the volume up on the radio dial because he has controls right at his fingertips on the steering wheel.

"Annie, what's going on? Where are you?" The lyrics, *So, Annie, are you okay? Are you okay, Annie?* are now blasting through the speakers. The music is so loud. I see his lips moving, but I'm not certain what he said. Did he say, "You should have asked me? It should be me?"

"Josh, turn it down now! This isn't funny." He's holding eye contact with me in the rearview. He doesn't see the light turn yellow. He doesn't see the large SUV that speeds up from the oncoming traffic to make the turn after their light turns red. He doesn't see the SUV that hits our small sedan on his side at full force.

The sound of metal crunching is deafening. I hear a horn blaring, and my stomach drops as our car rolls. There's more crunching before I'm thrown back in the opposite direction, and everything goes black.

"Annie, are you okay? Annie, Annie, are you okay?" God, I hate this song.

"Josh, turn off that fucking song." My throat feels like I swallowed glass. I cough in an attempt to clear it.

"Annie, ANNIE! What's going on? Are you okay, Annie?" Blake?

"Josh," I moan out. "Where's Blake?" I feel so groggy. What's going on?

"Oh god, Annie. Can you hear me?" I hear sirens in the distance, and everything fades out again.

My throat still feels like sandpaper, and a high pitch noise pierces my ears. Why can't I move my neck?

"Ma'am? Annie? Can you hear me? I need you to calm down. I know this is scary, but I need you to stop screaming." Screaming? Oh god. That high pitched noise is coming from me. My scream turns into a sob as I attempt to open my eyes.

"W-what happened?" I manage to croak out. There's a young man right in front of me wearing a blue uniform.

"You were in an accident."

"H-how bad i-is it?" Everything hurts, and I'm having trouble keeping my eyes open.

"The car is badly damaged, and it's on its side leaning against another car. You rolled at least twice. The car it's leaning against stopped you. We're gonna have to use the jaws of life to cut you out." Jaws of life? Cut me out? I try to look around at the damage and remember that I can't move my neck. I lift my hand to check it and feel the brace. I panic and try to claw at it, but instead of plastic, my nails scratch flesh that isn't mine.

"Shhh, Annie. It's going to be okay. My name is Justin. You've been in an accident. You have a c-collar on your neck. I'm holding your head stable in case you have a spinal injury. We're going to get you out of here. I won't leave you until we do. I'm here with you."

"Justin. Okay. I remember. How d-do you know my n-name?"

"When we got here, your fiancée, Blake, was still on the phone. She heard the crash on her end of the line and didn't want to hang up until she knew someone was with you. I spoke to her." With me. She didn't want me to be alone. I love her. My heavy lids drift close again.

"Ahhhhhhh! Stop, stop it. It hurts! Fuck stop, pleeease." Searing hot pain rips through my body. It feels like I'm being torn apart.

"Annie, it's Justin. I've got you. They're almost done. The frame bent around your leg. They had to make sure the car was secure and wouldn't fall over before they could get you out."

"I'm s-s-so cold." The sun looks like it's setting outside. How long have we been in this car? We. We...

"Josh?"

"Justin, my name is Justin. We're almost out of here, Annie. A few more minutes."

"Jo-" I clear my throat. "Josh, my d-driver." I glance in the

227

direction with my eyes. The front seat looks empty from the little I can see. They must have gotten him out already.

"Who?"

"Josh, my driver w-was with me." My voice is weak and raspy. The screeching of metal pierces the air, and I'm flooded with white-hot pain again. I can't take much more. Images of Blake and Cole flash in my mind. I need their strength. The pain takes over again, and my vision goes black.

Opening my eyes, I see I'm outside of the car, next to an ambulance, lying on a stretcher. I'm strapped to a flat board. What little I can see of the scene around me is devastating. There's glass and metal all around, reflecting the flashing blue and red lights of police cars, fire trucks, and ambulances. All I can see of my car is the undercarriage and all the support beams they used to keep it upright. Petals from the red roses I bought Blake are scattered around the ground of the accident scene. Off to the side is a blue tarp with two white sheets on it.

"Justin?"

"I'm right here, Annie. I told you I wouldn't leave you. I'm going to ride to the hospital with you. My partner, Spencer, is going to drive us. We just needed to secure your leg before we could leave." My leg. I try to wiggle my toes, but I don't feel anything. Justin must see the panic in my eyes. He lays a hand on my arm. "We've given you some of the good pain meds. If you're feeling numb, it's normal." Okay, it's normal.

"Justin, the white sheets? Is everyone okay?" He looks down at the clipboard in his hand.

"It was a bad accident, Annie. You're very lucky. Let's get you to the hospital and take care of this leg. You have some pretty bad cuts and bruises that need to be looked at, too." My eyes grow heavy as they lift my stretcher into the ambulance, and I start to drift into sleep once again.

CRACKLE: Dispatch we're enroute to Dov Memorial.
  "10-4. You good, Webb?"
  "Yeah, I'm good thanks."

Silence again.

37

Blake

It was such an incredible day. I told Annie what I wanted, and she let me pleasure her. She got her IUD out so we could officially start trying to conceive a baby with Cole. But then I called her to make sure her appointment went well, and she was arguing with...

Then I heard the most horrific sounds. Sounds that have given me nightmares and wake me up crying and screaming at night. Cole has been a godsend. He's hardly left my side since I called him and told him what happened. I was a blubbering mess. He could barely understand me through my hysterics. He picked me up from work and brought us straight to the hospital.

We got to the emergency room before she arrived. Three torturous hours before she arrived. She was unconscious when she got here. They wouldn't tell us much more than she was going straight to surgery, and we were directed to a waiting room on a different floor. That was two days ago.

"I can't live without her, Cole. She needs to come back to us." I bury my face into his chest and cry tears that haven't stopped in days.

"I know, Princess. I feel the same way. She'll come back to us. She has to." He's rubbing my back while slowly rocking me back and forth in his lap. "Has there been any new news from the doctors?"

"No, nothing since before you left. Thank you for the clothes." He kisses my forehead.

"You're very welcome. I talked to Nicole. Candy is all settled. She's loving Java and Beans, and can stay as long as we need her to."

"Good. I talked to Annie's dad today. He will take over until she can get back on her feet. He's out of the country right now, but I'm keeping him updated. He's going to work remotely unless he needs to come back. My boss said I could take as much time as I need, but...I think I might just quit. She's going to need a lot of help. A shattered pelvis could take 3-4 months before she's fully back on her feet. And her leg also. I'd rather be there for her than worry about her. She never wanted me to work anyway."

"I think she'd love having you home with her." His tone is soothing, and it mends a tiny part of my broken heart. My hand drifts down to the cuff I gave him the day after Annie's surgery, with ABC engraved on it. I wanted him to know that we were on this journey together, and he was a part of us.

When Annie came out of surgery, and we were finally able to see her, the first thing I noticed after her injuries was her missing bracelet. The nurse informed us all her personal items she came in with were in a bag in the closet. I searched the bag more times than I'd like to admit, and the bracelet wasn't in there. She also informed me that in the trauma field, during an accident, they will cut off clothes and, if necessary, jewelry, like necklaces and bracelets, if they are concerned for the patient's safety while being transported. But everything should have been in the bag, and it's not there.

"But first, she has to wake up. Why won't she just wake up, Cole?"

"Shhh, Princess." He runs a tender hand through my hair. "Remember the doctor said there was some mild swelling on her brain, and it might take her a little longer to come back to us. All of her tests look good. We just have to be patient."

"They came in and took more blood while you were gone. They said she had a low-grade fever, but it's probably normal. They're running tests as a precaution."

·∿∿·∿∿·

Three more days have passed. It's been five days since the accident, and there's been no improvement. In fact, she has an infection and had to go on antibiotics. I barely recognize her. Her blonde hair is dark with grease. The bruises on her face are starting to heal, but she has purple bags under her eyes.

Cole is asleep, lightly snoring in the reclining chair. I'm jealous he can sleep. I'm still having nightmares, and I'm afraid to close my eyes. I've been surviving on coffee. At least it's good coffee.

The perk of having money is being able to afford a private suite in the hospital—one with an actual coffee pot in the room. The room is large and resembles a hotel room with a desk and couch in the corner. The burgundy and navy colors from the curtains and furniture break up the starkness of the white walls and linens. The food has been good, and the rollaway bed is comfortable, but I'd happily drink day-old coffee, eat terrible food and sleep on a lumpy bed if she would just wake up.

There's a soft knock on the door, and the doctor comes into the room. I don't like the look on his face.

"Good morning, Ms. Rogers. How are you today?" I hate the fake cordial tone they always give. I know it's their job, but it never makes me feel any better, especially when he calls me Ms. Rogers after he's called me Blake, as I asked.

"What's wrong? Has something happened?" Cole stirs from his sleep, hearing the desperation in my voice. He comes over, wrapping his arms around me from behind for comfort. I melt into his embrace, needing the support.

"It's not cause for major concern yet, but her white blood cell count continues to elevate, indicating that there is still an infection that her body is fighting."

"Okay, so what does that mean?" I grab Cole's hand, attempting to stop mine from trembling so hard.

"It means we have to be more aggressive with the antibiotics. We want to take more images to ensure we didn't miss anything. There was a lot of shrapnel in her body from the accident. Even a small piece can cause the body to go into overdrive. We don't want her to go through any more trauma than she already has." This is all too much. I spin in Cole's arms and grab handfuls of his shirt. The tears have dried up after days of crying. All I can do is sob in his arms.

"Shhh, Princess." Cole rubs my back, trying to calm me.

"I need...I need to get some air. I need a break. Can you call Nicole and see if I can come by and take Candy for a walk?"

"Of course." He digs into his pocket and takes out his phone and keys. "She's at work. I'll text her and let her know you're stopping by. Take my keys and let yourself in. I'll be here and won't leave her alone until you get back. I'll let you know if anything changes."

I take the keys and watch him text his sister. Grabbing my purse, I'm about to leave the room when he calls my name. I turn to face him as he's walking towards me. His hands engulf my cheeks, and he stares deeply into my eyes.

"BlakeLynn, she *will* wake up, and we'll get through this together. I love you." I take a step back as tears well in my eyes. My hand comes up to my chest, rubbing the ache in my heart.

"I c-can't. I can't, Cole." Shaking my head, I take a few tentative steps back. My gaze moves to Annie's and then back to his. "I can't hear those words until she can hear them, too."

He steps forward and brushes a thumb over my cheek, wiping away a tear I hadn't noticed had slipped down.

"Okay, Princess" His tone is soft and tender. "It's okay. I get it. I'll tell her, too, as soon as she wakes up. Until then, I'll tell her every day, hoping that wherever she is within herself, she hears it and knows it's true." He brushes away another tear and kisses my cheek before sitting next to Annie and holding her hand.

Walking out of the hospital doors, I inhale a deep breath. I didn't realize how much I'd been missing the fresh air. I haven't left Annie's side since they wheeled her into the room from surgery. Cole has brought me clothes, and went to tend to his dogs that he walks, but I couldn't get myself to leave.

I rummage through my purse, looking for my phone so I can text Josh to pick me up, when I collapse to my knees. A wave of consuming guilt washes over me, taking my breath away. Josh. I hadn't thought about him this entire time. The

234

police informed me they notified his family. It was just him and his mother. I can't imagine how devastated she is.

Two lives were taken that day. Josh and the driver of the car that hit them, they both…I don't even want to think about it. It could have been three. Annie almost didn't survive the surgery. She lost so much blood. She's still not awake.

"Ma'am? Are you alright?" My eyes snap up to a tall man towering over me. I almost forgot I was on my knees.

"Yes. I'm sorry. My Annie…" The tears spill out again. He extends his hand to help me up.

"Did you say, Annie?" Taking his hand, I stand up on shaky legs. He actually is really tall. I try to focus on the face in front of me through blurry eyes. He has glasses, and a goatee, short dark hair, and a soothing voice.

"Yes, my fiancée, Annie, was in an accident. She's in there." I look up at the building behind me.

"Are you…Blake?" he asks hesitantly. He's holding onto my shoulder, helping me stay upright. I look up at him again, trying to recognize who he is, but I don't. "Are you Annie's Blake, from the car accident last week?"

Who is this man, and how does he know us? Oh god! I try to jump back from his hold, but I'm still unsteady, and he grabs my other shoulder.

"Are you a reporter? No comment. No, no comment." A billionaire in a major car accident involving multiple fatalities quickly made headlines. The hospital has done a fantastic job shielding us from the media, and I was stupid enough to walk outside without even thinking.

"No, Blake. No, I'm not a reporter. My name is Justin. I'm the paramedic you spoke to on the phone at the accident." Justin? I completely forgot I spoke with someone. I was so relieved when help got there. I asked where she would be taken and went straight to the hospital once Cole picked me up.

"Justin. Oh god, Justin." I throw myself at the man before me that saved the love of my life. "Thank you so much. Thank you for saving her. Thank you for being there. For not leaving her alone." My words are pouring out through my sobs, and I'm not even sure he can understand me, but I don't care. He needs to know how grateful I am.

"Blake, it's okay. I was just doing my job. How's she doing?" I pull away slightly so I can look at him.

"Annie had an open fracture to her pelvis, a broken leg, and lost a lot of blood. The surgery was long. Now she has an infection and...and she hasn't woken up yet." He's nodding, his face solemn. I drop my arms from his neck, my shoulders trembling in his hands.

"She was fearless. You probably didn't know this, but I think she was bringing you flowers. There were red rose petals all around the car when we got there." Hearing that makes my heart mend just a fraction. She was always thinking about me. IS. She IS always thinking about me. I can't think like that.

"I'm scared." My confession holds all the weight of my emotions.

"She was too, but it's your turn to be brave *for* her. She needs your strength."

"I truly don't know how to thank you for what you did."

"Just tell her how proud I am of her when she wakes up." He looks down at the ground and his brow furrows. "Listen, I don't usually do this, but I've been through a lot in my life and know how important it is to have people to talk to. Can I give you my number in case you or Annie need a shoulder or an ear?" Reaching into my purse, I find my phone and hand it to him.

"I think she'd love that. Thank you." He enters his number into my phone and hands it back to me. I hit call on the screen, and his phone rings in his pocket.

"Now you have mine in case *you* ever need a shoulder or ear." He nods and gives a shy smile. "Thank you again, Justin."

"Do you ever talk to her? They say that even unconscious people can hear what's happening around them in their subconscious. I talked to Annie the entire time I was with her. Especially in the car. I told her everything I was doing."

"I occasionally sing to her. My favorite song came on the radio the morning of the accident, and the lyrics resonate with our current situation. The song continuously goes through my head; sometimes, I sing it out loud or hum it to her."

"That's perfect. Keep doing that. Well, take care, Blake. I'll be thinking about you and Annie." He walks inside, and I stand for a few more minutes soaking in the sun and fresh air before pulling up my rideshare app and waiting for a ride. A different ride than I wish I were calling. Looking up into the clouds, a tear slips down my cheek.

"I'll miss you, Josh. Thank you for always being there for her and keeping her safe."

38

Cole

I've never felt panic like I did when Blake called me the day of the accident. She was still on the phone with Annie when she called me from work. The pure terror in her voice as I heard her screaming Annie's name had my knees buckling. I was leaving their house after walking Candy when my phone rang.

"Hey, Princess. Ho-"
"ANNIE! Annie, can you hear me? Cole. Come get me now. Annie, PLEASE ANSWER ME. Annie's hurt, Cole. She was in an accident. Come get me."

That's all she said before she hung up. I struggled to process the information through her yelling and crying. I didn't bother calling back. I knew it was an emergency, and it didn't matter what it was. I was going to get her.

I texted her when I was five minutes away, and she was waiting outside for me. She managed to tell me which hospital we were going to through her hysterical crying. I held her hand the entire way, giving her as much strength as possible.

I didn't have any answers about what was happening, but I knew it had to be bad for Blake to react the way she was. Once we were inside, I was able to piece together that there was an accident, but Annie had yet to make it to the hospital. They had no other information for us, and I had to fight with a hysterical Blake to keep her from taking my keys and trying to find her.

When the ambulance arrived with Annie three hours later, Blake was practically catatonic in my lap. Tears were still streaming down her face, but she was staring off into the distance and hadn't made a sound in over an hour.

When the nurse finally called Blake's name, she practically fell to the floor, trying to get to her. We spent six hours in the surgical waiting room. Blake cried. She paced. She screamed several times, and when she let me, I held her.

Seeing Annie for the first time after surgery was shocking. She had metal coming out of her hips and leg. The doctors said she was too unstable to do further surgery and would need more later to remove it all. Her body was limp and pale, and she had cuts, scrapes, and bruises all over her body.It shattered Blake all over again. How could this lifeless body in front of me be the same vivacious woman that I had spent all weekend worshiping?

Blake refused to leave the hospital, and I didn't blame her. I went to their house and packed a bag for both of them before taking Candy and heading home to pack one for myself. Nicole was more than happy to watch Candy for as long as we needed. I knew we had a long road ahead of us.

I've walked Mercy and Titus this week, and Nicole has taken care of Lucy and Candy for me. My sister has been an invaluable help. She's even brought us dinner and coffee at the hospital several times. She officially met Blake, and despite the circumstances, they hit it off. Nicole is excited I found two women to love. There's been no judgment toward our situation.

·ᴖᴖ˙·ᴖᴖ˙

As I sit here and hold Annie's hand I can't help but wonder what our future holds. When she wakes up we have a long road ahead of us with healing and recovery. I hear the door open and look up to see Blake walking in.

"Hey," she says as she walks toward me. She looks a little more refreshed than when she left earlier. It seems spending time with Candy was just what she needed. Rising from the chair next to Annie, I pull her into my chest and kiss the top of her head.

"I missed you. How was Candy?" She curls her body into my chest.

"I missed you, too, and Candy. That crazy dog was so excited to see me, but I'm a little worried that we might not get her back. When I was leaving, she was cuddling on the couch with Java and Beans. They looked adorable together."

"Nicole said they do that all the time. Do we need to get our dog a dog?" Hmm, our dog. I like the sound of that.

"Maybe. I do happen to know a great dog walker." The corner of her lip tips, and the small gesture warms my heart. I tip her chin up and lean down to give her a chaste kiss. She sighs in contentment and lays her head on my chest.

"Any new news?" We both look over to Annie.

"Nothing new. They took her for more tests but haven't

been back with any new information. I'm not sure they'd talk to me anyway. I'm not family." She looks up at me and this time she gives me the smallest of smiles.

"They would. You're one of Annie's emergency contacts." When did that happen? Blake sees my confusion and continues. "You really didn't read the contract, did you?" I shake my head. I was too excited. I trusted Annie and signed it without asking any more questions. "When you agreed to be the baby daddy, she added you as her emergency contact in the event that anything occurred while she was pregnant. She wanted to make sure you had a say in what happened. Pretty sure she didn't have anything like this in mind, but it works to our advantage."

"Guess I should read that contract. Any more surprises I should know about?" Annie and her lawyers really did think about everything.

"The baby would have your last name."

"What?" I'm in shock. I didn't even think to ask if that was a possibility. "Why? Her name carries so much power."

"The company is named after her father. Annie had some anonymity growing up because her last name differed from his. Eventually…" She looks over at Annie. "Well, *now* I guess, her last name will be synonymous with the business. She wants our kids to have as normal of a life as possible. With your last name, she felt like they could."

"Wow, I had no idea. She's incredible. You're incredible." I pull her impossibly closer to me, soaking in every ounce of her warmth. We hold each other for several long minutes. It's been an exhausting week, and we take comfort in each other's presence.

A small cough is heard in the room, and we both look to the

door to see it empty. Blake notices first and leaps from my hold. Annie's hand is rubbing her throat, eyes barely open.

"I'll grab a doctor."

39

Annie

I'm so cold.

Something smells funny.

What is that incessant beeping?

My head hurts. Actually, everything hurts.

I hear voices, but they sound far away.

I know those voices. It's Blake. And Cole.

My eyes feel heavy, but I want to see them. Opening them slightly, the room is bright. So bright. I peek out of a small slit in my left eye. I see them. They're right in front of me, holding each other. My people. They look so sad.

I open my mouth to speak, and my throat hurts. I lightly touch the front of my neck, and attempt to clear my throat. Instead, I cough, and it catches their attention. Blake jumps away from Cole as if he's on fire.

"I'll grab a doctor." Cole runs out of the room as Blake grabs my hands, sobbing into the pillow beside my shoulder. Reaching up with my free hand, I rub her hair, and she cries even harder.

"*Mijn Diamant.*" My voice is barely a whisper.

"Annie. Oh god, Annie. We've been so worried." She tentatively touches my face, and I lean into her hand. Cole returns with a doctor and stands next to Blake, grabbing our intertwined fingers and connecting the three of us.

"Hello, Ms. Poulsen. I'm so happy to see you're awake." As he logs into the computer attached to the wall, I open my mouth to speak, but it's too difficult. "Would you like some water?" I nod, and Cole pours some into a cup for me. I try to sit up to take a sip, but the doctor lays a hand on my shoulder to stop me.

"Ms. Poulsen, you've sustained some substantial injuries. Do you know where you are?" I look around the room. I'm in a private hospital room. Despite looking almost like a hotel room, there is insignia of the hospital logo on various things.

"H-hospital." Cole adjusts the straw in the cup so I can take a sip of water. It feels cool and soothing going down my irritated throat.

"Good. You're responding to me, so I assume you know your name. Do you know who these two are next to you?

Nodding, I answer, "Blake, my fiancée, and Cole, my...baby daddy." Cole and Blake give me small smiles but the doctor's eyes flash to me in confusion. He's clicking around on the computer.

"I'm sorry. I wasn't aware you had children."

"We don't, not yet," Cole answers for me. "But we're planning to." He squeezes my hand.

"I see." I don't like the look on his face. "Ms. Poulsen, do you know why you're here? Do you remember what happened?" I take another sip of water, then close my eyes and try to think of the last things I remember.

"Blake in the car." I look, and her cheeks flush pink.

"Doctor's appointment. IUD removed." Cole squeezes my hand again. "Red roses." Blake loves roses. "New car...no... we..." *Oh god.* "The song. The red light. Car crash...Josh. Oh god, Josh." I look at Blake and Cole, and neither of them is looking at me. "Where's Josh?"

No one is answering. I try to sit up again, and a lightning bolt of pain runs through the lower half of my body.

"Shit." The word escapes from my lips as a hiss. I grab the edge of the sheet covering me and flip it off my lower half. I'm speechless at what I'm looking at. I take a moment to assess what I'm seeing versus what I'm feeling.

"Baby, it looks worse than it is. You broke your leg and pelvis in the accident. There was a lot of damage." I still can't believe what I'm seeing. I look to the doctor for confirmation.

"We had to put the external brackets on you until you healed a bit. There was extensive trauma to your lower half. Your body should be healed enough now to remove them and have them replaced with a cast and hip binders." Okay, that sounds rational.

Digesting everything he just said, I think back to the accident and what I can remember of it. There's still an unanswered question. I remember the two white sheets I saw before they put me in the ambulance.

"Josh." His name is a whispered sigh. I look into Blake's eyes, and they're filled with tears. She shakes her head. She doesn't need to say the words out loud. A sob rips through my chest. We were arguing. He took his eyes off the road because I yelled at him. "It's my fault," I whine and bury my face in my hands. Cole's big hands wrap around my wrist and gently pull them away.

"Kitten, it wasn't your fault. The other driver ran the light.

Plenty of witnesses saw it."

"Don't call me that. I don't deserve it." I can't handle being his kitten right now. "Our light was turning red. We were arguing. He wasn't paying attention. He...he..." I'm overcome with grief. Josh was lying on the ground under one of those white sheets.

"Shhh, it's ok." Blake's hand runs across my cheek, and I flinch. She snaps her hand back.

"There w-were two sheets." I vividly remember two laying on the tarp.

"The driver of the SUV that hit you. He didn't make it either." Cole's use of the words "didn't make it" sounds like they missed a party, not that they died. Died. Josh died. Because of me. Because he was jealous of Cole. What was the last thing he said to me? I asked, no, I yelled at him to turn down a song on the radio. He said something I couldn't hear over the music.

I wish I could hide away right now, but I seem to be immobilized by all the metal keeping me in this bed.

"Please leave." Hearing those words come out of my mouth shatters me.

"I'll leave you all to talk-" the doctor starts.

"No. You stay, I want them to leave." A wave of shock and disbelief washes over Blake and Cole's faces. Blake grabs for my hand, and I pull it back. "Please. Please, Blake. Go."

"Annie, I-"

"Red," I whisper, barely loud enough for anyone to hear. I can't even look at her. I know she won't protest. She can't. I used my safeword. That's the way "red" works. No questions asked.

"O-okay. Okay, Danika. We'll go." Cole grabs her arm.

"Princess, what are you doing? We can't jus-"

"She said red, Cole." She looks at me with desperation in her eyes. "We don't get to object. Let's go." She tugs at Cole to get him to walk towards the exit. They're about to walk out when Cole comes bounding back in and kneels at my bedside, grabbing my hand. I try to pull away but his grip is firm.

"Kitten, Annie. You need to know, and then I'll leave. I need to tell you I love you. I love you, Danika. Please know that." I can't listen to his words. I'm not lovable. I manage to pull my hand away and look in the opposite direction.

He slowly stands and walks out of the room with Blake. I turn to the doctor and ask, "What's next?" He takes a moment to compose himself from what he just witnessed before he responds.

"Well, all of your tests came back normal today. You have an infection, but your white blood cell counts are already lower, so the antibiotics are working. As long as the decline continues, we should be able to get you back in for surgery in the next 24-48 hrs."

"Good. Let's get that taken care of. Do I have any personal effects here? Did my cell phone make it?" He walks towards a closet.

"Let me check what you came in with." He pulls a plastic bag out of the closet, and I see my phone. He brings me the bag and I pull it out. The screen protector is cracked, but it looks to be in working order. Of course, it has a dead battery, though.

"How long ago was the accident? How long have I been here?" I realize I have no concept of time at the moment.

"The accident was on Friday. Today is Wednesday. You've been here five days." Five days.

"Can you find me a charger? I have calls to make." He walks to a drawer in the room and pulls out a cord.

"It connects directly to your bed. Let me help you with it." He reaches behind my head and hands the cord to me.

"Thank you." My tone is dismissive, but he doesn't leave. "Is there something else?"

"You mentioned the young man was your 'baby daddy,' correct?" The doctor looks uneasy with this conversation.

"Correct. I had my IUD removed so we can start trying to conceive a baby in the near future."

"Ms. Poulsen, your injuries were extensive. The infection your body is fighting has inflamed all of your reproductive organs and many other major organs. We won't know for certain until the infection is gone, but with the trauma, inflammation, and antibiotics, there is a high probability that conceiving will be extremely difficult, if at all possible."

His words swirl around in my still-hazy brain. High probability, *if at all*. He didn't say "no possibility," but he might as well have.

"If there's nothing else, please leave."

"I'm so sorry, Ms. Pou-"

"LEAVE!"

I stare straight ahead, hearing his footsteps retreat and the door shut behind him. My breathing is erratic. My entire body is numb. Not from the broken bones, not from the pain medication I'm on, because of Josh, and because of the future that I just lost.

I killed a man. I might not have done it with my own two hands, but my words killed him. My distraction caused his death. He had a future ahead of him. Did he say...? What did he say to me right before we crashed? My head hurts from all the information it's trying to process.

Tears stream down my cheeks. My chest is starting to hurt from the weight of the grief. My overreaction most likely ended my future of ever being a mother to my own child.

"*Stop it, Danika.*" I chastise myself inside the empty room.

I have a company to run.

I have to call my lawyers and my father.

I have to determine how bad the media coverage is.

I have a game console to launch.

I have to get to work.

40

Blake

I t's been a week. A week since Annie used her safeword.
Five days since she had surgery to remove the external
hardware from her pelvis and leg. Four days since we
had any kind of meaningful conversation. And by meaningful,
I mean anything more than "How are you feeling?" and "Can
I get you anything?"

Cole and I stayed away the rest of the night after she told
us to leave. She's never used "red" with me before. The word
was a stab to the heart when I heard it. It shattered me.

I asked Cole to take me back to his house. I needed his
comfort and to see Candy. The three of us slept in his bed
that night and every night since. Despite having a private
room, Annie insists we keep to the hospital's visiting hours.

I put my notice in at work, effective immediately, and my
boss understood. Now, every day from 8 AM until 10 PM, I
sit in silence in Annie's hospital room. She works and leaves
the room to go to physical therapy.

The morning after her surgery, she spoke to me. I think
the effects of the anesthesia were still in her system. She

expressed her grief over Josh and how she felt responsible. It seems she also remembered him saying something that gave her the impression he was jealous of Cole, but her memory was still foggy, and she couldn't recall exactly what he said. We cried together before she fell back asleep, but when she woke again, she went back to ignoring me.

Cole has been in and out. He's struggling with her silence. She seems to completely ignore him as if he's not even in the room. He drops me off in the morning, then returns around dinner, and stays until he drives me back to his house.

·∿∿·∿∿·

I keep telling myself that today will be different. Today is discharge day from the hospital. Annie is being transferred to a rehab facility for a week, and then she will come home. A home I haven't been to since the accident.

Cole has gone by to get more clothes for us and made sure the downstairs guest room was all set up. Annie won't be able to climb stairs for at least 4-6 weeks, so we will need to sleep downstairs.

We. I hope she allows me to sleep in there with her. I don't know what's going on in her head, but I can tell she's battling demons.

Cole dropped me off 20 minutes ago, but I haven't gone to her room yet. The morning sun feels like a warm hug as I sit on a bench outside the hospital. I know the woman I love is still in there, but she won't let me in to help her heal. I don't think I can sit in silence another day and listen to her talk on the phone and do work. I'm not even sure how she got her laptop.

I'm about to pull my phone out of my purse to have Cole come back and get me when a shadow blocks my sun.

"Blake? How are you?" I recognize the voice, but the glare of the sun won't allow me to see the man standing in front of me. He moves to the side and sits on the bench next to me.

"Oh, Hi, Justin." It's Annie's paramedic.

"Hey. Is everything okay? You don't look so good." I don't feel so good. It seems like my outside matches my insides.

"Um, that's probably more of a loaded question than you want to get into, so I'll just say I'm fine." He looks at me with sympathy.

"How about we go inside, and I treat you to a bad cup of coffee, and you can tell me how 'fine' you actually are?" That causes me to snicker. The coffee maker in Annie's room is practically gourmet, but somehow a cup of terrible hospital coffee with a new friend sounds like exactly what I need.

"Sure. After you." He smiles, and we head inside.

Sitting in the quiet cafeteria reminds me that Annie is in an actual hospital. Smelling the sterile air, being surrounded by white walls, and the hustle of the passing employees as they quickly grab their meals brings me back to the reality that there was an accident and Annie could have died. We've been in our little private suite bubble for nearly two weeks, and I haven't left her room.

"How's Annie?"

"We're jumping in with the big guns, huh?" I take a tentative sip of my coffee. It's not gourmet, but I actually appreciate its normalcy.

"Would an easier question be asking how *you* are?" My eyes flashed to his. The hazel color looks so comforting and inviting. He genuinely seems like he cares. Taking another sip of the lukewarm coffee, I sigh.

"Annie is doing physically well. She's transferring to a rehab facility today for a week and then should come...home." I still don't even know what that will look like. I've spent every night in Cole's arms while Annie pushed us away.

"And mentally?" He caught that.

"She's...hiding, ignoring, withdrawing...I don't know. She won't talk to me. We had to tell her about her driver dying. She blames herself. They were arguing, and she said he wasn't paying attention when the light was changing." I can't imagine the guilt she feels despite it not being her fault.

"Does she know that the driver of the SUV was under the influence? He was drunk in the middle of the afternoon. He would have run that light whether her driver noticed or not."

"No. I didn't know. I don't think Annie does either. At least not that she's mentioned to me. Like I said, she really isn't talking to me or anyone outside of work."

"Have they brought in a therapist yet?" I scoff at the thought.

"They've offered. She's refused."

"How about you? Have you talked to anyone?" The laugh that bursts out of me is erratic and hysterical. No one has checked in on me since the accident. Cole and I are doing our best to hold each other up, but we're fighting a losing battle. Justin places his hand on my shoulder, and I jolt back.

"Sorry." He throws his hands up in surrender, and I feel guilty for my reaction. My laughter quickly fades.

"No, I'm sorry. I'm in uncharted waters here. Annie has always been the strong one in our relationship. I'm having a hard time adjusting to everything. I haven't talked to anyone, but maybe I should. Got any good suggestions?" My question was meant as a joke, but judging by the tortured look that just passed through his eyes, he's not taking it as one. He reaches into his back pocket and takes a business card from his wallet.

"Actually, yeah." He hands me the card, and I look it over. "She's really good with trauma survivors and their families. Survivors' guilt can be just as bad as the trauma itself. She could be good for both you and Annie."

"It sounds like you're speaking from experience?" He looks to the floor and shakes his head.

"It comes with the job." He brushes off my question, but I can tell there's more to it than just his job.

"Thanks for this." My phone buzzes in my purse, and I pull it out, seeing a text from Annie.

Annie: I'd like to speak with you.

Well, that's a first. She wants to talk. I apologize to Justin for being rude with my phone and explain that I have to go.

"Please reach out if there's anything I can do for you or Annie." He squeezes my shoulder, and this time, I don't flinch.

"Thanks for the not-so-terrible coffee and the card." We exchange smiles, and I head to Annie's room.

Knocking on the door before I walk into her room feels awkward, but there's been such a rift between us I don't feel like I have permission to enter unannounced.

"Hey. How are you today, Baby?"

"Oh good, you're here. Please have a seat." Okay. Apparently business Danika is here. Taking a seat as she instructed, Annie starts typing on her laptop. I hear a mechanical sound and look to see a printer spitting out papers. When did that get here? "We have a few things to discuss before I go to rehab this afternoon." She's so formal and emotionless.

"Okay, like what?"

"Would you get those papers for me?" She gestures to the printer. "My lawyers will be here this afternoon to notarize everything, but I wanted to give you a chance to read it all over and make any changes you see fit." What is she talking about?

"Changes to what??" I cross the room, retrieve the papers from the printer and sit back down.

"As you know, when I proposed to you, there were reasonable expectations of the life that we were planning together. Circumstances have changed, and I want to make sure you have the opportunity to live the life that you were promised prior to my accident." All I can do is stare at her. She's talking to me like I'm a stuffy businessman in a suit.

"Annie, I don't understand. What are you talking about?"

"I can't reasonably expect you to want to continue a life with me knowing I can no longer provide you with a vital part of your future."

"What? What do you mean? What can't you provide me?"

"Oh, I'm sorry. It seems I've glossed over an important piece of information. The doctors have informed me that, due to complications from infections, there is little to no chance I could ever conceive a child." Tears immediately flood my eyes, and I swallow a gasp in my hands.

"Oh my god, Annie. Why didn't you tel-" She puts her hand up to stop me from speaking any further.

"No reason to dwell on what we can't change. As you can see there is a sizable severance package for you, along with a monthly stipend. If the amount isn't sufficient, there is plenty of room for negotiation."

"Annie, what the fuck are you talking about? Severance

package? Am I your fiancée or an employee?" The tears have stopped, making way for the rage boiling inside me.

"I can no longer provide you with the future that you expected. It's better we part ways amicably."

"Are you breaking up with me? Danika Liv Poulsen, if you think for one second that your ability to have or not have children changes how I feel about you, you're wrong." She completely ignores me and continues with her monotone businesswoman attitude.

"There is a clause in there that permits you to continue your relationship and allows you to procreate with Cole. My lawyers have a similar contract for him and one that supersedes my original one with Cole." I can't even process what I'm hearing right now. I stand up and throw the papers to the ground. Now I'm pissed off.

"Annie, Cole and I are people. We aren't some business deal you made that you can just dismiss because you don't like the terms anymore."

"Aren't you? I have signed contracts with both of your signatures on them." *Bitch.*

"That's not fair, Annie, and you know it! We are nowhere near the same people we were when I signed that contract to be your submissive. We fell in love. You proposed. Does that mean nothing? You conceiving a child was never a condition of my love for you. Never. I can carry our children. We can adopt. We can have a surrogate. Our possibilities of creating a family are endless, Annie. Or we don't have to have any children at all, and it can just be us." Once again, she dismisses me.

"Of course, you can keep the ring and any purchases I've made for you over the course of the relationship. There are housing allowances for both you and Cole. If you choose to live together, that's fine as well. Your rents or mortgages will be taken care of, as well as any vehicles, including a new vehicle every five years."

"Fuck, Annie. What the actual fuck. Red. Fucking red. Do you hear me? RED!" Again. She dismisses me *again*.

"The lawyers will be here at 2 PM to notarize all the documents." I drop to my knees at her side of the bed and grab her arm, pleading–tears of anger, heartbreak, and frustration stream down my face.

"Annie, don't do this. Oh god, please don't do this. I love you. Cole loves you. We don't care if you can't carry a baby." She glares at me with rage in her eyes.

"I DO! I fucking do, BlakeLynn." Finally, some emotion from her, even if it is anger. "I killed a man, and my punishment is taking away my ability to give birth to my own child. You don't want me anymore. You won't. He won't.

I'm not her anymore. I can't be. I won't be. And I won't hold you back. Go be with Cole, or don't. It's not my concern."

I can hear my heartbeat whooshing in my ears. My fingers are tingling with the rage and adrenaline coursing through them. I stand and knock the chair over as I stumble back towards the door.

"I won't. I won't sign any paperwork. I'll never agree to any of that."

"You don't have to." She isn't even acknowledging me. She's talking to her computer screen. "The notarization is just a formality. The accounts have already been set up. It's already finalized."

I'm horrified. I leave the room, run down the hall past the elevator to the door for the stairs and fling it open. Taking

the stairs as quickly as possible, I don't stop until I'm outside.
I pull out my phone and dial Cole.

"Hey, Princess. How's yo-"

"Cole," I manage to hiccup out. "She's throwing us away."
The sobs are wracking through my body. It's hard to breathe
through the tears.

"What? Blake, where are you? I'm coming to you. Just tell
me where. Are you still at the hospital?" I hear him call out a
command through a muffled hand. He must be out walking
a dog.

"Y-yes, but I can't stay here. I have to move. I'm gonna
w-walk. Come find me, Cole. Please."

"Princess, I'm on my way. Do you want to stay on the
phone?"

41

Cole

This has been the most challenging couple of weeks. Annie moves to rehab today, and hopefully, having some independence will increase her morale. Dropping Blake off this morning and seeing the tortured look in her eyes almost broke me. Annie is her entire life, and she's been giving her the cold shoulder since she woke up.

I laugh to myself as I watch Candy and Lucy play in the dog park together. I've started walking them at the same time because they get along so well, and it's less time away from Annie and Blake. My phone rings in my back pocket, and I pull it out.

"Hey, Princess. How's yo-"

"Cole." A sobbing hiccup escapes her lips. "She's throwing us away."

Blake is a mess on the other end. I cover the mic on my phone and call for Lucy and Candy to come. I guess we're going on a ride all together. She needs me, and I need to get to her. I'm not going to waste time returning them home.

"Princess, I'm on my way. Do you want to stay on the

phone?" Her sobs are breaking my heart. What does she mean by Annie is throwing us away?

"N-no. Call me when you're close. I'm heading uptown."

"Okay, I love you. Be safe, and I'll be there soon."

I text Lucy's mom to let her know we're going on a field trip. I don't want her to worry when we don't return on time.

Blake texted me and said to meet her at a coffee shop named S'morgasm. The GPS shows me there's a park nearby, so hopefully, she's up to continue walking so the dogs don't get antsy.

·∿∿∿∿·

Candy sees Blake before I do. She's sitting outside the coffee shop curled up on a wrought iron chair with her coffee, looking small and helpless. Candy lets out a bark, and Blake looks up.

Her tortured expression from this morning has changed to despair. What did Annie say to her? I let go of Candy's leash, and she quickly approaches Blake, who melts out of the chair, throws her arms around the dog's neck, and starts sobbing again.

"I'm so sorry. I should have known you were working." Crouching down next to her, I stroke her hair and look into her sad brown eyes.

"Hey, don't ever apologize for needing me. I'll always come when you call. What would you like to do?" She sighs and leans into me, wrapping me into her hug with Candy. Lucy lets out a little yip wanting to be included. We both chuckle, and I pick up the little furball.

"How about we take them home and go out to lunch? We

have a lot to talk about, but I'm still processing." I kiss her forehead, and we stand.

"Whatever you need, Princess."

She's quiet in the car while we return the dogs home. She lets me hold her hand in my lap but mostly stares out the window or silently cries. I feel so helpless, not knowing what she needs.

I received a text from Annie wanting to speak to me just before Blake called. I instantly knew whatever Annie wanted to talk about must be the same reason why Blake was upset. Hopefully, she sheds light on the issues, and we can work it out.

She directs me to a parking deck then we walk to a restaurant with bright neon signs on the front.

"What's this place?"

"Somewhere that makes me smile." She squeezes my hand and leads me inside.

Walking in, I see it's decorated to be a 50's diner. There's a guy dressed like a biker with slicked back hair and a leather jacket at the front counter.

"Sit wherever you want. I don't care." He dismisses us with a wave of his hand, and I follow Blake, wondering what that was all about. We sit at a booth with a stage or catwalk next to it. I've never seen anything like this place before. A guy in some kind of scout uniform comes to our table.

"Drinks." His tone is bland and demanding.

"Green mountain soda." She turns to me. "Quick, what are you drinking?"

"Um. Coke, I guess."

"Do we look like we serve Coke? You'll get Pepsi and like it." What the hell? This server has a bad attitude.

"We'd like some outrageous fries with chicken," Blake blurts out before he walks away.

"It's nice to want, isn't it?" The scout guy walks away, and for the first time in 2 weeks, Blake has a smile on her face.

"What just happened? Why was he so rude?" Her smile gets wider, and my heart expands. I've missed that smile so much.

"That's his job. It's the premise behind this restaurant. Just wait. You'll have fun. I promise." They can be as rude as they want if it keeps that smile on her face.

Blake tells me I need to quickly decide what I want to eat. When Scout, that's what his name tag says, comes back with our drinks, I order a Roadside Burger with onion rings, and Blake gets a Grown Up Grilled Cheese with sweet potato fries. He dismisses us with a flick of his hand and a "Yeah, Yeah" before walking away.

Reaching across the table, I grab her hands. She looks at our joined fingers and smiles at me sweetly.

"Are you ready to talk, Princess?" Her head shakes before she looks away.

"Let's enjoy this first." I'm about to say okay when the servers all stand up on the catwalk next to us and start singing and dancing to the YMCA. Joy. The look on her face is pure joy, and I soak up every second of it. I have a feeling when we do finally talk, I'm not going to like what she has to say.

We watch the server's performance, and when the song is over, they all scramble away. Scout returns with our appetizer and our food at the same time. I ask for ketchup, and Blake slaps a hand over her mouth, laughing. I'm confused by her reaction until Scout grabs a bottle of squeeze ketchup from the counter behind him and proceeds to draw a camping scene on our table in ketchup. A tent, a tree, and a sun decorate our tabletop. He plucks a sweet potato fry out of Blake's basket, pops it in his mouth, then turns on his heels and walks away.

My heart is soaring seeing her so happy. There's been such a dark cloud hanging over her. Over us. I want to stay in this bubble as long as possible. She's giggling, and it's heaven to my ears. We don't talk much while we're eating. Instead, we enjoy the atmosphere. I can tell she's trying to savor it. We pay for our meal and step outside.

"What now, Princess?" She places her hand in mine and leans into my side.

"Let's go home." I love the thought of Blake and me at home. But...

"Where's home?"

"The same place we've been for over a week." Back to my house. To my bedroom. She still doesn't want to return to the home she shares with Annie. I kiss her forehead, and we walk toward my car.

Safe under the covers in my bed, not caring that it's still the middle of the day, she finally opens up. She tells me about every appalling thing Annie said to her. I listen in silence, part in disbelief, and part in anger, but I know speaking it out loud is helping her process.

Annie sent us both a text around 3 PM informing us that everything was taken care of with the lawyers and that she didn't need us to accompany her to the rehab facility. It turned Blake into a blubbering mess again. She fell asleep curled in my arms, and we stayed that way all night.

The next morning I wake up before my alarm to a beautiful angel in my arms. It makes me sad to see worry lines on her forehead, even in sleep. I kiss her forehead, trying to soothe away her worries, and she stirs.

"Morning, Princess. What do you say about showers? Then I'll take you out for breakfast. If you'd like, you can come with me to walk the dogs today." She's had me take her to see Annie every morning. I'm sure she feels lost, not having a purpose now.

"That sounds wonderful. I'll jump in first, and you make coffee?" She's blinking her long lashes at me. I squeeze her hip and peck her lips before crawling out of bed.

"Coming right up."

Both freshly showered and caffeinated, we head outside to get breakfast, and I stop in my tracks.

"What's wrong, Pup?" My adrenaline spikes at her use of the word Pup. It feels like she hasn't called me that in forever, but I can't dwell on that right now.

"That's where I parked last night, right?" I'm looking around the parking lot for my little sedan and come up empty. She finally sees what I see and gasps.

Sitting in my parking space is a brand new Jeep Wrangler JL with a big red bow.

"Princess, tell me you did this?" She shakes her head. I already know she didn't. Approaching the car, I see a note attached to the bow.

~Coleman
I hope this vehicle is suitable for your dog-walking business needs. If not, don't hesitate to get in touch with my financial advisor, and we can get you something more to your liking. The keys are in your mailbox.
~Danika Poulsen

"She's joking, right? She bought me a new car?" Blake sighs and shakes her head in her hands.

"She said the contract had a car allowance for a new vehicle every five years. I guess it starts now."

"But that's a forty thousand dollar vehicle." I can't take my eyes off this brand-new Jeep that apparently belongs to me now. Blake huffs next to me.

"Probably more, knowing Annie. I'm sure it has all the bells and whistles."

Peering in the windows, I see she wasn't wrong. The inside has every feature imaginable. There's even a gate installed along the back seat to help transport my dogs.

"So, what do I do?"

"You get the keys out of your mailbox. Don't ask how she got them there, you probably don't want to know, and we go to breakfast." I'm about to respond when both of our phone notifications ding. Blake opens her phone first and sighs. Her eyes well up with tears, and I pull her into me.

"Oh, Annie." She buries her face into my chest.

"What is it, Princess?"

"Check your phone," she mumbles into me. I open the notification and drop my phone in shock. Blake chuckles.

"Don't worry. I'm sure you can afford a new one if that one just broke. Have you checked your email? A copy of my contract was sent to mine last night." My mind is having trouble digesting the amount of zeros I just saw on the screen.

Pulling her closer into me, I rest my chin on the top of her head, pondering this weird situation we find ourselves in.

"Blake, I don't want anything from her. I never have. It's never been about the money for me. I just love her. I wish she would let us love her."

"I know, Pup. She's hurting. She needs to control every aspect of her life, but she can't control her grief. I've watched it consume her while sitting in that hospital bed. This is the decision she's made, and unfortunately, for now, we need to respect it."

42

Blake

Two weeks later

S'morgasm used to be my favorite place to come. This was my happy place before Annie, and it only got better once she started coming with me. I didn't even know about the back room before her.

She doesn't think I know, but I started falling in love with her the day I found out she set up an account for the free coffee cups. The owner thanked me the next time she saw me, not realizing Annie hadn't told me.

"Blake." I turn to see Justin approaching me with his coffee.

"Hey Justin, thanks for reaching out." He gazes at the floor before taking the seat across from me at our high-top table.

"I shouldn't have, but I felt like you needed some answers." He still isn't making eye contact.

"Justin, what's going on?" He fiddles with the lid of his coffee cup before finally looking at me.

"Let's just say that I've found myself spending some time with Annie." My hand flies to my chest.

"Oh my god. How is she? She hasn't returned any of my calls or texts." I haven't seen or spoken to her since the day I left the hospital. She hasn't reached out to Cole about bringing Candy back to her either. It's been complete radio silence other than business emails or bank deposits.

"That's why I asked to speak with you. Blake, she isn't doing well. I'm not sure if you're aware, but she's still at the rehab facility." She is? That explains why we still have Candy.

"No. I had no idea. I moved out. She, um...she broke off our engagement." I unconsciously spin the ring that I refuse to take off.

"I figured as much. She...We happen to be in a group together. A group of people with similarities." He's being extremely cautious with his words. I reach across the table and place my hand on his forearm.

"Justin, you don't have to tell me anything you shouldn't." I see a rush of emotion flash across his face.

"I know. But she's being ridiculous. She obviously has a support system and isn't using it. She pushed you away!" I'm taken aback by his outburst. He takes a moment to compose himself as if he's surprised as well. A look of remorse flashes in his eyes. "I'm sorry, Blake." He pauses for another moment. "To my understanding, she should have only been at rehab for a week, right?"

"As far as I know, yeah. The day I had coffee with you was the last time I've seen or spoken to her."

"She's not allowing herself to heal. From what I've heard, she refuses her physical therapy sessions and works all day. She's using her room as a hotel slash office with room service. Hell, she's had some woman coming and going bringing her meals." God bless Sarah.

"Wait, you said you were in the same group. Has she said anything to you about the accident?" His head shakes.

"It's common for trauma victims to forget some, if not all, parts of a tragedy. Their brain blocks the negative things to protect them. I go by Jay when I'm there. I'm kind of the leader of the group. And honestly, she doesn't pay much attention to me, let alone anyone or anything for that matter."

"So she has no idea who you are?"

"No. It was a bit of a surprise to me, too. On a few occasions, I've caught her eyes lingering on me, maybe trying to figure out who I am, but she hasn't said anything. Blake, she's still in her wheelchair, which isn't uncommon, but she isn't even trying to use a walker. Her attitude is going to hinder her healing. I know it's not my place, but she could really use someone to talk to. Something to raise her morale."

"I want nothing more than to be that for her. Cole and I have tried everything, and she ignores all attempts to contact her."

"Cole? I haven't heard her mention that name."

"Oh well, he was, is, our um...boyfriend." I'm afraid to look at him. What will he think of us now?

"That's incredible. So Annie has two people to support and encourage her. That's even better." Okay, that went over well.

"I'm not sure how much help either of us can be, though. She's shut us out completely."

"She's buried herself in work. She isn't dealing with her trauma, which hurts her physical healing process. She hasn't once mentioned her driver, not that she's talked much at all."

"What do you suggest, Justin?"

"She needs to be reminded she isn't alone. How did you meet? Maybe something from that time can help her remember when things were good." I can't help but laugh.

"We were colleagues and became…more. The beginning of our relationship was a little unconventional."

"Okay, hmm. Is there something she likes that's just between you and her?" I can feel my cheeks heat as a memory comes to mind.

"Little One, I'm going to use this blindfold on you. Use your safewords if you need them. Do you understand?" I look up at her from my kneeling position on the floor.

"Yes, Danika." She rubs her knuckles along my cheek.

"Tell me."

"Yellow is good. Orange is wait. Red is stop."

"Good girl. Now, go lay on the bed, hands above your head." I stand then crawl to the middle of the bed. My body is electrified with anticipation. We've never done sensory deprivation play before. This relationship is still new, and she's learning my likes and boundaries.

"I'm going to tie your wrists to the headboard and place the blindfold over your eyes." Annie explains every new thing we try as she does it. Trust is the foundation for a relationship like ours. Once we've tried something once, she won't explain it again.

I feel the cool silk as it's tightened around my wrists and the tug as it's secured above me. Another piece of silk is tied around my eyes.

"I have three very different objects that we will play with. I'm not going to tell you what they are, but none of them will inflict any physical pain. You may speak freely only to guess what the object is. Do you understand, little girl?"

"Yes, Danika." The room is silent other than the occasional rustle of the sheets as she moves around. I hear the bedroom door open

and momentarily panic that she's leaving me here alone, but I remind myself that I'm here for pleasure, not pain.

The door opens and closes again, and the bed dips as she sits beside me. A gentle hand caresses from my wrist to my elbow.

"Shhh, Little One. My apologies. I should have told you I was leaving the room." I didn't realize my body was reacting to her absence until I felt my arms trembling under her touch.

I feel her lean over and grab something from the bed. A silky sensation whisps over my collarbone, and I gasp. It's gone as quickly as it appears. The silkiness brushes over my nipple, and my back arches off the bed as it trails from one to the other. The object is soft and smooth, and I can't even begin to guess what it is.

The other objects that night were ice and a vibrator. Both brought me to new heights of pleasure, but it wasn't until my blindfold was off that I found out what the first one was. The excitement of the unknown and it being the first object we ever used has stuck with me.

"Red roses."

"That's perfect. Why don't you send her some roses. She may not take your calls, but all deliveries get signed for at the front desk and brought to the rooms. Would you be willing to send some?"

"Of course. I'm willing to do anything to help her." I look down into my almost empty coffee cup. If he's going to help, he should probably understand our dynamic. "That's why I've stayed away. I said our relationship was a little unconventional. Annie isn't just my fiancée." I look up, and his face shows no emotion. A mask I'm sure he's perfected from his time in the medical field. "Annie is my Domme, and

I'm her submissive. But we fell in love." I look back down into my coffee, wondering what he's going to think of us now.

"Blake, I'd never judge you for your relationship. Please don't be ashamed or afraid to talk to me freely. I'm a safe space in all aspects." His words are so sincere. I'm glad Annie had his comfort through the worst event of her life.

"Thank you." I smile at him through the tears threatening to spill over my lashes.

"Now, let's get your girl back because I think you both need each other."

43

Annie

One month later

Why can't people be more competent?

"Is everything ready for the launch? Yes. No, those aren't the numbers we agreed upon. I want them corrected two hours ago. There's no time-"

"Good morning, Ms. Poulsen." Slamming my phone into my lap in frustration, I glare at the intruder.

"Don't you people knock? I'm on an important call." I don't know why they think they can just walk into my room at all hours of the day. I pay good money for this suite.

"Ms. Poulsen, it's time for group therapy."

"I can't go. I have a meeting. Jack, I'll call you back."

"Ms. Poulsen, you've been told if you don't participate in therapy, you can't continue to stay here." Dammit. I thought if I threw enough money their way, I could stay without going to their ridiculous group therapy sessions. I already go to their physical therapy sessions.

"Participation was never a requirement. Just attendance.

273

Bring me my wheelchair."

"No."

"Excuse me?" Who does she think she is? I pay her salary.

"I said no. You need to use your walker. It's been almost eight weeks since your surgery. Doctors orders. No more wheelchairs."

"I need my wheelchair."

"You NEED an attitude adjustment, and you NEED to have faith in yourself. You CAN do it, and you will. It's time." I turn my head away from her, and my eyes land on the table with several bouquets of red roses in various stages of decay. They've come every other day for weeks. Always from Blake, and always a variation of song lyrics from her favorite song. The song she sang the morning of the accident after giving me an orgasm in my car.

~Annie
I will never stop marching to find you
In the middle of the hardest fight
It's true, I will rescue you
I love you,
<3 Blake

Despite my rejecting them every time they bring a new bouquet into my room, the staff members tell me, "If you don't like them, throw them away yourself." They also insist on reading me the notes every time. Yesterday's lyrics were tough to hear.

~Annie
I hear you whisper underneath your breath

I hear your SOS, your SOS
I will send out an army to find you
I love you,
<3 Blake

I wish I could. I fucking wish I could throw them away myself. I'm so overwhelmed with guilt and grief that I can't do it. My leg doesn't want to work the way I want it to. I'm weak and powerless to my body.

I killed Josh. I threw away Blake. I let Cole go. I miss Candy. I have no one, and I can't blame anyone but myself. It's easier this way. Now I can't disappoint anyone.

"Come on, Ms. Poulsen. Up you go." She reaches for my legs to help me shift them off the side of the bed, and I swat her away.

"I can do it," I tell her in a clipped tone. I swing my left leg off the bed and physically push my right leg over to join it. My muscles are stiff and achy. Planting both feet on the ground, the nurse hovers next to me, waiting with the walker that has the ridiculous tennis balls on the bottom.

I brace my arms on either side of my hips on the bed and slide to the edge. The nurse places the walker in front of me so I can grab it. I lean forward, wrapping my hands around the bars, take a deep breath and concentrating on the cool floor soaking through my socks.

I hate these stupid ugly yellow socks with grips that they force me to wear. The swelling in my leg hasn't gone down entirely, and my shoes don't fit. I'm forced to stare at my favorite color, which I'm beginning to loathe because of the constant reminder of all the despair in my life.

"You can do this," I mumble to myself. With all my weight

pressed against my arms, I slowly lift to my feet. As I stand upright, I give the nurse a smug smile.

"Okay, you proved me wrong. Now, let's walk." I know I'm lying to myself. I'm standing with the majority of my weight on my good leg. Walking requires two legs. I lead with my bad leg to take the first step and place it down about six inches in front of the other.

Baby steps. You can do this, Danika. You're a strong woman. Men fear your power.

The more weight I put on my bad leg, the more confident I become. See, I didn't have anything to worry about. With my weight evenly distributed between my two legs, I put more pressure on my bad leg to be able to lift my good one and complete the step. When my left leg finally leaves the floor, I collapse. My knee buckles, and my body lurches forward. My face hitting the front bar of the walker with the entire force of my weight.

The nurse catches me before I fully hit the floor and pushes the call button on my hospital bed for help.

Embarrassment.

Frustration.

Guilt.

Two more nurses come rushing in and help me back onto the bed before assessing the knot growing on my forehead.

"I'm FINE. Leave me alone." One of the nurses leaves and comes back in with a wheelchair.

"Your chariot, Ms. Poulsen." He makes a foolish bowing gesture toward the chair.

"Where do you think I'm going in that?"

"Group therapy. You're perfectly fine. No reason you can't attend."

"You're kidding me, right?"

"Not in the slightest. And I will make sure your doctor is aware of this incident. I have a feeling there's extra PT in your near future." Feeling defeated because I know I've been given more leniency than I should have, I don't resist when I'm helped into the wheelchair and pushed to group therapy.

As if showing up at all wasn't bad enough, my little incident made me 10 minutes late. I hate being late.

"Danika, glad you could join us. Come on over." *As if I have a choice.* I'm wheeled into the circle, the nurse moving a chair out of the way to make room for mine. Before she leaves, she bends down and presses lightly on my forming bruise.

"Call a nurse if you get dizzy or have a headache."

"Apparently, I'm told I'm fine. Now let me suffer in silence." She nods and leaves.

"We have some new faces, so we were just doing a round of introductions. You haven't missed much. Would you like to do yours?" Looking around the room, I don't recognize anyone. Not that I expected to. I've been flying under the radar, but my fall this morning will undoubtedly stir things up. Four other people are sitting in the circle beside the leader. What was his name again?

"Fine. My name is Danika. I was in a car accident about three months ago. Here I am." What more do they need to know? I just need to do my time and get back to my room.

"Would you care to share any of the details of the accident? Like your injuries and why you're here?"

"Don't you already know why I'm here?" His head tilts, and eyes squint. He's assessing me. "You have my file, right?" His face falls to neutral again.

"I do, but not everyone here has that information. Would

you like me to share it for you?" Is it worse saying it out loud or having to listen to someone else say it? I sigh, realizing I can give the version I'm comfortable with if I say it myself.

"Three months ago, I was in a car accident that killed my driver and crushed my right leg and pelvis. I've had two surgeries to correct all of the bones." Do I share the last part? No, I'm not ready. Losing a part of a future I didn't even have yet is not something I want to talk about with strangers. Sensing I'm done speaking, he continues.

"Thank you for sharing, Danika. Okay, let's get started. Everyone here has lost someone in a traumatic way."

"Including you?" My curiosity got the best of me. Something about him is so familiar, and I can't place it. As much as I hate coming to these sessions, I always feel calmer when I leave.

"Yes," he says with hesitation in his voice. "Including me." He's looking at me intently now. I wish I could figure him out.

"Jay?" an older man with ill-fitting clothes speaks up. Jay. That's his name. He doesn't look like a Jay.

The two men speak, and the rest of the meeting continues around me. When the session ends, Jay walks over to me.

"Can I give you a lift back?" His tone is sincere. I look around and don't see anyone else waiting for me.

"Um, sure." He rounds my chair and sets a leisurely pace back to my room.

"Can I ask what happened to your face?"

"You can ask. That doesn't mean I'll answer." He doesn't look disturbed by my attitude. I respect him a little more.

"Okay. Fair point." He pauses, seemingly wondering if he should ask anyway. "So Danika, how did you get that bruise? It looks fresh. Does it have anything to do with this wheelchair you should have been out of weeks ago?" I snap my head up and back to look at him.

"How do you know that?" He shrugs.

"You're not the only one that knows people." He winks at me. His statement seems so ominous. We approach my door, and again I look up at him.

"How did you know what room I was in?" He dips his head and chuckles as he pushes me to the edge of my bed.

"An answer for an answer, Danika?"

"Fine, you go first." He offers his arm to help me stand, and I begrudgingly accept it.

"Nope. I hold all of the power here. I could just as easily look up your file, but I'm giving you the opportunity to tell me instead."

"Well, didn't you just give away how you know all about me?" He gives a noncommittal shrug.

"Maybe. Maybe not. There's more to knowing someone than just what's on a piece of paper. Or, well, a computer screen." He steps away to place the wheelchair by the door. When he turns, he must see my discomfort. I'm even more sore now because of the fall, and my hip doesn't have the strength to lift my leg onto the bed. "Can I help you?"

"It doesn't seem like I have much of a choice. My body doesn't want to cooperate." He helps me sit back farther on the bed and then guides my leg until I'm in a comfortable position. "Thank you."

"No problem. Now are we going to trade answers?" Curiosity is getting the best of me. He obviously works here, but I didn't think he had the type of job to have full access to my medical records. He just runs the support group.

"Fine. I tried to use my walker before the meeting, and I fell. My leg wasn't strong enough to support me." I expect to see pity in his eyes. The sad little rich girl can't get her shit together. Instead, I see compassion. Understanding. Empathy.

"I'm sorry you're struggling, Danika." His head tilts in the direction of the dozens of roses across the room. "Who are those from?" I don't even want to look at them. They stir up more grief inside me.

"You owe me an answer before I give you another one."

"You're correct. Okay." He sighs and sits in the chair next to my bed. "I own this wing of the rehabilitation center. The mental health wing." He owns it. That's what he said. Not at all what I imagined he'd say.

"Wow. You aren't usually speechless. I must have really shocked you."

"You did, actually." I honestly have no idea what to say. He owns the room I'm sitting in. The room that I'm paying for. I was initially in the Physical Therapy wing, but after being here for two weeks, they moved me to this section when it became apparent that I probably wasn't leaving anytime soon. Once I was moved, they forced me to start group therapy.

"Did you have me moved to this wing?"

"Who are the roses from?" Damn. It seems I can't get anything past him. "An answer for an answer."

"I don't want to talk about it." I don't even know what I would say. My feelings haven't changed for her, for either of them. But I can't allow myself to feel anything. "So, I guess you won't answer any more questions for me until I answer yours?"

"It's an answer for an answer. I can ask a different one, but

I'm not sure you'll like that one either." Several minutes go by without a response from me. Nodding in understanding, he stands, and I sense my social time is over.

He walks to the door but stops with his hand on the knob. He looks at me and hesitates, deciding if he should say what's on his mind.

"Go ahead, Jay. You won't hurt my feelings."

"Don't dismiss your support system. Be happy you have them and lean on them. It's a luxury some don't have." Before I can process his words, he opens the door and leaves.

44

Cole

Being in a constant state of bliss and depression is agony. Blake and I are happy together, but there's a gaping hole in our relationship. A void that no matter what we do, is always there, like a tickle at the back of your throat that won't go away.

Laying on our brand new plush navy couch in our new townhouse, Blake and I are enjoying each other's company while some chick flick drones on in the background. Candy is curled up on the couch to my left, and Blake's head is in my lap while I mindlessly stroke her hair.

We've been here for two weeks, and despite being fully furnished with everything we could possibly need, it feels empty. Blake and I don't have to work, but together we walk the dogs. I left my job working for PC Madness because, after everything with Annie, it didn't feel right to continue working for her.

"Do you think she's depressed?" I look down to see the sweetest brown eyes looking back at me.

"Who, Princess?"

"Candy. She's had a lot of change. First Annie and then Java and Beans. She just sleeps all day." She has seemed off. I've been wondering the same question. "I know we joked about it, but do you think she needs a friend? Should we adopt her a dog?"

Annie is still in rehab, and Candy is staying with us for now. I continue to receive a weekly deposit in my account that she set up for the fee to walk Candy.

"It's definitely something to think about." She looks so at ease laying on me. It hasn't always been this way. She had nightmares constantly for weeks after the accident and would wake up crying and sweaty. She was always screaming Annie's name. At first, it upset me that she was in my arms and screaming hers, but I quickly realized she was reliving the sounds she heard over the phone the day of the crash.

Our emotional relationship is the strongest it's ever been. Our physical relationship is growing day by day. It was a while before we did anything besides passing kisses because of our guilt. Closing my eyes, I shake my head, reliving the memory of our first encounter.

After spending hours laying on the couch in my apartment comforting each other, Blake has fallen asleep next to me while we were watching a movie. The sexual tension between us has been growing, and the feeling of her soft skin has me on edge. I need some relief.

Gently removing myself from the couch so as not to disturb Blake or any of the three dogs curled up together, I make my way to my bedroom and quietly close the door. My pants are hastily removed and tossed aside as I climb onto my bed and lay on top of the charcoal gray duvet. My cock is already semi-hard at the thought of relieving the pressure that's been building up.

Reaching into my boxer briefs, I give myself a few firm tugs and groan at the sensation before reaching into my side table and grabbing the lube. I remove my boxers and with the click of the cap, my cock is slick. The easy slide of my hand along my shaft has my body tingling with want. I close my eyes and think about the first night I met my girls and how sexy they looked in their masks. My breathing increases as my hand makes circles around the tip of my cock. I'm lost in the few memories I have with them together when I hear the door click and a small gasp.

"Pup," escapes her lips in a breathy whisper. I'm frozen with the shock of being caught and the exhilaration of the situation she found me in. I stare into her eyes as she slowly walks to the bed and climbs in next to me. "Please don't stop." I smile at her, but she's not looking at my face. Her eyes are fixed on my slow-moving hand, still stroking.

"Princess, why don't you join me." I see her hesitation as she thinks over my request. "Just...next to me. Pleasure yourself while I pleasure myself. We don't have to touch." Her relief is visible as her guilt melts away.

Tentatively, she lays down next to me on her back and spreads her legs. She watches my hand stroke a few more times before lowering hers under the elastic waistband of her sleep shorts. I see the motion of the fabric and wish it was my hand.

"That's my good girl. Are you wet, Princess?" She hums in response, eyes closed as she gives in to her touch. "Will you let me watch?" She opens her eyes and tilts her head to look back at me. Her other hand rims the band of her shorts, and she slowly pulls them down. She drops her knees to the bed so I can see her hand moving between her slick lips.

"Tell me what to do. Imagine it's your hand around my cock.

What would you be doing? If that were my hand on your pussy, I'd be gathering the wetness from your entrance and gliding it toward your aching clit. Swirling around it but not touching it yet. I'd want to drive you wild, so you're aching for me. Are you aching?"

"Yes." Her answer comes out as a moan.

"Tell me what to do. I want your commands. Please, BlakeLynn." I know I'm practically begging, but I yearn for the loss of control. For her control over me.

"Circle your thumb around your tip." I obey. "Are you wet for me, Pup?"

"Yes," I hiss out.

"Let me taste. Give me your thumb." She reaches across me, grabbing my hand and drags it to her until her lips wrap around my thumb. A low growl escapes me as her warm wet tongue circles my thumb, and my dick twitches on my stomach. I savor the feeling, wishing for so much more. She gives one last suck before she pops my thumb out of her mouth.

Her eyes stare back at mine, hooded with as much lust in them as I'm sure I'm returning.

"Are my fingers circling that swollen clit? Are there little shocks being sent to your core?"

"God, yes. Stroke your cock. I want you to use a firm grip. I want to hear how good my hand on your cock makes you feel. Tell me."

"It feels so fucking good. I wish it were your soft, plump lips taking me in your filthy mouth. Do you want me to lick that pussy? Can you feel me flicking you with my tongue? Sucking it into my mouth." Her back arches off the bed as her fingers increase their speed. Her soft moans are driving me wild.

"Fuck, Pup. I feel you. You feel so good. I'm close. Are you close? I want you to come with me."

285

"I'm right there with you, Princess. Your hands are bringing me to ecstasy."

"Oh god. Oh fuck, fuck, Cole. Come with me. Come with me now." Her body convulses into itself as she's panting with her release. My balls tighten, and I squeeze hard for the last few strokes before I'm coming all over my stomach, muscles spasming and her name spilling from my lips.

"Pup?" I blink a few times before looking down at Blake. "Whatcha thinking? I swear my head just raised a few inches." She chuckles as I realize my dick is hard under her. Grasping under her arms, I pull her up to me until she's straddling my lap. Squeezing her hips in my hands and smiling, I lean in for a gentle kiss on her lips.

"Thinking about how much I love you." I nuzzle my nose to hers as she rolls her eyes.

"I love you too, but it takes a lot more than that to raise the monster in your pants." She swivels her hips to make sure I know what monster she's referring to. Dropping my head to the back of the couch, I groan out my frustration.

"You are the devil. You know that, right?" Her returning smile is bright and full of mischief.

"Yep." She pops the P as she slides off my lap.

"Hey tease, I'm gonna go have dinner with Nicole. Would you like to join?"

"I was going to meet up with Justin for coffee. Maybe we can all get something together?" I'm glad she's been hanging out with Justin. The glimpse into how Annie is doing has helped her more than anything I've been able to do.

"That sounds great. Let's coordinate."

·෴˙෴·

The girls hijacked our casual dinner/coffee evening. Justin and I currently find ourselves at Midnight Moonshine, dressed for a long night of drinking and debauchery. I warned Justin of Blake's love for the Kickin' Cowboy shot. I knew there was no way she would let Nicole get through the evening without participating in at least one.

When we got here, I was able to convince them to sit and have dinner in the restaurant before heading out to the dance floor. My hope was to pump them full of carbs to help soak up the alcohol.

Before we left the house, Justin and I had flipped a coin to be the designated driver but were instantly vetoed. Blake hasn't been here since her engagement, but she was determined to replace that memory with some new ones using alcohol.

"Absolutely not. You're not driving." Blake walks out of the bathroom, hands firmly placed on her hips. She looks sexy in a sleeveless black dress, with her hair bouncing in soft curls around her face. The bottom of her dress is flowy, and the V in the front plunges below her tits. I haven't seen her look this dressed up since before...

"Princess, it's alright. I don't need to drink. I want to make sure everyone gets home safely. And how the fuck are your tits supposed to stay in that dress all night? You aren't supposed to be the show." She slaps me on the chest.

"That's what rideshare apps are for, Coleman." Nicole steps out of the bathroom behind Blake. "And double-sided tape." She grabs two handfuls of Blake's breasts and jiggles. My jaw drops. "These girls aren't going anywhere."

"You both look beautiful." I almost forgot Justin was here with the show my sister was putting on. Nicole is wearing red daisy duke shorts and a crop top vintage band shirt. Her blonde hair is curled similarly to Blake's.

"Big sister, would you mind not manhandling my woman, please?" She releases her hold on Blake's chest and I step up to rescue her.

"You do look beautiful. And I'm sorry for my sister's wandering hands. She's a virgin and can't control her urges."

"Shut the fuck up, Coleman. You know I'm not a virgin."

"Hey Coleman, why don't you watch your virgin sister do this!" Poor Justin. The girls have been drinking heavily. Truthfully we all have.

I watch as Nicole grabs his chin and forces it up. He knows what's coming, so he opens his mouth. She pours the shot in, and gives him a moment to swallow before she splashes him, slaps him, and to everyone's surprise, she pulls him in for a deep kiss.

She has her arms wrapped around his head in a vice grip. He's being a gentleman, and keeping his hands firmly planted on the bar, while Nicole is controlling the kiss completely.

"Okay, there, Miss Non-Virgin. Let the poor guy have some air. You've proven your point." She's already slipping off the bar when I step up to help her. She pokes Justin in the chest as he's staring at her in shock.

"That was fucking hot. Raincheck for later." She winks and grabs Blake's hand. "Come on girl, lets go freshen up in the bathroom." I palm my forehead before turning back to him.

"I'm sorry, man. My sister can be a little feral. Her filter is slim most days, but add alcohol, and it's a recipe for disaster.

Usually a comical disaster, but that…that was new. You're welcome to crash at our place tonight if things get weird." Justin and I knew we would be more sober than the girls, and it was best to keep an eye on them tonight. He's planning to crash in my old room at her house.

"It's all good. She doesn't scare me." I arch a brow at him.

"Famous last words." I shake my head at how naive he is to my sister's antics. "Justin, I know we haven't talked about it yet tonight, but how is she?" He pushes his glasses further up his nose and sighs.

"She's getting there. She's walking now with the walker. Soon she'll only need a cane. I've gotten her to open up some, but mostly outside of the group. It's become my routine to walk her back to her room after. She won't talk about the roses. I try every day. You and Blake seem to be off-limits to talk about, but I'm trying to get through to her." I clasp his shoulder and look him directly in the eyes. I want to make sure he understands me.

"I know you are, and we appreciate everything you're doing for us and for her. Thank you." He smiles and almost looks embarrassed.

"We'll get through to her. I have something up my sleeve, but I'd rather not use it unless it's an absolute last resort. We aren't there yet."

Our drunken charges come bouncing back to us from the bathroom and exclaim they're ready to go home. I guess the evening is over.

45

Annie

My hip is sore today. I need to stop favoring it and try to distribute my weight between my legs evenly.

"Alright, see everyone tomorrow." Jay's voice snaps me out of my mental chastising. I say my respectful goodbyes as the other group members leave past me.

"You look uncomfortable today. Is everything alright?" Jay extends his arm to offer support as I rise from the chair with my cane. "Just sore. I started a new stretch in PT yesterday." He stands beside me until I'm steady on my feet, and we start walking toward my room.

"I heard you've been working hard. I'm proud of you, Danika."

"Thank you. I'm ready to get back to the office. I think it's time. I'm trying."

"Don't push yourself too hard, though, okay?" He offers me a sincere smile. "When you finally leave, I think the nurses will miss Sarah's fresh baked goods." We laugh.

"I'm sure she'll miss having all of them to bake for. Compared to the requests she's been taking from the staff here, I'm pretty boring to cook for. She's an amazing cook, and I'm lucky to have found her."

We reach my room, and Jay opens the door for me. As I'm about to sit at the desk, there's a knock and a nurse enters.

"Good morning, Ms. Poulsen. Your delivery is here." The nurse walks in with a frustratingly large bouquet of red roses. The sizes of the bouquets have changed. Some days just a single red rose; others, like today apparently, there seems to be three dozen.

"I don't want it."

"Sorry, Ms. Poulsen, I'm required to deliver all packages to their appropriate room."

"I. Don't. Want. Them." The nurse places the bouquet on the table with the half dozen others sitting there. "Take them away. Take them *all* away."

My frustration is at a boiling point. Day in and day out, I stare at the reminder of the things I've lost. The red roses remind me of the first sensory scene with Blake. The rose tattoos on Cole's arm. The car accident. Josh's death. I can't take it anymore.

Approaching the table, I grab the new flowers she just delivered and smash them on the floor. I pick up a single bud vase and throw it across the room.

"Fucking. Reminders." *Smash.* "I did this." *Scream.* "I ruined everything." *Bang.* Glass shatters everywhere around us. I see the nurse try to approach me. Jay stops her, says something in her ear, and she leaves.

"I can't do this anymore." *Scream.* "I don't deserve their blind faith." *Crash.* My body, overcome with exhaustion, collapses to the ground, wracked with sobs. "I...can't..."

hiccup, "do...thi-is...anymore." I don't even recognize the shell of the person I've become. I'm hyperventilating from the wave of emotions.

All around me, I see the now wet note cards with the lyrics written on them. The reminders that have taunted me for weeks with their support. The stupid lyrics that haven't let me forget I have help. The song that reminds me I'm not alone.

"There's never been a moment you were forgotten"
"You are not hopeless"
"I'll be your shelter, I'll be your armor"
"I will rescue you"

I'm numb to my hip's pain as I curl into the fetal position, surrounded by shards of glass, rose petals, and lyrics. I hear the crunch of glass as a blanket is placed on top of me. Strong hands wrap around my feeble body, lifting me from my carnage.

I'm carried bridal-style out of my hospital room and I hear Jay speaking to someone about cleaning up the mess. My face is buried into his chest, and my hands clutch his shirt like it's my last lifeline. It might very well be. I've pushed everyone else away.

He opens a door and steps into an office.

"This is my office, Danika. We're going to wait in here while your room gets cleaned up. Would you like the door open or closed?"

"Closed." I've suffered enough embarrassment for a life-time.

"Okay. I'm going to set you down on your feet so we can

get this glass off of you, and then we can move to the couch. Wrap your arms around my neck. I've got you."

He bends and gently places my feet on the floor while I tightly grasp his neck. I can hear the rain of glass as he unwraps the blanket. My grip falters, and he grabs my hips.

"Annie, I've got you. I won't let you fall." *Annie, I've got you. I've. Got. You.* Annie. He called me Annie, not Danika. I gasp as memories from that dreaded day flood me.

"It's going to be okay. My name is Justin. We're going to get you out of here. I won't leave you until we do."

"Annie, it's Justin. I've got you."

"I'm right here, Annie. I told you I wouldn't leave you. I'm going to ride to the hospital with you.

Eyes wide and brimming with tears, I look up at the man who saved my life. The man who promised not to leave me while I lay hurt and broken in my car. The man who's allowed me to live in his rehab facility far longer than I should have.

"J-justin."

"Hey, Annie. I wondered when you'd put the pieces together in your memory." His smile is the most heartfelt, genuine thing I've ever seen.

"But how?"

"A story for a story? Are you ready to really talk?" I don't have any strength to object, so I stay quiet. Am I ready? "Are you ready to talk about Blake and Cole...and Josh?" I'm so shocked by his question that I release him and take a step back. Carefully, I turn and walk over to the couch before sitting.

"You did it again." There's awe in his tone and a smile on

his face.

"Did what?" My tone is clipped. There are so many emotions swirling around in my brain, and anger chose to surface in my answer.

"You just walked away from me without your cane and sat on the couch. In your room, you walked from your desk to the table to smash the roses. Without your cane, Annie. You got out of your head and did what your body has wanted to do all along."

Holy shit. Justin is right. I wasn't even thinking. I do a mental check of my body, and nothing feels off or wrong. Was that what I needed this entire time? Did I just need to get out of my own head?

"I did it?"

"I think you're ready, Annie. But first, I want to give you something." He opens his desk drawer, then comes and sits down next to me and takes my hand. He flips my palm up and deposits something small and delicate into it. When he pulls back, I'm consumed with emotions. My bracelet. Our bracelet. I haven't seen it since the crash. I had looked through my personal effects bag repeatedly, and it wasn't there.

"How?"

"I needed to remove all your jewelry in the ambulance because I knew you were going directly into surgery. The bracelet had to be cut off, and I must have missed your bag when I was putting it all in. I found it in a corner a few weeks ago when we were deep cleaning the ambulance, but I knew you couldn't handle it yet if I gave it back to you. Blake told me to hold on to it until you were ready."

"Blake? How do you know Blake?"

"I'm going to tell you my story now, and then you can tell

me yours. Deal?"

"A story for a story. Okay. Deal." I'm ready.

46

Blake

Annie went home over a week ago. She had Justin come and retrieve Candy, which was heartbreaking. Not because I miss Candy, which I do, but because she didn't even ask Cole or me to bring her back. Cole still goes to pick her up for her walks, but Annie never comes to the door.

Honestly, we aren't even sure if she's home. There haven't been any new cars in the driveway, and when Cole brings Candy back inside to check her water, he hasn't seen her. The door to the room set up for her downstairs is always closed.

This morning Cole received a text from Annie. It was business related but still the first communication in months.

Annie: You won't need to walk Candy today. She's taken care of.

"What do I even say back?" Neither of us could believe she had reached out.

"Just tell her, 'okay.' Unfortunately, we both know she

probably won't say anything back." And I was right. There was no response after his "Okay, I'll see her tomorrow" text.

"Princess, let's take Lucy to the dog park today." Cole is making our to-go coffees as I finish getting ready in the bathroom. "She's gotten so used to walking with Candy that she'll probably be lonely without her."

"Sounds like a great idea."

·ᴎᴎ··ᴎᴎ·

Walking hand in hand, we stop to open the gates of the small dog section of the park. Unlike the big section, which has boulders and tree stumps, the small area has tunnels for the dogs to crawl through and a few agility ramps. Lucy takes off, immediately exploring her new surroundings. We use the large dog section when we're here with Candy, so she hasn't been in this area for a while.

Taking a seat on the bench, I curl into Cole when he places his arm around me. He kisses me tenderly, lingering for a few long moments, and I toy with my cuff on his wrist.

"I'd really like to get that dog we keep talking about, Pup."

"I think that sounds like a good idea, Princess. We can look online when we get-" He stops when he feels my body stiffen under him. "What's wrong?"

"Listen."

"*Kommen.*" His back straightens when he hears it. I discreetly peer over his shoulder to see Annie and Candy walking away from the large dog section of the park. WALKING. She has a slight limp, but she's on her feet doing it.

"She's so beautiful." I can hear the awe in his voice. God, I'd forgotten how beautiful she is. She walks far enough away that Cole can fully turn around and look without her noticing. He wipes my cheek, and I feel the wetness from the tears I didn't know had spilled over.

"She is. Do you think she saw us?" I wonder how she would feel if she did see us cuddling on the bench together.

"I have no idea, Princess. Look at her walking. She looks so strong and healthy. So unlike the frail, broken woman who kicked us out of her hospital room months ago." He squeezes me tighter into him. "I fucking miss her."

"Me too, Pup." More than anything. We sit for a while longer as we digest having just seen Annie for the first time, before we take Lucy home.

·∿∿··∿∿·

"I'm going, Cole, and I won't let you stop me." I'm stomping around our living room like a toddler, gathering my purse and keys. Seeing Annie yesterday was a knife to the heart and I can't handle the silence anymore. "I've already called her secretary, and she's in her office today. I'm going to see her. I need...I don't know what I need other than to see her. To be in the same room as her. To breathe the same air as her."

Strong hands grab my shoulders, stopping me from my frantic wandering pace around the house. "Okay. Okay, Blake. But I'm going with you. Someone needs to be there to pick up your pieces if things go bad. I'll always pick up your pieces, Princess. You don't have to do this alone. I want to see her as much as you do." He sighs and pulls me into his chest. I can feel his erratic heartbeat under my cheek, and I know mine must feel the same. "Come on. I'll drive."

"Do you think she will see us?" My nerves are evident in

my shaking voice.

"I guess we're about to find out, Princess." I was surprised when my keycard still worked at the back parking deck. I thought for sure she would have deactivated it by now.

My fingers nervously tap on my thigh as the elevator climbs to the top. As we pass each floor, I watch the numbers light up, and my stomach drops with each new light. Cole grabs my hand to calm me.

"Listen to me. No matter what happens up there, I'm here, and you're coming home with me. Got it?"

"I love you." I lean my head on this arm and squeeze his hand.

The elevator dings at the top floor, and the doors open. I divert my eyes from the glaring marble floors but hear Cole's "Shit" when he doesn't.

"I forgot about the blinding floors."

"Ms. Rogers. Mr. McGrath. Is Ms. Poulsen expecting you?" The receptionist quickly stands, and sounds panicked by our presence.

"She's about to." I shock myself with the confident tone of my voice as I proceed down the hallway. The receptionist picks up the phone, and I hear her telling Annie we're coming.

My confidence wanes with every step I take closer to her office. I stop in front of her door and take a deep breath, gathering all of my strength.

"I'm right here, Princess." Cole rubs his hands soothingly down my arms. As I'm about to reach for the handle, the door opens.

There she is. Staring back at me in all of her stunning beauty. She's wearing a gorgeous deep green pencil dress with bright white sneakers.

"Hi." My word is a breathy sigh as the tears instantly stream down my face. I have to stop myself from reaching out to her.

"Can we come in, Annie?" Thank you, Cole, for rescuing me. "Hi" was the best I had. She steps back, and we walk into the familiar office. My soul crushes as her scent fills my lungs. The vanilla scent that used to be *our* scent. I haven't been able to use it since leaving the hospital. It evokes too many raw emotions.

I move across the room and sit on the couch, shoving my hands under my thighs to stop from even thinking about touching her. Cole sits next to me and palms my knee. I'm enraptured by her as she gracefully walks across the room, her limp barely noticeable, as she sits on the chair across from us.

The air around us is thick, and the silence is awkward.

"You look beautiful, Annie." Once again, Cole speaks, breaking the silence. "We've missed you. Thank you for letting us in."

"Well, I'm not sure I was left with much of a choice, but…" She looks away from us and folds her hands in her lap.

"But?" She wants to say more, but she's unsure. It's not an expression I'm used to seeing on her.

"But I've been wanting to reach out to you. Justin told me about the roses. I know he asked you to send them. At the time, I didn't appreciate them. I couldn't. They were a reminder of things I wasn't yet ready to face. But now, thinking back, I realize I looked forward to them as much as I hated them. The lyrics written on the notes made me think of the hard things I was trying to run away from. Justin…well, let's say we have a lot more in common than I ever expected, and he's helped me work through many of the things I was

300

feeling. And, more importantly, those things I was avoiding."

Hearing her words knocks the wind out of me.

"Annie-"

"Please, let me finish." I nod. "I don't- I can't expect you to forgive me right away for the things I said and did. I was horribly cruel, and I realize it now. Fuck. I can't believe the way I treated you, like just another problem I could throw money and a contract at."

"Kitten, it's alright." She closes her eyes at the sound of her pet name. He says it out of love and habit, but she recoils at hearing it. My heart breaks a little at the sight. She must know how much we still love her.

"It's not, and you shouldn't forgive me so easily. I'm...I'm in therapy, and I'm working through my issues."

"Annie, I'm so happy for you. That's amazing, Baby."

"It's necessary. I don't deserve the recognition." Another awkward silence fills the room.

"I'm sure you're busy. We should go, Cole." I don't want to go. I want to sweep her into my arms and never let go. "I miss you, Annie." Her honey-colored eyes lock on mine, staring right into my soul.

"Come to dinner this week. Wait. No." She shakes her head and scrunches her brows. "Let me try that again. Would you like to come to dinner soon?"

"We'd love to, Kitten. Name the time, and we'll be there."

"I'll talk to Sarah, but three days notice should be plenty. How does Friday sound?"

"We'll be there." She wants to see us again, and my insides are doing somersaults with excitement.

We all stand and walk towards the door. Cole reaches up and places a hand on her cheek. Her eyes close as soon as she feels his touch. In a low gravelly voice, he whispers into her ear.

"Do you have any idea what it's like to want you this badly and be unable to do anything about it? It's destroying me." He kisses her forehead and walks out. She stares down the hall at his retreating body in shock at his words.

I can't control my restraint any longer and throw my hands around her neck and bury my face in her hair. I haven't felt her in so long, and my body instantly releases some of the stress that's been bottled up.

I pull away before she has a chance to return the embrace and kiss her cheek.

"I love you, Annie. Nothing has changed." I squeeze her hand before following Cole down the hall. I feel lighter than I have in months.

47

Annie

The feel of Blake's embrace lingered with me all day. The heat from Cole's kiss still brands my forehead. My heart soared when I saw them together at the dog park. I was so happy that they still had each other. I couldn't help but mourn the loss of them for myself. My mind and body still longs for them.

The rideshare driver pulls up in front of my house, and I thank her before walking inside. I'm still not comfortable driving to work, and I haven't been able to hire anyone else to drive me. I still carry that guilt.

Candy greets me at the door, happy to see me. I've noticed a difference in her demeanor. I feel terrible that she had to bounce around for months because of my selfishness. I can tell she's lonely being home by herself all day. First, she had Nicole's crazy little dachshunds, and then she was home all day with Cole and Blake.

Cole and Blake. I barely survived their visit today. I wanted to collapse into their arms and forget the last three months. They're still so deeply ingrained in my soul. Blake was still wearing her bracelet and ring. My ring. The engagement ring I gave her when I asked her to be my wife. My hand involuntarily rubs my bare wrist. When I returned home from rehab, I placed my bracelet into my jewelry box and tried not to think about it. Its absence is felt often.

I can't believe she hasn't taken either of them off. It's obvious she and Cole are a couple. I noticed the cuff on his wrist and can only assume it's the one Blake bought for him that I never got to see. They share a townhouse together. A townhouse that isn't too far from here. It's just on the other side of the dog park that we frequent.

"Hey, Candy. Want to go for a walk?" I don't know what I'm doing. Well, I know what I'm doing. I'm purposely walking in the direction of Blake and Cole's house with the intention of walking by. What I don't understand is why. I know my reasons are selfish. I don't deserve to see them again so soon but my entire being aches for them. The need to get even a tiny glimpse into their life together. Maybe I want to punish myself. Maybe this is some masochistic way to torture myself by seeing something that I can't have.

Whatever the reasoning, halfway through our outing, it becomes evident there's a fatal flaw in my plan. The sky is starting to darken, and the clouds look heavy. My weather app says the rain will begin in 5 minutes. *Shit.* All of my options involve me walking in the rain. Fuck it. I'm not a quitter. I came all this way to walk by, and I will do it.

We round the corner, and I can see their townhouse down the road as a loud clap of thunder shakes the ground. Candy yelps and tugs on her leash hard enough that I have to let go. I can't take the chance of her pulling me down and injuring me. She shouldn't go too far.

I'm correct. She doesn't go far at all. She runs down the road straight to Cole and Blake's front door. Obviously, she would recognize their house. This was such a stupid idea. Another loud clap of thunder, and the sky opens up. I'm soaked in seconds as I see Candy scratching at their door, whining for them to open it.

"Candy, *Kommen.*" I shouldn't be surprised that she ignores me. What she does do is grab the attention of the residents of the townhouse. Cole opens the door, and she runs right inside. I'm only a door away, getting soaked to the bone as he steps outside to see where Candy came from.

"Annie?" Cole spots me, disappears inside, and immediately comes back out with an umbrella. He reaches me, and I cling to him like a moth to a flame. "Annie." My name is a sigh of relief from his chest. His warmth seeps into the cold chill of my body caused by the rain.

"Cole?" Blake stands at the door, wondering where he went. She spots us, and her hands fly to her mouth. Cole bends down, and with his free arm, he picks me up and carries me inside.

Candy, the traitor, is already curled up on the couch asleep. Cole carries me into the kitchen and sits me on the counter. I don't let him go. I can't. My body won't allow me to, even though my mind screams that I'm crossing too many boundaries.

My dress is clinging to my every curve. My sneakers are soaked, and my makeup is running down my face. Cole sweeps wet hair off my forehead, and I can feel the trail of heat left behind by his fingers.

"Kitten, what were you doing out in the rain?" Hearing my pet name soothes me, unlike this afternoon when it was

ANNIE YOU'RE OKAY

painful to hear. I nestle into him further as Blake walks into the room with a towel and wraps it around my shoulders.

"Annie." She puts her forehead to mine and sighs. The heat from her body causes me to shiver, and Cole rubs his hands along my wet dress. "Can we get you out of these wet clothes? I can give you something to wear."

I nod but make no move to get off the counter, too content to have them surrounding me again. They feel like home, and I don't want to give up this feeling. Cole lifts me again and carries me through their bedroom and into the bathroom, placing me on the counter.

"Kitten, change your clothes, and I'll make you some hot tea. How does that sound?"

"Okay."

He leaves, and Blake enters the room with an oversized t-shirt that belongs to Cole, yoga pants, a thong, and a sports bra. She lays them on the counter next to me.

"Do you need any help?" Her voice is timid.

"Could you help me off the counter?"

"Of course." I gesture for her to stand in front of me. Using her shoulders for support, I slide down until my feet touch the floor.

"Thank you. Um, one more thing."

"Anything, Annie." I pick up the thong. "Do you have something with... more coverage?"

"Oh, yeah, of course. Would boyshorts be good?" She's giving me a quizzical look.

"That would be perfect. Thank you again." She leaves to change out the panties, and I attempt to clean the smeared makeup from my face.

"Is there anything else you need?" Handing me the

306

boyshorts, she smiles the sweetest smile, and I hate how formal this conversation feels.

"I...no. I'm okay. I'll be right out." I wanted to tell her how much I've missed her. How much I just wanted to hold her. To bury my nose in her hair and see if she still smells like vanilla.

She closes the door, and I look around the clean white bathroom. I see Blake's familiar products mixed with more masculine ones. What catches my attention is the cinnamon toothpaste. I know Blake hates the flavor, and when asked, Cole wanted mint too. My heart skips a beat at the thought that this toothpaste is here because of me.

I remove my wet dress and undergarments, and without any other choice, I sit down on the toilet seat. I'm not steady enough on my feet for balance to put my underwear and pants on without sitting.

I look down and see my new reality. The 8-inch scar that starts just above my pubic bone and wraps around my hip. Along with the four holes, two on each side of my pelvis, where the stabilizers were. The scars that remind me of how mangled my body was from the accident. But also remind me of how far I've come. That's the reality I need to focus on. There's a light knock on the door, and I realize I zoned out longer than I thought.

"I'll be right out."

"Okay, Kitten. Just checking in. Your tea is ready." I get dressed as quickly as my body allows. Using a towel, I sop up as much water from my wet hair as possible before grabbing a hair tie from the counter and piling it on top of my head in a messy bun.

Taking a deep breath, I place my hand on the doorknob and

exit the bathroom toward the kitchen. I pause to look around the bedroom and can tell Blake did most of the decorating. The bedspread is a burnt orange color with dark gray sheets and cream-colored throw pillows. The black chair in the corner is plush and soft looking, with a knitted orange throw blanket draped over the back. Even the curtains are shades of orange and gray. Her personality shines in this room.

Entering the kitchen, Blake and Cole are waiting for my return, each holding a steaming mug. I smile inwardly as I notice more pops of orange in here as well. The teapot, dish towels, and cookie jar bring a cheerful presence to the room.

"Hey." I give them each a smile and Cole hands me a mug and slides the box of tea options across the counter.

"Hey, Kitten. Are you ready to tell us why you were standing outside our house in the rain? Is there something wrong?" I'm momentarily flooded with sadness at the realization that "our house" doesn't include me.

"Wrong? No. Nothing's wrong. I just...I couldn't stop thinking about either of you after you left my office today. I felt like I needed to be near you, even if it was just walking by. I know I sound pathetic, but I couldn't help myself. I got caught in the rain, and the thunder scared Candy. She came straight here." Cole puts down his mug and walks up to me.

"May I?" He stops in front of me and extends his arms out in an offering. It's my choice to accept his embrace or deny it. Taking a moment too long, he starts to drop his arms before I take the step forward and crash into him. Large, warm, tattooed arms engulf my body. This embrace is different than earlier. He's changed his shirt, most likely from the wetness that I caused. He smells like fresh laundry and him. A smell that my body knows well.

"Hey, Kitten?" I hum into his chest in response. "I always knew you'd look fucking amazing in my shirt." I can't help but smile at his inappropriate comment.

Blake's tiny frame steps up behind me, and her arms wrap around my front. I feel her chest shaking on my back, and I can't tell if she's laughing at Cole's comment or crying. I spin around and wrap my arms around her. Cole's arms encircle us both, and I never want this feeling to end–this euphoric feeling of calm and serenity. I'm home.

48

Cole

Fuck, it feels so good to have her in my arms again. When I opened the door and saw Candy, I almost panicked. I know we aren't far from Annie's house, and I was worried something happened with her causing Candy to run to us.

I was relieved and confused to see her standing there in the rain. She felt so frail when I picked her up, and she clung to me. Blake was equally as confused and expressed as much when she left Annie alone in the bathroom.

As frail as she may seem right now, this woman holds all the power to my heart and soul. Her body may be healed, but her mind still isn't. It's evident by how she's desperately clinging to us right now.

"Kitten, what do you need? What can we do for you?"

"I need you both. But..."

"Whatever you want, Baby, it's yours." I'm glad to hear Blake and I are on the same page. Annie turns and looks me in the eyes.

"I can't give up control, Cole. I can't give it to you. For

months I felt powerless, and I'm finally feeling like myself again. I'm not ready to give that up. I understand if you can't handle that. I know I'm asking a lot. " I reach up and clasp her cheeks with both hands.

"Annie. YOU. Are. Enough.

Releasing my hold on her, I take a step back and fist my shirt behind me before pulling it over my head. My socks and shoes go next, then my pants. She's staring at me in awe. When I'm down to just my boxer briefs, I drop to my knees before her. Heels under my butt, back straight, hands in my lap, and eyes down; the list ingrained in me to be a proper submissive. The same way she taught Blake to submit.

Annie brushes her fingers through my thick hair and trails them down my jawline, lifting my chin to look up at her.

"How?" Her question is breathy and awestruck. I don't respond because it wasn't a direct question, and I don't want to talk out of turn. She realizes my hesitation and encourages me. "You may answer me, *Mijn Vrede.*" I forgot to ask her what that means but now is obviously not the time.

"BlakeLynn." One simple word, and she understands everything. She turns her attention to Blake, and they have a silent conversation with their eyes. Annie nods, and Blake removes her clothes, kneeling beside me, thigh touching mine, in just her blue thong.

I can hear Annie's deep, even breaths as she walks around Blake and starts braiding her hair. Once done she steps back in front of us and caresses our cheeks.

"Look at me." Blake and I both obey her command.

"I'm going to be honest with you both. There are parts of me that have changed, both mentally and physically, that I'm not yet comfortable with. I know deep in my soul that being here right now is what I want. Seeing you both on your knees, willingly submitting to me, reminds me of our bond of trust. Knowing I still have that is more arousing than any physical activity we could participate in."

She is our queen standing above us. My mind is screaming for me to dominate her, to reject being on this floor at her feet. But my soul wants to give her everything she needs to heal herself.

"I have a question for you both. Have you maintained a physical relationship in my absence?" I hear Blake's quick inhale and move my pinky over slightly to caress her thigh. One of us needs to answer her since she asked a direct question, and I can tell it makes Blake uncomfortable, so I do it for us.

"Yes, Danika." Blake's thigh trembles in anticipation of Annie's response.

"Good boy, Coleman." A growl threatens to escape my throat, but I contain it. She knows what it does to me when she calls me Coleman.

"Little One, did he take good care of you?"

"Yes, Danika."

"Good. And it seems you've also taught him well. You've done an excellent job." She mewls at Annie's praise.

"We're going to move this into the bedroom. My mobility isn't one hundred percent, so I'm going to be the puppet master tonight. Up." We rise and follow her to the bedroom, where she instructs us to get in the middle of the bed.

"*Mijn Vrede*, how many orgasms does our little girl need to have? Tell me what your personal record is with her?" Blake told me about her submissive relationship with Annie. I know their record is 13.

"6, Danika."

"Hmmm? Good job, but I think that's too many." *Too many?*
"She can have one now, and then not another until I say so."
I'm not sure what she has in mind, but I have a feeling this
will be pleasurable torture for us both.

"Little One, what's your personal record with Cole?"

"4, Danika."

"Twice as many as you seems like a fair exchange to me."
Oh. Fuck. So, I need to edge Blake with only two orgasms,
but I have to blow my load four times. Pleasurable torture,
indeed. "Cole, show me how well you eat out her pretty pussy.
Make her come so hard that she screams your name." She
doesn't have to tell me twice.

I've perfected this woman's pleasure in the months we've
been apart from Annie. The guilt of having sex without her
had us doing everything but completing our connection for
a long time.

I lay between Blake's legs, and Annie sits on the end of the
bed to watch. My cock is hard, knowing she'll be watching
what I'm doing. I waste no time and dive right into my happy
place, lapping up her wetness that proves she's as excited
about this as I am. Both women moan, and it's music to my
ears. I forgot what it sounds like for Annie to be aroused.

"Kiss me, Coleman. I want to taste her." *Fuck yes.* I've been
dying to taste *her* again. Sitting up on my knees, I lean in and
kiss Annie's soft, plump lips. Her mouth opens, allowing me
access to sweep my tongue in and savor her.

She tastes like cinnamon, like her toothpaste. She must
have brushed her teeth when she was in the bathroom earlier.
I started using her toothpaste as a way to be close to her
however I could. I knew it was silly, but in her absence, I felt

313

like she was with me for those few minutes every day.

Her kiss is taking as much from me as I'm taking from her. There's a silent exchange of power, but I'll let her win. A flat hand pushes my chest away.

"Make her come."

Back between Blake's thighs, I sink one finger inside of her while circling her clit with my tongue. She's on the edge, and I know she'll come as soon as I add another finger and rub just right.

"Make her come, Coleman. Stop teasing me. I want to see her lose control." I growl into Blake's pussy. I couldn't stop the feral sound caused by her dirty demand. Sliding the extra finger into her weeping pussy I twist precisely as I know her body needs, and she screams with pleasure, bucking against my face and spreading her arousal all over it.

"That was fucking beautiful." Annie's hand is caressing my lower back. "You ate her pussy so fucking well. You're such a good boy. Now flip her over and slam that big cock into her until you come. But remember, little girl, you don't get to come again until I say so."

Flipping her onto all fours, I thrust into her and I angle my hips to not hit her g-spot. I'm already so worked up that it doesn't take long before I'm roaring her name and spilling inside her. Blake is a panting, sweaty mess from holding back her release. She collapses on the bed, and Annie lovingly brushes the hair from her damp forehead.

"How are you doing? Check in." Annie caresses her cheek, and she leans into her hand.

"Yellow."

"Good. It's my turn to eat your delicious pussy. I want you to sit on my face while I eat you, and I want you to devour

Coleman's cock. Make him come again."

Annie removes her shirt and lays down on her back near the edge of the bed, gesturing for Blake to take her place on top. I will always be in awe of the exquisite picture they make together.

I step up to Blake and enjoy the look of pleasure on her face while stroking myself. She grabs my cock, leans over, and swallows me to the back of her throat. The pleasure is euphoric and I have to concentrate to stay on my feet as her tongue massages the bottom of my shaft. I watch as Annie's hands slide up Blake's body and grab handfuls of her heaving breasts. I know the stimulation is driving her crazy, and the moan that escapes her, vibrating my cock, confirms it.

I want to hold onto this memory of the three of us coming together for the first time after our tragedy.

"Fuck!" The word escapes me as Blake starts massaging the spot behind my balls. She gave me no warning before her assault, and despite having just come a few minutes ago, I feel like I'm about to explode again. The more relentless Annie is to her, the more torture I receive. She adds more pressure on her massaging finger and I lose it, coming down her throat while forcing my knees not to buckle.

I collapse on the bed, careful not to land on either of them, and Annie taps Blake to get up.

"You cheated, little girl." Blake sits on the bed next to me as Annie sits up. She looks between the two of us, and her face changes into an expression I don't understand. Her face falls, and her eyes gloss over.

"Blakey."

49

Annie

I thought I could handle it. I thought holding onto all the control would make things easier for me, but it's not. I want them. I want to give myself to them, but how can I expect them not to see me differently? My body has changed. I don't even like to look at myself in the mirror anymore.

Seeing the two of them next to each other makes me reconsider everything.

"Blakey." One word, and she understands. I see the confusion on Cole's face as she crawls across the bed and takes me into her arms. I guess she never shared our end scene word with him.

"Baby. God, Annie. I've missed you so fucking much." She's peppering me with kisses along my neck and jaw. I motion for Cole to join us, and he sits closer.

"What just happened, Princess? Is everything okay?" Blake giggles on my neck, and it makes my stomach flip.

"Our Annie is back." She inhales deeply into my hair. "Vanilla. I missed this smell."

"Missed?"

ANNIE

"She couldn't smell anything vanilla without it reminding her of you so she changed her products. I'm a little partial to her new apple smell, though." He twirls a strand of her hair between his fingers.

I lean in and nuzzle her neck, inhaling the scent of apples on her skin. I smelt it when her thighs were wrapped around my head, but now I understand what I was smelling.

"I like it, too."

"Kitten, are you good?" That feels like a loaded question, and in a way, it is. This is the best I've felt in months, but there's still something holding me back.

"I need to share myself with you. Show you something. My biggest insecurity. My...my scars." Cole laces his fingers in mine.

"Nothing you could show me would make you any less beautiful in my eyes."

"Our eyes," Blake corrects him.

We shuffle around until I'm standing in front of them.

"I need to sit down to do it myself, but Cole, would you take off my leggings? Just my leggings."

"Of course." I palm his shoulders to stay steady as he slowly pulls them down to my calves, and I step out of them one at a time. The anxiety coursing through my body, knowing there's only a thin piece of fabric between them and my hideous scars, has my hands trembling. To give myself a few more moments, I raise my arms, and Cole understands my silent gesture. He fingers the band of my sports bra and pulls it over my head—one more layer.

"I'm going to explain to you what you're about to see before I show you. I have four dime size scars, two on either side of my hips, from the stabilizers you saw. They are slightly raised and a darker red color," I close my eyes and feel them each take one of my hands to give me the strength to continue.

"My pelvic surgery was extensive. I have plates and screws. The scar is a deep purple color and raised." I pause before giving the last description and feel Blake squeeze my hand. They are so incredible, letting me explain this at my own pace.

"This scar spans from my pubic area to the side of my hip. It's ugly and angry looking and my constant reminder of everything that happened that day."

Cole stands up and grabs my chin. The slight force and control of the action, makes me shiver with desire.

"No matter what you're about to show us, it's a sign of your strength, and will to survive and persevere. You're alive. You're here with us. We love you because of and despite your scars, and your beauty is only amplified by them." His thumb swipes a tear falling down my cheek. Grabbing his wrist, I lean his forehead against mine.

"I love you, Coleman McGrath."

"God, I love you too, Danika Poulsen. So much. I've been waiting to say those words to you when you would actually hear them. I've been waiting to hear you say them back to me. I want to be with you. Both of you. I want to live the life together that was robbed from us all those months ago before we even got a chance to start it. I want to be the first thing you touch in the morning." He pauses and gives me a devilish grin. "And I want you to be the last thing I taste at night." There's a little snicker next to us. "You too, Princess."

He sits back down on the bed and trails his fingers along the waistband of my boyshorts. His eyes peer into mine, silently asking for permission, and I nod.

I close my eyes, not wanting to see their reaction, as the

fabric slides down my legs. My body is hyperaware of his hands as they brush my thighs. My ears intently listen for gasps of horror or groans of disgust, but I hear nothing. I gradually open my eyes, focusing my attention on their faces. I'm surprised to see tears streaming down Blake's face.

"Please don't cry. I know it's ugly, but it doesn't hurt anymore."

"It's not ugly. It's beautiful. And I'm crying because I feel like a horrible person. You went through all of this alone. I should have ignored what you said and pushed harder. I should have let you know more that we were here for you no matter what." Blake leans over and sobs into Cole's shoulder.

"*Mijn Diamant*, I felt your silent support every day when I looked at those roses and heard the nurses read the lyrics. If you had pushed, I would have pushed back harder and fractured our relationship. You did nothing wrong, and I appreciate you for not giving up on me. I love you so much."

"They read you the note cards?" There's a glimmer of hope in Blake's eyes.

"They did, despite me not wanting to hear it." Cole takes my hand.

"We never gave up on you, Kitten. We knew you needed time to heal on your own terms. We struggled with it every day, but we are so glad you're here now."

"So, neither of you is disgusted or horrified by my new body? It comes with limitations as well."

"Never, Kitten. Tell us how we can help you?"

"Well, kneeling of any kind is difficult. It will get better with time, but I'm still working to improve that mobility."

"So, standing blow jobs and bending you over counters. Got it." Cole's smile is bright and playful. I push his shoulder, and the lack of give sets me off balance. I start to tilt forward, and he catches me with a firm grip on my waist.

"I've got you, Annie. I'll always have you." His words are so sincere. If he weren't already holding me up, my knees would buckle.

"I want you, Cole. But I'm scared. Will you...can we figure this out together?"

"We absolutely can. We can figure this out together and at your pace. What do you want me to do?"

"As boring as this sounds, I think missionary is the best position to start."

"Staring into your eyes while I make love to you isn't a hardship, Kitten. I promise."

We adjust ourselves on the bed and decide to prop a pillow under my hips. It feels like I'm about to lose my virginity when Cole asks me if I'm ready.

"Use your colors...no. Fuck that. Use all your words. Talk to me and let me know if anything hurts, and we can adjust. Okay, Kitten? Are you ready for me?"

"Okay. I'm ready." He toys with me by rubbing the tip of his cock between my lips, gathering my wetness. I'd forgotten how much I love his piercings.

Slowly he penetrates me inch by inch, occasionally pulling out before sinking back in farther. I can feel each barbell as it enters, and it feels incredible. He stills when fully seated, giving me time to adjust and assess my body.

"I'm okay. I promise. Just go slow." Blake threads her hands through my hair and trails kisses along my neck and collar. Her soft hands feel delicate on my skin. It's a stark contrast from Cole's large rough hands, but I've missed them both. I feel the rotation of his hips as he slowly pushes in and out of me. The feeling of fullness consumes me. His gentle touch shatters my heart into a million pieces and glues them back together, shard by shard.

"Talk to me, Kitten. How are you doing?"

"Fucking wonderful. Can you, maybe, lift my legs? I want to feel you deeper." He glides his arms under my legs until my knees are in the crook of his arms. I wait for any sensation of pain, but it never comes, only more pleasure as the position allows his cock deeper into me.

"Fuck, Kitten. You feel perfect. I've missed this sweet pussy wrapped around my cock. Blake, play with her clit. It's been far too long since our girl had a proper orgasm."

I expect Blake to slide her hand between us, but instead she crawls over my body, and uses her tongue to tease me.

"God dammit, Princess. Are you going for the gold medal licking both of us?" Her tongue is dipping from my clit to my entrance, where Cole's thrusts are picking up speed.

"Kitten, I hear your sexy fucking moans, but I need to know you're doing okay. I'm doing my absolute best not to pound into you. I want to tear you up and claim you as mine." Blake moans at his dirty words, and the vibration shoots sparks to my toes.

"Un-fucking-believable. But I don't think I can take it harder yet."

"Shh, relax. I promise I won't do anything more than you can handle." His reassurance expands the love I have for him.

Blake takes that opportunity to suck my clit into her mouth. My back involuntarily arches, pushing Cole deeper into me.

"Oh fuck. Fuck. You still good, Kitten? Damn, you feel like heaven."

"I'm so close. Keep going." Grabbing a fistful of Blake's hair,

I hold her in place. Her tongue is doing everything I need it to do. She nips down on my clit, and I feel my inner walls clamp down on Cole's cock. The orgasm rips through me like nothing I've ever felt before. I'm simultaneously flying and falling at the same time. My mind is thrust into the dark, but there are bright sparks of light behind my eyes. The sounds I'm making are animalistic. I feel Cole spasm inside me as his orgasm overtakes him, and he comes with a deep growl, chanting my name like a prayer.

Spent and sated, Cole gently lowers my legs, removes the pillow, and climbs next to me. He wraps an arm around my back and pulls me into his chest. Blake snuggles up behind me.

"Kitten, are you in any pain?" Pain? That was the most pleasurable experience of my life.

"No. Why would you ask that?"

"Because you're crying."

"I'm just so fucking happy. I didn't realize I was crying." I curl up into him and lace my fingers through Blake's hand wrapped around me.

"I love you, Kitten. Love you, Princess."

"Love you, Pup."

"Love you, *Mijn Vrede.*" I hear Cole quietly ask me what that means, but I'm already drifting to sleep.

·∿∿·∿∿·

I'm woken up the next morning by a dip on the bed and a wet tongue on my feet.

"Good morning to you too, Candy. Do you need to go out?"

"I've got her, Kitten. Go back to sleep."

"Some of us have jobs we need to get to." I gently jab him in the side with my elbow.

"Baby, isn't that supposed to be the perk of being the big boss?"

"Our big launch is soon, so I'm busier than usual."

"Well then, Sugar Mamma, you better get ready for work, and I'll take care of Candy. Princess, want to start the coffee for us?" Blake can't answer him because she's too busy laughing over his use of the term sugar mamma. I roll over and look him straight in the eyes.

"Cole, my pockets are deep. I could make your body disappear, and no one would ever find you."

"Touché, Kitten. You're adorable when the claws come out." He pops a kiss on my nose and hops out of bed before I can retaliate.

"Do you need any help, Annie?" Blake's sweet voice chimes up from behind me as I watch Cole pull on a pair of jeans and a T-shirt before walking out with Candy.

"He's so pretty." That man's body was sculpted for magazines, and his tattoos only further his attractiveness.

"He sure is." She hums in appreciation. "Coffee, Baby?"

"Please." She kisses me on the cheek before getting up and pulling clothes out of the drawers to get dressed. "Of course, you're welcome to anything in my closet, or one of us can drive you home if you'd rather wear something of your own."

"I'm not sure if your daisy dukes and mini skirts are appropriate for work, but I'm sure I can find something here that is suitable." She shoots me a joking glare and sticks out her tongue.

"I know. It's not like I ever had a real job working in a lawyer's office or anything." She finishes getting dressed before giving me a heated look. "I like the idea of you wearing my clothes all day." Sitting on the bed next to me I see the shift in her demeanor.

"Last night was probably different for your body." Her hand glides gently over the covers across my hip. "Can I help you with anything this morning? Some pain meds? An extra hand getting up? You don't have to do this alone anymore, Annie. We're here for you. Please lean on us for support."

She's right. Mornings are usually the most challenging part for me, and my body got a workout last night that was different from anything I've dealt with this far. I have them now. It's okay to ask for help from the people that you love. *I am not a burden.*

"Hey." Blake rubs her thumb along my forehead. "What are you thinking? Your forehead got all scrunchy." I blink at the beautiful woman staring down at me in concern.

"I'm thinking that you're amazing, and I'd love the help." Blake allows me to use her for support until I feel stable, then we walk to her closet.

"I have the perfect dress. It's a little casual, but you can pair it with a blazer, and it will be perfect." She pulls out a pale yellow sleeveless dress. It has a ruffled collar and buttons down the front to the waist, where a bow sits on the left hip.

"It's beautiful. I've never seen it before." She's correct. It will look perfect with a blazer.

"Cole bought it for me as a little pick-me-up." She leans into me, and with an exaggerated whisper, she excitedly exclaims, "IT HAS POCKETS!" I love how the simple things in life excite her.

I'm in the bathroom putting on makeup when I see Cole standing in the doorway, staring at me with a cup of coffee in his hand.

"May I help you, Cole?" He walks up behind me, and we lock eyes in the mirror. He places the coffee on the counter and reaches up to sweep the hair off of my left shoulder. Without breaking our eye contact, he kisses the side of my neck. I jump as his hand roughly grabs my ass cheek. As I open my mouth to speak, his other hand winds across my chest and grips my neck. He's entirely in control of my body at this moment, and the panic I expect to feel isn't there. His hand contracts enough to make me gasp.

His blue eyes stare back at me in the mirror, daring me to react, but I don't. I won't. I recognize this for what it is. This is a claiming. I can see the spark of dominance in his eyes. I feel safe with his hand around my neck. His mouth brushes against the shell of my ear, and I shudder.

"Be good today, Danika." One more pulse of his hand around my neck, and he walks away without another word.

50

Blake

I t feels unreal how quickly everything has gone back to normal. Well, our new normal. Cole had never lived with us before. As Annie and I lay here in bed, legs tangled together, wrapped up in the comforter, Cole continuously shoots us looks and makes off handed-comments.

"That's unrealistic. No one actually acts like that." I toss a pillow at him. "Listen or leave, buddy. We are having book club." Annie and I have been reading out loud to each other before bed and it's my turn to read tonight. We're close to the end of *Hazel's Harem,* and I'm currently reading a group sex scene. We both like reading why-choose romances, and one of the men in this book has a dick piercing that we enjoy reading about.

"I want you all to mark me. Make me yours, I want you all to come on me."

"Fuck, Alice. Keep talking like that, and I won't last much longer."

"Make me your dirty girl. Make me filthy. Claim me."

"Oh, come on. It doesn't actually say that." I show him the lines I just read out loud, and his eyes shoot up to his brows.

"No fucking way. So you're telling me this single mom got three dudes to fall in love with her, and they didn't make her choose between them? That's way too unbelievable." Annie looks at me and smirks.

"Mijn Vrede, do you expect us to ask *you* to choose between us?" *Oh shit.* She's got him now. His mouth is opening and closing like a fish out of water, unable to come up with a good excuse. "That's what I thought." Annie's smile is smug and he jokingly scowls back at her.

"Do you think Hazel and Dellah ever hooked up? They've known each other forever."

"Hmm. I don't know, Little One. But I hear Dellah is getting her own book, so maybe we'll find out soon."

"Wait, who's Dellah again?" I giggle at the idea of Cole trying to keep up with the story.

"Dellah is Hazel's spunky best friend. And, before you ask, Hazel was the one that was just about to get drenched in come." His face. His adorable face is a mix of confusion and wonderment.

"It's too bad there's only one cock in this relationship. Not too much come to go around." His jaw drops, and I gently close it with two fingers under his chin.

"Oh, I've got plenty of come for the both of you. Do you need an example?" He grabs his cock through his sweatpants and shakes it. I pat him on the head.

"Down, Pup. I wasn't trying to bruise your ego. I think we should tell Annie our little surprise."

"A surprise?"

"Kitten, Blake mentioned something to me a while back that she asked you to do. I set it up because I know a great photographer, and he's usually booked."

"A photographer?" She has no idea what he's talking about, and I'm amused.

"You can tell us no if you're uncomfortable, but we wanted to do something to show you how much we love your new body and think you are even more beautiful."

"Baby, we set up a boudoir photo shoot for the three of us."

"All three of us?" I see the confusion crease across her forehead.

"Yes, Kitten. This photographer specializes in intimate photos." She clears her throat and sits up straighter.

"Intimate photos? As in pornography?"

"Annie, I know what you're thinking." I run a soothing hand across her leg. "We've already spoken to the lawyers; the photographer has seen and signed the NDA. Even if you decide not to do it, he still gets paid. There's no reason for his indiscretion."

"Kitten, he's a friend of Nicole's. She cuts his sister's hair and recommended him. He's been fully vetted by your lawyers."

"Wow. You've both done your research." She pauses and looks between us. "Okay. I'll do it. When and where did you set it up?" Cole and I exchange a look, and she catches it. "What am I missing?"

"We want to do it in your office at work," I tell her. Cole reaches out and takes her hand.

"We thought since it's your place of power that it would empower you to be your true self and open up to us. No one in your business life will ever see you the way we see you."

"I think I like the idea. When is it?" He gives her a shy smile.

"We thought a Sunday would be the best day. Your office would be mostly empty. His next available Sunday happened to be this one."

"This Sunday? As in 3 days from now?"

"Yes, Kitten. What do you think?" I can see the turmoil on her face as she decides if this is something she's comfortable doing. I grab her cheeks. She needs to really understand what I'm about to say to her.

"Annie, you are wanted. You are loved. We love you without conditions. You are enough. You're enough right now. You were enough yesterday, and you'll be enough tomorrow. Just because your story has some bad chapters doesn't mean it can't still be beautiful. You're enough, even on the days that you don't feel like it. You're enough on the days you stand in front of the mirror and don't want to look at yourself because of your scars. You're enough on the days you don't recognize this beautiful human you've become in light of everything you've been through. Everyone deserves a person like you, but it's too bad because you're ours. You're ours, and we get to be selfish with you. We get to love and cherish you, and we are better people because of the love you give us back in return. I will spend every day for the rest of my life reminding you of all of this if I have to, but you need to know that the demons in your head that are making your forehead crease are fucking assholes, and they're wrong. You. Are. Enough. Period."

Tears are streaming down our faces, and the air in the room is thick with emotion. She inhales a shaky breath, and when she exhales, she closes her eyes.

"I. Am. Enough." She takes another breath in and out and opens her eyes. "Thank you." She intertwines her finger through mine, still holding her cheeks. "I love you. Both of you. Thank you. Let's do it."

51

Annie

I've always been a confident person. I've never wanted for anything in my life. Despite being born into money, my father instilled in me a good work ethic. I've been involved with mergers, the deconstruction of companies, launches of games and consoles, and everything in between. But, standing in my office bathroom, staring at myself in this red silk robe with the tiniest of outfits underneath, is testing my resolve.

I woke up this morning to a note from Blake telling me she and Cole had some last-minute things to take care of before the photo shoot, and they would meet me at my office in time for the pictures. Next to the note was a beautifully wrapped black box with a red bow and another note that told me to bring it to the photo shoot but not to open it until I was here.

Inside the box were two outfits. On top was a beautiful deep purple corset with black lace detailing and a black thong and garter set. A small piece of paper read "Outfit 2." The length of the bodice makes it full coverage and will hide my scar.

Underneath the corset was a layer of tissue paper with another small piece of paper that read "Outfit 1." Removing the tissue paper revealed the red silk robe. As I lifted it to admire the material, my eyes caught on what was under it. I gasped, dropping the robe to the floor. The pieces in the box were breathtaking.

I stare in the mirror at the woman before me, reminding her she is enough. Slowly I untie the belt of the robe. I dressed without looking in the mirror. I was too afraid of what I might see and change my mind. With my eyes closed, I let the robe slide off my shoulders.

"Fuck." My eyes snap to the bathroom door where Cole stands with his mouth open.

"Is it that bad?" I try to reach down to retrieve the robe, but he gets to me first, placing his hands on my hips.

"Bad? Not in the slightest. You took like my fucking wet dreams, Kitten. Let me get a better look at you." He steps back and assesses my outfit. My matching bra and thong set are sheer and nude in color, but it's the details that took my breath away when I first saw it. Intricate red lace roses and green vines line the cups of the bra and the front of the thong. Red roses. A reminder from Blake that she's always with me.

I squirm in his hand under his scrutinizing gaze. The unease creeps in the longer he stares.

"Danika. Stop." My body instantly responds to his commanding tone, shoulder pulled back, eyes to the ground. A gentle finger lifts my chin. "You are a fucking goddess, and I will accept no other opinion, and neither should you." The kiss that he gives me expresses all of his words and love. It's tender and forceful at the same time, leaving no room to question his intentions.

"Are you ready? The photographer is here."

"I am, thanks to you." He picks up the robe and helps me put it back over my shoulders. Taking my hand, we walk into my office to see big lights set up around the room and Blake lying on the couch being photographed.

Her lingerie set is similar to mine, except it's sheer green with yellow flowers. She looks gorgeous. She's sitting on her heels in the middle of the couch with her back to us. Her feet and butt are slightly hanging off the edge, back arched, and the photographer instructs her to play with her hair while looking over her left shoulder. As she does, she spots me and bounces off the couch towards us.

"You look..." Her fingers trail the hem of the robe between my breasts. "Can I?" I nod, and she fully opens the robe, Cole catching it before it hits the floor.

"Oh, Annie. It's perfect. I knew it would be." I take the same opportunity to peruse her body, and my knees buckle as all the air leaves my lungs. Luckily Cole catches me and holds me upright.

"What...You..."

"Looks like the cats out of the bag, Princess. Should we show Annie our little errand this morning? Have a seat, Kitten." He leads me to the couch, and they stand in front of me. Cole slowly unbuttons his pants, shifting them down a few inches, then lifts his shirt. Blake moves the string of her thong down her hip.

Tattooed on both their right hips, spanning the same length as my scar, is an intricate design of red roses and green leaves. There are no words to truly describe the depths of my love for these two. They did this for me. To fully drive home that they love me for who I am now.

333

I can hear the soft click of the camera, and I'm so grateful that this moment is being memorialized on film.

"Thank you." Two words that aren't enough to express the depths of my gratitude for what they did.

"You're very welcome. But, Baby, I'm dying to get to the next portion of this photo shoot. I saw this video-"

"Porn!"

"Porn."

Cole and I speak simultaneously, sending us all into a fit of laughter.

"Okay, okay, fine. I saw this *porn* where the three of them were on top of a desk."

"Let's do it, Little One. Whatever you saw, let's do it."

"Really?" She sounds apprehensive and excited.

"Yes, *Mijn Diamant.* Let's do whatever your beautiful, porn-loving heart desires." She jumps up and down, clapping her hands like an adorable child. I hear the photographer chuckling to himself. "Is there anything specific you need from us?"

"No, ma'am. Pretend I'm not here, and enjoy yourself."

Blake tells Cole to help me sit on the desk. She stands between my legs and runs gentle fingers up and down my arms, light caresses across my collarbone. Cole stands next to her and begins peppering me with kisses on my neck. My nerves are lit up like a Christmas tree.

"What now, Puppet Master Blake?" Cole's words are a whispered breath on my shoulder.

"Here's what I'd like. This is about worshiping you, Annie. You lay back on the desk, head hanging off the edge. I'm going to devour your sweet pussy down here, and you're going to let Cole fuck your mouth from up there. How does that sound?"

"Sounds fucking fantastic to me, Princess." I roll my eyes at him as he begins stripping his clothes. "I believe she was talking to me, playboy. It sounds wonderful, Little One." They help guide me down onto the desk, and without warning, Blake nips my clit through my thong.

"I'm keeping these on you. They look too good on you to sit on the floor." Her finger slides between the fabric to tease my slit, and she pushes it aside. She stares at me as she leans down, and the lower half of her face dips between my thighs. I feel the heat before her tongue sweeps up my core. My hips buck at the intrusion. Cole brushes my cheek.

"Are you ready for me, Kitten?"

Peering down my nose from my upside-down position, I open my mouth and stick out my tongue in offering. Cole rubs his tip in circles around my outstretched tongue and throws his head back in a moan.

"Every part of your mouth is heaven to my aching cock. Fuck." My lips stretch as he guides himself into me inch by inch. Barbell by barbell. This angle is different from anything I've ever experienced before. I wait for the pressure when he hits the back of my throat, but it never comes. I feel his hand wrap around my neck and gasp.

"Easy, Kitten. Breathe from your nose. You just swallowed my entire cock." He gives my throat a squeeze and groans. "I can feel my cock down your throat. I never want to leave."

Blake, who had paused her ministrations to watch the show, pushes a finger inside me, and I moan on Cole's cock in my throat.

"Holy mother fucker, Princess. Keep making her moan like that and I'll be spilling down her throat in record time." Blake enters another finger, and the feeling of fullness is almost more than I can handle. They combine their efforts and set an in-and-out rhythm with their thrusts. As my body begins to tingle with an impending orgasm, Cole squeezes my throat as he pulls out of my mouth completely.

"I need inside of you, Kitten. How about we move to the couch? Let our Princess sit on your face while I fill your pretty pussy?" I'm more than excited about his suggestion. They help me climb off the desk, and we pass the photographer as he's adjusting his camera. I really had forgotten he was here.

Laying on my back, I get situated so Blake can climb on top of me. Cole gently grabs my leg.

"I want to try and rest your leg on the top of the couch. Let me know if you feel any pain or discomfort." I nod. I like the idea. My hips will be supported, and he'll have both of his hands free. He removes my panties before easing my leg to lie over the couch.

"How's that?" I close my eyes and shift my hips to see if there's anything unpleasant, but there isn't.

"Feels great." I smile at his handsome face. I watch as he grabs his heavy cock, aiming toward my entrance. Blake leans over and swings her leg above me, exposing her glistening pussy. "Perfection, *Mijn Diamant.*"

As I get my first taste of heaven, Cole thrusts into me. The last time we were in a similar position, Blake wasn't allowed to come. Right now, that is my only goal. I feel her shift on top of me, and I can hear them kissing, connecting all three of our bodies.

Fingers start to strum on my clit, and they're too delicate to be Cole's. It appears Blake's focus is also to make me come. Cole shifts his hips and knows he's found my sweet spot based on the noises I'm making.

"I'm close." His voice is gravely with his desire.

"Me, too. Oh, Annie, keep going." I've been close. I was waiting for them. I swirl my tongue the way that drives her crazy, and she smothers my face as her orgasm takes over her body. I let go and clamp down on Cole's cock.

"Fuck me, Kitten." He growls his release as he spills into me.

Cole lifts Blake off me before pulling out, and walking to the bathroom to get supplies to clean us up. The photographer continues to take pictures through the entire process, and I know they will be images I'll cherish for the rest of my life.

Pictures of the two people that took my broken pieces and gently put them back together. My lovers that remind me every day that I am enough. That I'm okay.

Epilogue Nicole

Sitting in my car outside the house that has become my brother's residence, I look over the invitation again.

> *You are cordially invited to a*
> *"No Reason" BBQ.*
> *Your hosts, Annie, Blake & Cole*
> *Welcome you to their home to celebrate*
> *BEING ENOUGH.*
> *Please join them to eat, drink and*
> *Swim. Bring yourself, your smile and*
> *A bathing suit. Friendly dogs are welcome.*

I know this has nothing to do with Annie and everything to do with Cole and Blake. I step out of my little rundown sedan that I've had since college. Even then it was a used car. I open the back door with a squeak, and two little heads pop up at the noise.

"You ready, ladies?" Java and Beans, my crazy dachshund sisters, wag their tails as I grab their leashes and my hair bag. Although I'm a guest, Blake, and Annie asked if I would come early to do their hair.

"You can do this." I pep myself up. "You're a big girl. A big, *'you make stupid decisions when you're drunk'* girl, but still, you got this." I pat my pants pocket and listen for the crinkle of

338

my wrapped peppermints. They have been my lifesaver lately when I get nauseous.

I'm about to ring the doorbell when it opens. A gentleman in black bathing suit trunks and a Hawaiian shirt stands before me.

"Good afternoon. Name, please?"

"Nicole McGrath."

"Ah, yes. Welcome, Miss McGrath. Your brother is near the living room. The ladies are upstairs in their bedroom. They are expecting you." *Near* the living room. What does that mean?

"Thank you." He gestures to what I assume is "near" when Java and Beans pull on their leashes. I look up to see Candy standing just inside the doorway. Her little tail wags so hard that her entire butt swings in the breeze. Bending down, I release them off their leashes, and craziness ensues. Candy spins and takes off toward the back of the house while my two attempt to chase her as quickly as their little legs allow them.

I can't help but laugh at their antics. I place my bag at the bottom of the stairs. I know their bedroom is upstairs, but I want to say hello to Cole before I go up. I continue further into the house toward the sound of music and stop in my tracks.

"Oh my god, Cole!" My brother is hanging upside down on a stripper pole, wearing barely any clothes. "What the hell are you doing?" He rights himself and slides down the rest of the pole.

"Hey, big sis. You're early." He walks towards me; arms outstretched for a hug.

"Eww, gross. I can see your sweat from here. Stay back."

"Aww, you don't want a hug?" He's wiggling his fingers, taunting me.

"Ugh, I should have gone straight upstairs. This is what I get for wanting to be a nice sister and say hi first. What the hell were you doing? How can you climb the pole like that, and why are you doing it almost naked?" He drops his arms and cocks a brow.

"Which question would you like me to answer first?" His smile beams with his teasing tone.

"How about wha-"

"Hey man, that pool is amazing." I freeze. I haven't heard that voice in almost two months. The voice my sober brain is having trouble connecting with the eager, breathy tone the last time I heard it. Cole senses my change in demeanor and closes the distance between us.

"What's wrong, Nicole?" Before I have a chance to answer him, my name is repeated again by someone else.

"Nicole?" He starts walking in my direction, and I back away.

"I, um. I have to go do the girls' hair. I'll catch you later, Cole. It was good to see you, Justin."

I scramble back towards the stairs and hear their confused mumbles as I pick up my bag and find my way to their bedroom. I hear strange sounds as I walk down the hallway. Is it crying or moaning? After what I already witnessed downstairs, I hope it's not moaning. As I get closer, I can hear part of their conversations.

"How is it possible?"

"I-I have no idea. They said it wasn't completely *impossible, but the chances were extremely slim."*

"Baby, this is incredible."

340

"I'm not sure I believe it."

"Believe it! What made you test?" Test? What are they talking about? I hope Annie isn't sick. *"Why didn't you say anything?"*

Stepping into the doorway, I see them embracing each other in the bathroom.

"It was an impulse buy at the store today. I've felt 'off' in a way I couldn't describe. Someone walked by me, and their perfume was so strong I almost lost my breakfast in the middle of the aisle." That sounds familiar. *Wait, What?*

"I just...I peed on the stick, and almost instantly there was a plus sign. I couldn't believe it, so I tested with all three in the pack and got the same results."

They both jump when my bag slips from my shoulder. My body is trembling, and I have to lean on the doorframe to hold myself up. I want that—the enthusiasm and support for a new life.

"Oh my god, Nicole. Are you alright?" Blake got to me first and helped me walk over to the bed.

"I'm so sorry. I didn't mean to eavesdrop. This was a private moment, and I ruined it." Annie runs a soothing hand along my arm.

"You didn't ruin it. Although, your brother might think differently when he finds out you knew before he did." She laughs at the thought. I'm so happy that they found their way back to each other. He was so lost without her.

"My baby brother is going to be a dad. That's wild to think about."

"And amazing, and exciting, and monumental. You did it, Annie." There's so much love between them.

"How do you think Cole's going to feel about being an uncle?" That's the first thing I've said out loud, acknowledging my situation.

"No, silly, you'll be the Aunt, Cole's the dad." I'm staring at the floor, lost in the flashes of my lonely future.

"Darling, I think Nicole understands that she's the aunt. I don't believe that's what she was referring to, though. Was it Nicole?" I slowly shake my head in response to her question.

"Wait, what? If Cole is our baby's daddy, and Nicole is its aunt, the only way he could be an uncle is if…"

"…if I were pregnant." Those three words crush my soul. Pregnant. I'm so stupid and pregnant. "I'm pregnant…" I look over at Blake, "And it's Justin's."

Candy Bonus Chapter

What's that smell? Something smells fruity. I'm so bored being here alone. Mama left the doggy door closed, so I can't even go outside and chase the squirrels through the bushes. I've already checked, and the pantry door is closed, but I smell something sweet somewhere around here.

I love the sound of my nails echoing in the house. It sounds like I'm making music. I need to find the delicious smell. It's time to turn on my turbo sniffer. Taking a big inhale on the ground, I follow the scent up the stairs. I can feel my nostrils flare and my nose scrunch as I try to pinpoint where it's coming from.

Is it in the office? The door is always locked unless Mama is in there, but she's not home. A deep inhale at the door crack, and the smell isn't getting any stronger, but I know I'm getting close. Maybe it's further down the hall? Nope. The smell is getting fainter—time to turn around.

Oh. It's getting stronger towards Mama's room. Let me stop at the door and get a good sniff. Yep, definitely in here. I knew I was close when I was at the office door. Now, what are they hiding in here from me? Following the smell, I jump onto the bed. The scent is even stronger now, but I still can't figure it out.

Wait! The table...well shoot. There's something in the drawer giving off the mouth-watering smell but I can't get in there. Mama is always hiding the good stuff behind doors and inside drawers.

Hanging my head, I walk toward the door, disappointed to miss out on a potential treat. Is that...I smell it again. Nose to the ground, I'm determined to find whatever is making that fruity aroma. Ah-ha. It's in here. Once I get to the bathroom door, I'm positive I've found it. The smell is coming higher than the ground. Craning my neck and smelling the air, my chest pulses with my rapid sniffing.

THERE! Did Mama buy me a new toy? Did I ruin a surprise because this looks just like a bone?

Carefully lifting onto my back legs in front of the counter, I place my front paws on the edge. I've finally found the source of the scent that's been teasing me all morning. I tilt my head to grab the bone into my mouth and hop off the counter. Trotting over to my bed, I relax to enjoy my treat when I hear the doorbell ring and the front door open.

"Candy, *Kommen.*" It's Cole. It must be time to go outside. Maybe we can go to the dog park, and I can show off my new toy. "*Kommen,*" I hear him call again. Trotting down the stairs, he must hear me.

"There you are, Candy. Are you ready for your walk?" I walk around the corner into the kitchen and give him a little bark to let him know I'm ready. He looks happy to see me, but then his face scrunches up, and he looks upset. "What the fuck! Candy, what are you doing? Put that down. Oh my god."

Oh, he must want to play. I'm not giving my new toy up that easily. He's going to have to try and get it from me. I crouch down on my front legs. *Let's play tug-o-war, Cole.*

"Abso-fucking-lutely not. Drop it. What's the damn

344

German term for drop it." Hmm, I guess he doesn't want to play. Or maybe he wants to play a different game?

"*Lass es fallen*, Candy. *Lass es fallen*. Dammit, drop the dildo." What is he saying to me? I don't understand those words. Oh, well. Cole takes a step towards me. He wants to play chase. I love this game. He takes another step, and I step back. We do it again, and just as he looks like he's getting close, I spin and dart up the stairs. I hope he follows me!

Well, darn. He didn't follow me, and now he's on the phone. I guess he didn't want to play after all. He's so confusing. Why did he act like he wanted to play if he didn't? I guess I'll go back downstairs. It's time for our walk anyway.

Coming down the stairs, Cole is pacing the floor, talking on the phone. He sees me and repeats those funny words.

"Candy, *lass es fallen*, pleeeeease." What is he asking me "please" about? He's asked me to drop it, but he doesn't play back when I try to play. Why is he sending me mixed signals? Men are so complicated. I'll just lay on the couch with my toy. Cole seems to be upset about something.

This toy tastes terrific. Mama is so good to me. Cole is walking back my way, looking like he wants to play again. Let me grab my toy. What is that strange face he's making? He's getting closer. JUMP! Over the couch, I go.

He's finally playing with me. Yay! Around the corners, we race. Oop. He thinks he's slick trying to jump over the couch. I'm faster than you, Cole. Gotta try harder.

"Fuck, fine. But, if I get fired, I hope your next dog walker is ugly." Oh man, he's giving up again and talking back on his phone. That wall doesn't look like a comfortable seat. Maybe he's just tired from our game of chase. I'll sit back on the couch and enjoy my delicious toy.

"I'm so sorry, Annie. I didn't know what else to do but call." My ears perk up. He said, Annie. Is he talking to Mama?

A big yawn takes over my entire body. Maybe I'm tired too from all the activity. I think I'll take my new toy upstairs to my bed. It doesn't seem like Cole will want to play again anytime soon. He's still sitting on the wall, and he doesn't seem too happy.

Trotting up the stairs, I hear a noise. Was that a car door? I reach my bed, lay down, place the toy between my paws, and relax. I hear Mama Blake talking to Cole.

Mama Blake is coming upstairs. I know the sound of her footsteps. They are similar to Mama's, but they're a little bouncy. Maybe she wants to play now. She reaches the doorway, and her face doesn't look like she wants to play.

"Oh, Candy. Why this one, you sugar whore?" *Uh oh*. She doesn't look happy. She took my toy away. Maybe I ruined the surprise. Let me give her my sad face. Resting my head on my paws I look up at her.

Oh well. It was fun while it lasted, and it sure did taste good.

Hazel's Harem

Interested to know what Annie and Blake were reading? Flip the page to get the first chapter of Hazel's Harem. Available in paperback and in Kindle Unlimited.

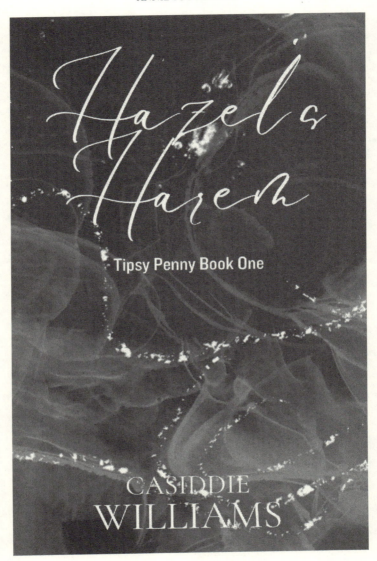

Tipsy Penny Book One

CASIDDIE
WILLIAMS

Hazel's Harem Chapter 1

13 years earlier

"Has it been 3 minutes yet?" I asked my best friend, Dellah, as I paced the small bathroom in her dorm room. The space has white walls, a white tub, and white floors. Who decided white was an appropriate color for a college dorm room? It feels sterile here, which is ironic because I may see the inside of many doctor's offices soon.

How is this happening? It was a random party with one gorgeous guy and a few too many red cups of punch. Well, duh, Hazel, I think you just answered your own question. I just wanted to have fun and let loose for one night. Depending on what that test says, it may have been my last night of fun for the next nine months. Hell, probably the next 18 years.

"Hazel, stop pacing. It's not going to make the timer go off any sooner." Pfffhh. Easy for her to say. She's not the one who's a week late for her period during her senior year of high school.

Dellah, my petite blonde spitfire of a best friend, graduated last year and has been living her best life at college this fall, getting started on her graphics design degree. Thankfully she's only an hour away and took my panicked phone call this morning when I looked at my calendar. In true Dellah-style, by the time I drove to her dorm, she had a test waiting for me. She also had tissues, ice cream, and a few wine coolers that she bartered from her roommate. She's prepared for either outcome.

"Which guy was it again?" she asked. I shot her an incredulous look, and her hands raised in surrender. "No judgment, girl, there were some hot as fuck guys at that party. I was just trying to remember who it was."

"Well, it sure sounded like judgment." I stop pacing and assess the girl looking back at me in the mirror. Do I look different? I don't feel any different. Same auburn hair and hazel green eyes. Same freshman fifteen I managed to earn four years ago during my freshman year of high school instead of college.

I glance at the reflection of my best friend, anxiously waiting for the timer to go off. She's the reason I got into this mess. She invited me to spend the weekend at her dorm, and of course, we ended up at a party. What else is there for an 18 and 19 year old to do on a college campus?

"The Mad Hatter," I replied.

"The who?" she asked, eyebrows raised.

"The Mad Hatter from *Alice in Wonderland*. He had a tattoo on his forearm of the Mad Hatter's hat with a playing card and a pocket watch. You know how much I loved that story growing up. It's what made me spark up a conversation with him in the first place. Well, that and the liquid courage." Besides his obvious tall, dark, and broodiness, of course. Dellah stared at the wall momentarily, brows pinched, trying to remember my mystery guy.

"I never got his real name. I kept calling him the Hatter. In fact, when I walked up to him, that liquid courage took hold of me. I grabbed his arm with the tattoo, looked right into his cornflower blue eyes, and asked, 'Why is a raven like a writing desk?' Without hesitation, he looked back and said, 'I haven't the slightest idea, Alice.' "

Our conversation flowed easily. We talked about my mother and his grandmother and little sister and our collective love of *Alice in Wonderland*. He was so excited to be able to talk about it to someone who had as much of a passion for it as he did. Many drinks later and we're bouncing off of walls, mouths fused, trying to find a room with an unlocked door.

My mystery man, my Hatter, had me panting his 'name' while calling me Alice and turning our one night stand into the strangest evening of role-playing. And before we parted ways for the evening, he kissed me one last time and whispered, "Fairfarren, Alice."

I shake my head, bringing myself back to the present. It was all too easy to fall back into the memory of those piercing blue eyes as my nameless Hatter wooed me with our mutual love of a fairy tale. I never expected I'd have a memorable and meaningful conversation at a college party.

Now here I am, five weeks later, impatiently waiting for the longest three minutes of my life to pass. The timer goes off, and Dellah and I stare at the test, neither of us brave enough to look at it. With a long sigh, I finally turned it over. Dellah doesn't need to see the two pink lines I'm staring at to know it's positive. My collapse to the floor and immediate sobs give her all the answers she needs.

"Now what?" Dellah asks as she crouches down to the floor embracing me in her arms. "We can go back to the house where the party was and see if anyone knows who he is. He looked older, so someone must know him."

"No. No. I made this mistake, and it's my burden to bear. I'm going to be a mother, and you're going to be the most kick ass aunt in the world." We both chuckled slightly because what else was there to do in this situation?

"You better believe I am, bestie! We will get you through this together, and this baby will have the best life he or she will ever know."

About the Author

Cassidie is a single mother to 5 children living South Carolina. This is her second novel and she is excited to produce more works of fiction for her readers to enjoy.

You can connect with me on:

f https://www.facebook.com/casiddiewilliams

@ https://www.tiktok.com/@casiddiewilliams_author

Also by Casiddie Williams

Welcome to my little corner. I hope you've enjoyed reading about Annie, Blake, and Cole. I have 2 more books planned in Annie's world as well as 2 more in Hazel's. I hope you'll join me again to read about Dellah's adventures.

Hazel's Harem
A new job opportunity brings curvaceous, single mom Hazel Gibson, back to her hometown where she finds her hands full with a little more than just her 12 year old daughter.

When two gorgeous men offer her a six week proposition to be with both of them together, no strings attached, Hazel decides you only live once, and why choose if you don't have to?

But life has a habit of throwing Hazel curve balls, and she finds herself having to make some major life decisions to protect her family. Curve ball #1: When you're already juggling two men, what's one more?

Dellah's Delight

We are returning to hang out with Dellah and learn more about her relationship with Collin. Dellah's book will span before and after Hazel's, so you'll get a glimpse of how Hazel and her Harem are doing—release date planned for the end of November.

Casiddie Williams